WITHDRAWN

I
SEE
YOU
SO
CLOSE

Also by M Dressler

The Last to See Me
(The Last Ghost Series, Book One)

The Deadwood Beetle
The Medusa Tree
The Floodmakers
The Wedding of Anna F.

I
SEE
YOU
SO
CLOSE

A NOVEL

M DRESSLER

ARCADE PUBLISHING • NEW YORK

First Edition

This is a work of fiction. Names, places, characters, and incidents are either the products of the author's imagination or are used fictitiously.

Arcade Publishing books may be purchased in bulk at special discounts for sales promotion, corporate gifts, fund-raising, or educational purposes. Special editions can also be created to specifications. For details, contact the Special Sales Department, Arcade Publishing, 307 West 36th Street, 11th Floor, New York, NY 10018 or arcade@skyhorsepublishing.com.

Arcade Publishing® is a registered trademark of Skyhorse Publishing, Inc.®, a Delaware corporation.

Visit our website at www.arcadepub.com.
Visit the author's site at mdressler.com.

10 9 8 7 6 5 4 3 2 1

Library of Congress Cataloging-in-Publication Data

Names: Dressler, Mylène, 1963– author.
Title: I see you so close : a novel / M Dressler.
Description: New York : Arcade Publishing, 2020. | Series: The last ghost series; book 2
Identifiers: LCCN 2019050016 | ISBN 9781948924894 (hardcover) | ISBN 9781948924900 (ebook)
Subjects: GSAFD: Ghost stories.
Classification: LCC PS3554.R432 I2 2020 | DDC 813/.54—dc23
LC record available at https://lccn.loc.gov/2019050016

Cover design by Erin Seaward-Hiatt
Cover photos: © Alina Prochan/Getty Images (woman on the left); © Anouchka/Getty Images (woman on the right); © Saso Novoselic/Getty Images (forest); © Alxey Pnferov/Getty Images (night sky)

Printed in the United States of America

For my mother

MJK Bellamy

we did it

Let no one tell you what form you can take.

PART ONE

THE GHOST

1

"So what do you do for a living, hon?"

For a living. Such a curious expression. The woman beside me, driving the car, means what work is it that I do to keep body and soul together, as they say.

I don't know how to answer that. When you're dead, you don't work in the usual way.

My job is to keep always one step ahead of the ghost hunters. Of course, the woman sitting next to me doesn't know that. She picked me up by the side of this mountain road, where I'd raised my thumb to her, because I look as alive as anyone, as alive as she does in her downy white jacket. If you look a certain way, you're seen as no threat. She pulled the car over and leaned across to open the door, and by her face I saw she'd even taken pity on me, because this body I wear, with its thin blue coat, makes me look small and weak, under a haircut bobbed blunt and short, like a child's. She likely thought: I needn't be afraid of this girl standing at the edge of the woods. I might even help her.

3

And it's true that if you, the living, are kind to me, and treat me well, you'll have no reason to fear me. But if instead you decide a young woman standing pale and cold and all alone and small and needing a lift is someone to take advantage of, well, you're going to run into a bit of trouble. The last driver who stopped for me—a grubby, grabby man who thought me an easy mark—I left making better acquaintance with the bottom of a lake, his hands pounding against the window glass.

Such beautiful lakes and trees they have here, so high up in the mountains, much like we had on the coast. The leaves and the pine boughs quiver and quake as the sun drops its work for the day. It makes me feel right at home.

"I'm in housekeeping," I answer the pleasant woman beside me. "I tidy and clean things."

"Hard work?" she asks, nodding and turning her wheel on the twisting road.

"Sometimes. Sometimes not."

"I'm an office manager," she tells me.

"Is that good work?"

"Used to be. Not so much anymore. They've got me doing the jobs of two younger assistants who left. Plus my own job. You know, what can you do? Things change."

They do. I used to be an ordinary ghost—a spirit tied to a place, a haunt. Now I have this body, this flesh to call my own and to travel and touch the world with. Imagine what that's like. How it might feel, after being invisible, erased, holding on only with your will, for a hundred years and more, to at last find you have a way, again, to fill space. Though, to be sure, when I wear this body I can't flit or fly as easily as my ghostly self can. I can feel the scrape of this veined armrest beside me. The cloth of the seat at the back of my head. The folded collar of this coat. But I feel the weight of this skin, too, and the pressure of the one who died so that I could take it. She was young and bright and she didn't deserve to die. No more than I did.

"All you can do is take a break from life now and then," my new, unknowing friend goes on, "so me and some of my girlfriends, we're taking off work and meeting in Reno, gonna let off some steam. Do you like to gamble?"

I took a chance and stole a body to escape a hunter. I'd say I do.

"Yes."

"Come with me the whole way," she says, nodding certainly. "If you want to. No trouble."

She's one of the kind living. Though she seems suddenly tired, clutching the wheel. She sighs and says, after a moment, "Don't mean to be pushy, though, hon. Everybody's got their own way they're going. I know that."

I thank her and tell her that at the moment I'm looking for something peaceful and out of the way.

"God, I hear that." She laughs a little. "I need that sometimes, too. Just want to cut myself off from everything, check out, lie low. You're in the right stretch of the Sierra Nevada for some good down-time. There're such pretty little towns hidden up here. Just let me know where you want to jump out, Miss . . . I'm sorry, is it okay for me to ask your name?"

I don't say: I'm Emma Rose Finnis. Irish born and Irish stubborn, raised to be staunch in the face of wounds. I don't tell her I came into this world in 1896 and died in 1915, drowned unfairly against cold, black-rocked shoals. Nor that I haunted a mansion beside the sea for more than a hundred years, until a hunter came along and thought he was strong enough to put me down. He wasn't.

"My name is Rose," I say. "And you're Sheila."

"That's right, how did you know?"

"Your luggage, in the back seat."

"You read that tiny tag? You must have twenty-twenty vision."

Yes, these eyes and ears are as keen and quick as mine once were. I might draw no real breath, but this nose, it scents the powder clinging to the soft, sagging cheek beside me, and the weary sweat at the heavy neck. I may have no heartbeat, yet my soul still pounds in furious answer to what's right and what's wrong, and knows light and dark; which is how I know this woman laughing beside me is only laughing on the outside, and that under the powder and the hands rubbed with lotion to make them feel softer, she's hard, she's worn. She's a servant in someone else's mansion, just as I once was. It can make you feel beaten down.

I say, "I noticed your luggage because I like to get away, too."

"Where'd you come from, Rose?"

"The ocean."

"Nice. I always wanted to live on the coast. It's hot down in the valley where I'm from. I could use more rain, fog, mist in my life. You come from the north coast or the south? The north? Did you mind the cold?"

"No. I'm used to it." Also, it helps disguise me. If the temperature is freezing, and someone living accidentally brushes against my skin and feels how icy I am, then they aren't startled and I'm not given away. There's a risk I face, taking on this body so that I can take in the world. Someone might touch me and wonder. Even I wonder at it, how my icy soul lifted and keeps this body fresh. *It's because I willed it,* I think, *when I saw this flesh fall,* remembering all my anger at being felled myself.

My friend Sheila says, "I guess you know, Rose, it gets pretty brisk up here, this time of year. Ever been this high before? There's no snow yet, but it'll come. Later than it used to. When I was a kid, we used to drive this pass and by now everything would already be blanketed. But nothing's like it was, anymore, anywhere. I tell myself it's still pretty, though."

It is. The aspen trees, the higher we've climbed, have soaked in the distant gold of the setting sun, lighting up the dark places between the towering pines. Stony peaks shrug all around in deep grays and blues, half-skirted with boulders and flounces of deadfall.

When I was a little girl, growing up along the seashore, I imagined such mountains rising from the long valley. At school we studied a map on the wall to learn about the great ranges of California. The Sierras were so high, our teacher excitedly told us, that droves of pioneers died trying to cross them. She was a dramatic one, Miss Camber. The great Sierra Nevada in winter could be so deep in bitter snow, she said, that even the tallest man would be buried by it. She'd paced and shivered and clasped her arms as she moaned: A mountain blizzard, why, it could be so cruel, it could take your hands and feet, and even your eyes.

I'd raised my hand and stood beside my desk, politely, as children—especially poor children—are supposed to do.

I asked her, "How can snow take your hands and your feet and even your eyes?"

She'd flashed an impatient look at me and said of course it froze and then rotted your flesh. All of it. And the cold, it was terrible, like all the pangs of hell.

"But Miss, is hell a fire, then, or ice?"

"You will sit down, Emma Finnis, for asking such a foolish question! You should *know* there is earthly pain and there is the pain of damnation, and of course they are *different*, as I *do* know."

Yet it seemed to me that all pain must be the same—or else how could you recognize it, from one place to the next?

I was sent to the corner for that little remark.

"And stay there, foolish girl, and count in silence to five hundred. You won't move until I say you may."

It was good practice, it turned out, for being dead.

"My parents," Sheila beside me goes on, "used to bring me up here when I was about eight or nine. We'd go sledding, just pull over by the side of the road where there was a good hill or a ravine, and take off. I have the best memories of this byway. That's why I decided to take it."

I have some fine memories of my childhood, too. Of running away from my work as a servant to dance a reel in the music hall with the bearded lumberjacks. Of climbing up a sandy slope to meet secretly with a boy who loved me. Of laughing with my best friend, a housemaid like me, as we sloshed each other with soap and scrubbed wooden floors together. When you die and become a ghost, you remember everything, from before your death and after, too. And so I remember the lighthouse I climbed, and slipping and clinging to the edge of it. And how you might fight and fight and fight, as hard as you can, to hang on and keep your head above the waves, and still sink. And I remember rising from my watery grave and haunting the place that had killed me.

Then the ghost hunter came, a man who said ghosts don't feel the way the living do, that we were nothing but unthinking waves, beating dull against a duller shore.

But if that's the case, how did I manage to beat you, Mr. Pratt? For I have. For the time being, at least.

Though it's over my shoulder I'm always looking, now.

"I miss the old days," Sheila is saying, sadly. "My mom just passed away. In summer. In June."

"I'm so sorry," I say, knowing how hard the crossing can be. "How did she die?"

"Emphysema. She smoked. It was hard, at the end. But she did the right thing, and let go. She followed the law. She didn't make any fuss. She died and she stayed dead, the way you're supposed to."

It takes a strange will not to go where they tell you to go.

"What burns me up are the cheaters." Sheila lowers her voice and shakes her head. "The lawbreakers. Everyone knows what the rules are now, right? When you go, you have to go. There's not enough room in the world for everyone and all their problems, not with everything this poor planet's already dealing with. So why do we still have some people staying when they shouldn't? I've heard there's even some kind of new thing running around, some kind of freak that's part ghost and part body-snatcher."

Pratt, the ghost hunter, has dared to tell the world about me, then? If that's true, I must find a way to get off this road, and quick.

"What I want to know," the voice beside me says, rising angrily, "is if the cleaners have their weapons, then why aren't they using them? I'd be fired from my job on the spot if I didn't do it as fast as I'm supposed to do it. But they can just let any kind of ghoul run around free now?" Her voice cracks, her powdered, sagging face turning suddenly ugly. "How about I just lie down and do nothing? Take this little vacation and never come back?"

I could make that happen, I think, my own anger rising.

They always disappoint you, in the end, the seemingly kind ones.

All at once, holding the wheel tightly, Sheila starts to cry. It's a soft sound, and she's dropped her chin, as though trying to hide it in the down of her coat. *All pain is the same, all pain is the same*, I try telling myself, but my rage still blights and burns. I'm no ghoul, as she called me. I never was. It's just that, when you're dead, you can suffer from the same black moods as when you're alive. And the darkness, it can come so fast and easy, it shocks you. Then the spirit has to decide what to do with it.

Give her a chance, I decide. *Give her a test. The one the last driver failed.*

"I'd like to get out now," I say. "Before it gets too dark."

"No. What you oughta do is come all the way with me, to Reno." She swipes at her tears, ordering me. "Traveling alone like you are, like this, what you're doing—hitchhiking—it's not legal, and it's not safe. Not with the way the world is."

"I know. I'll still get out at the next town, please."

"Fine. Well—fine, then, whatever," she sputters. "There's a turnoff to a little place, just ahead. White Bar, the town's called. It's not right on the road—you'll have to walk a ways, over a bridge—it's out of the way. Not nearly enough action for me, no slots or craps."

"Good. You can just let me off there."

She stops the car on the shadowy verge of a lane and watches me as I get out and peer down toward thickening woods.

"Guess you'll be all right?" She leans from her seat toward me. Her headlights whirl through a flighty dust.

"Yes. You've done enough, Sheila." *Now, for the test.* "One question, though. You're right that I'm traveling alone, and it's not safe. But it's safer than the place I left at the coast and the man I left there. If I tell you that I'm on the run from him, and that no one knows where I am, no one in the world, and that I don't want anyone to know—what would you say to that?"

She looks at me. Her mouth opening. Taken aback. Then she nods her head, slowly. "Oh, hon. No wonder you were so quiet. My God. I've been there, too. With a guy. I *never* want to be there again. I'm sorry. I'm so so sorry. Sorry I got all riled up in here for a minute, and never even noticed that . . . I won't say a single word. I promise you. I don't even remember your name, okay? I never saw you."

"Thank you, Sheila. You'd better go on now."

"Sure you won't stay with me?"

"I'm sure now."

"You take care of yourself, Rose."

"I will. You too."

I let her go.

Pain is all the same. It can make you do things, if you're not careful.

I turn toward the lane, careful not to look back at her and change my mind.

Forward is the only, and trickiest, way to live.

2

A little marker in front of me reads:

TOWNSHIP OF WHITE BAR

¼ MILE

Nothing and no one on the lonely iron-railed bridge just on the other side of it. I go forward, these feet stepping on a walkway matted with pine needles, these eyes watchful in the fading light.

If there are other eyes peering from the trees around me or from behind the lights glowing at windows nestled at a distance, I can't make them out. I walk on, and the air smells of chimney smoke and of fire licking against dry stones. Past the iron bridge the lane drops, then rises and falls toward the sparks of a town, appearing and disappearing between rough-barked trunks.

I pass a locked white building that looks like a church and a few gray cabins, shuttered. The trees thicken overhead and then thin. The way flattens before me, and a narrow valley opens out as the road leads to a flagstone square, trimmed with glowing, hooded metal lamps. A blockish metal statue stands quiet in the center of the town, like a bell unrung, with quiet buildings upright, all around. Some have peaked roofs trimmed in white lights. Others show tall false fronts with empty balconies.

A low mutter of water runs somewhere past the square, under the shadow of the mountains. A soft sound, like steel chimes, fills the air. No other sound stirs under the covered porches, and nothing moves, not the trees, nor the empty cars parked along the high granite curbs.

There's something familiar here, I think.

There's no sound of the sea, nor a tang of salt in the air, and the shadows of the mountains crowd close, like shoulders touching. But though I've never seen this place, I know the world better than I used to and am growing accustomed to its samenesses and its differences. All at once, this makes me happy, this knowing what it means to travel. We Finnises, we're Irish immigrants, wanderers. I was born to see the world, not doomed to haunt one corner of it. Yet how many souls, I wonder, believe they have no other home than where they've lived and died and have been told they must keep to? Or is that only a story a body tells itself because it's afraid to be free?

I see shapes flickering between gingham curtains that brighten a brick building at one corner of the square. I move toward them, wondering if I'm far enough from the coast now that no one will see in me the *freak* the ghost hunter has begun talking about.

A chorus of little bells jingles atop the door as I push it open. Inside the café, four faces turn to stare at me. They look pleasant enough, and not at all surprised; as though they're used to strangers coming in at any hour. Two of them perch on stools at a polished red counter. One, a white-faced man, wipes his hands on a smudged apron. In a booth near the gingham curtains, an elderly couple stares and stirs their coffees. All the other seats in the café are empty. The man in the apron stands. Not quickly, not slowly. His face is smooth and looks younger than the wiry gray hair on his arms.

"Well, hello," he says, "and welcome to White Bar! Didn't hear you pull up."

"Thank you," I say, and smile and keep my face smooth in return. "Are you still open?"

The aproned man turns toward a woman still seated at the counter. She's short and sturdy, with hair the color of salt and steel, and she wears a quilted, puffed vest, like a pillow.

He asks her, "Are we open, Mayor?"

"We certainly are, Bill." She slides off her stool. She nods at me. "Booth okay?"

"Please."

"Pick any one you like. Menu's on the stand."

The elderly couple sitting quietly side by side go on stirring and tinkling their spoons in their cups in front of them, their faces full of wrinkles, their hair white as snow. *They're living long lives*, I think, *and maybe lucky ones, too.* They wear warm, braided sweaters with high necks that prop up their chins.

"Coffee?" the mayor asks as I take a booth across from them. "It's cold out, and that thin jacket can't be doing you much good."

"That'd be lovely," I say. It's always best that I seem to eat and drink. I shiver to pretend I'm chilled.

"Bill?" She turns to the man. "Hit all of us again with the hot stuff, would you?"

"Coming right up."

So delicious the coffee smells, like life itself. I stir the blackness and must remember: it's too hot yet to pretend to drink. When I look up from my cup, the mayor is sitting down with the white-haired couple and the man named Bill is standing beside them, holding the coffee pot in one hand. They're all smiling at me, in a measured sort of way. *As though I'm a pot*, I think, *and they're not yet sure what I hold.*

"So what brings you to us?" the mayor asks, and the elderly couple across from her nod. "On your way to Reno? Thought you'd make a little side trip?"

"Yes," I say, silky as cream. "Someone told me this town was very beautiful and quiet, and I had to stop. Are you all so lucky as to live here?"

"We are." The old woman crinkles her eyes at me, delighted with the compliment.

"This is Mary and John Berringer," the steely-haired mayor says, lifting her mug toward them in a toast. "We're lucky to have *them*. They run the Berringer Inn, right next door."

"And Martha, here," the old woman says quickly, "we're fortunate enough to call our mayor. This is Mayor Hayley."

The old man named John shouts, as if a little deaf, "Mayor Hayley's the owner of this hoppin' place!"

She laughs and bows to him, then turns and points her cup toward the counter. "I might be the owner, but Bill over there does all the work, keeps it going. My place across the way keeps me busy. The White Bar Hotel—if you're looking for a place to stay the night."

"We're all competitors!" the old man shouts toward me.

His wife, Mary, shakes her head, a bit embarrassed. "John is joking. We're nothing like! Besides, we're already closed for the season, and Martha's still open. If you're needing a room, Miss . . . ?"

I smile, watching all of them. So they know nothing yet about a ghost, a *freak* wearing borrowed skin. Or, if they've heard of it, they don't see her in me. For though I wear the skin of a dead woman, it's the light of my eyes that shines from her face, and the shadow of my cleft, my father's jaw, that lies across this chin.

15

"I'm Rose," I say. "If you do have any rooms—?"

"Plenty!" Mayor Hayley says. "Spring and summer are our big seasons here, but fall tapers off big-time. Lots of room tonight. Though you're lucky, we're about to shut down for the year. I go on a bit longer than most, holding out for a few more latecomers like you. Folks looking for some quiet and not the bright lights and big action—since we don't have any slot machines or a ski lift. You do know that about us, I mean about White Bar, right?"

"Not that we didn't try, Martha!" Bill calls from the kitchen.

"Yeah, well," she calls back. "Failure is only reaching for the wrong spoon."

"We tried," the old woman leans over and whispers toward me, "this past summer, to have a view-tram built, you see. To bring more people in."

"But it all went to hell in a handbasket!" the old man barks. "That's what happens when you try to fix what ain't broken!"

"Anyway," the mayor says. "What do you do, Rose, that you can get away in the middle of a week, if you don't mind my asking? Or are you visiting from abroad? Is that a bit of an Irish lilt I hear in your voice?"

"Irish American, yes," I congratulate her. "I'm between places at the moment. Looking for a place to stay for a while. I'm traveling. Hunting for a bit of relaxation. Off the beaten path, you know."

"We certainly do. Didn't see your car out there, though." She peers through the curtains. "How'd you get here?"

"Someone dropped me at the top of the road. Before the bridge."

Now they study me oddly. Me with no luggage to my name, and only this thin blue coat on, and these flat, workaday shoes. I ought to have thought of such details before. But then, I've never before asked for a place to stay. Besides, how many lives and deaths would a soul have to number before she never made a single mistake?

16

"The truth is," I say quickly, for the trick always is to be swift when you've taken a wrong turn, "I wasn't planning to come to White Bar, Mayor Hayley. But I saw your sign, and all at once I felt . . . drawn down this pretty little road. As though my spirit were called to this place, somehow. As though I knew it. I know that must sound odd to you. Only, I trust it when I feel something, and especially when the something is so pretty and seems . . . so welcoming."

Their faces relax.

Flattery. It isn't so much a trick as it is remembering what it's like to be loved.

"That's really nice!" Bill calls from the kitchen.

"It sure is. And"—the mayor sets her coffee mug down, pleased—"I tell you what, you are absolutely right, Rose. We might not have any slots or runs here, and we don't pan for gold, not anymore, and we don't have any fancy shows like the big casino towns have, and we sure don't have all the crowds and the excitement. But what we *do* have is the beauty of this little valley, and serenity, and yes, a welcoming way. We're kind to each other, here."

"And to others, too"—old Mrs. Berringer smiles at me—"who are kind."

"And who are quiet!" Mr. Berringer shouts. "We don't like disturbances of any kind! Nothing banging the furniture!"

"He means the dead, the departed," his wife sighs. "Because of course everybody worries about that in an old town like this—we were established in 1852. But we're not like that. We promise you. We did have some trouble, back in the day, didn't we, Martha? But we've been quiet for years and years and years now."

"No ghosts, then?" I say, and pretend to be relieved. Though with a rush a dark mood comes over me. I'm saddened to think of all those now vanished, and admit to myself: it's been lonely, all these weeks, traveling with no company. I've yet to find a single, solitary soul like mine. Hiding somewhere. Hiding her rage, to keep herself safe.

"Ruthie"—the mayor turns and checks with her neighbors, then turns back to me—"Ruthie would know the date of our last cleaning. Ruth Huellet. She's not here tonight, she keeps our town museum, across the square. Back when the hunters first came on the scene—when was it, 2000, 2001?—we did have some poor strays we had to get rid of. John and Mary here even had one hiding in an armoire in their dining room."

"The doors on it," the old woman says, shaking her head, "were forever sticking, and oiling the hinges didn't do the trick. We found out something didn't *want* us opening the doors. So sad."

"And Bill, you had something knocking over the wood in your woodshed, didn't you? And stealing your boots?"

"Yep," he calls. "They figured out that was a Donner ghost just trying to get warm."

"Right," the mayor says, nodding. "Some of them wandered this way, the poor, lost things. It was painful." She faces me. "But when the cleaners came along, we did what we had to do—so don't you worry about a thing. We don't have disturbances here at all. Peace is what we have to offer in our inns and cabins and chalets. Peace and relaxation is what we all want, too. Even if you have to blast strays, when you find them. Rose, you look cold. Bill, turn up the heat, will you? Gal, you really don't have the right clothes for this altitude, you know. You're looking a little pale. Can we get you something to eat?"

I'm not cold. I'm feeling my rage, and wondering how long it will keep.

"I'm not hungry for my supper just now, thank you," I manage to say.

"More coffee?"

Bill comes and bends to fill my cup. He notices it's still full. He

18

blinks, embarrassed. He's worried his brew is no good. He thinks that's where the trouble lies.

Old Mr. Berringer says, as if he's been having a faraway conversation in his head all along, "Thing about life and death is, you can never be completely sure about it."

"John, dear"—his wife pats his shoulder—"we're talking about *supper* now."

"Already had our suppers!" He turns, wide-eyed, toward me. "What *I'm* saying, is, you never know what'll happen, when you pull on a door. What's inside it. Or outside, even. Look at all of us, just sitting here, minding our own business—and you show up out of nowhere. Or look at you, coming in, out of nowhere, saying a friend dropped you off, just easy-breezing in. What I want to know is, what is it you were thinking you'd find up here at the Bar? What are you looking for? Or what is it outside, there, that chased you in to us?"

"I'm so sorry, Rose." His wife blushes. "He gets like this, sometimes. John. Please! You're not making any sense."

Yet she's watching me closely, too, from her booth.

And so is the mayor.

And Bill at the counter.

I'm the one being tested now, it seems.

I'll have to calm my anger or be discovered. Anger gives the ghost away.

"It's a good question, Mr. Berringer," I say, this body smiling. So often a soul has to pretend and manage, as best she can. "I suppose I should tell you the truth. I do feel as though I'm being chased by something out there in the dark. Though it's hard to say exactly what it is. Have you ever felt like you're searching for company?" I ask them, for it's best to keep close to the truth, when you want to deceive. "Or that you want to run, not really away, but *to* something? Even if you don't

19

know where that something might be? That's how it is with me, you see. I'm running and searching, at the same time. But I don't want to be any trouble to you." I start to rise. It might be the prudent thing. "If I've come at a bad time, too late in the season, or if my coming seems strange to you, I could just take my coffee and go."

Their faces fall in a flash, disappointed.

"No, no, stay!" Bill urges. He calls to the mayor. "We're not ones to turn away someone who needs company, are we, Martha? And like you said, we're still open."

The mayor's eyes check in with the old man and woman, who nod quickly.

"Rose, say no more." She stands. "Plenty of room at my place, as I told you. We don't pry here—but we sure can offer you rest from searching for one night. If that's what you need. Would you like that, hon?"

"If you would be so kind, yes." There may be no friends nor ghosts here, but there's no Philip Pratt, either.

The mayor reaches for a row of hooks by the door and takes a heavy coat from it.

"Why don't you come on over and check out my hotel, and see if it suits you for the night?"

"How nice. I'm sure it will. Thank you, truly."

"Now Rose, dear," old Mrs. Berringer says, still seated at her booth but reaching a spotted hand up toward me. "I'm positive you'll feel safe and comfortable at Martha's place. And I want you to know we *do* welcome you, and it's good to have you here, dear, and—oh my goodness, your poor hand, it's so cold! Martha, you be sure and give her some warm things for the evening, if she needs them!"

"I will."

The old man stares at me. "No hard feelings, girl? Got to be careful, in a small town like ours. Hope you'll enjoy hunkering down in that old saloon of Martha's."

Bill smiles as I pass him, a helpful, yearning look on his face. A bachelor, I imagine. He has a lonely man's way about him. The dead know loneliness when we see it.

"Are you certain I can't get you anything to eat, to go?" he asks.

"Come on, Rose," the mayor says quickly. "Before Bill makes you think we never let a customer leave."

3

The cold seems uncomfortable for Martha Hayley, even under her thick coat. She trembles. Her breath blows out in thin white smoke. No steam passes from my lips, so I keep behind her. The balconies around the square are dark as we cross. Against the tall curbs, the cars seem to lean.

"I'm just across the way," she says, pointing. "This is our town square. We call that old bronze statue over there the Old Prospector. We were a gold rush boomtown called Eno Camp, back in the day. The Eno River—hear it?—that's where the miners panned. We've still got a nice little waterfall just outside of town you might like to go and see in the morning. Watch your step now, okay, this is a high curb. Everything was elevated, even in mining times, for the snow and also for the mud."

She unlocks a pine-wreathed door. Inside, a snug parlor awaits. She rubs her hands together before turning up a pink-hooded lamp. A fringed rug lies soft under the soles of my shoes. The walls are papered in a scrolled velvet. She goes to stand behind a burled desk with rows of heavy brass keys hanging behind it. Another parlor opens to my right, with a stone fireplace readied with logs and kindling. An archway beyond it leads to a dining room with empty tables and spindle-backed chairs, and a staircase rising.

The mayor takes off her coat and hangs it behind the desk. "Now! Let's get you settled in. Welcome to the White Bar Hotel, formerly the Eno River Saloon. That's what ol' John Berringer was cackling about back there at the café, just so you know. The Berringers are old-timers around here. Sometimes that makes them a bit . . . Anyway." She turns to the glowing tablet in front of her. "What kind of room would make you feel cozy for the evening, Rose? A king bed? Queen? You're such a small thing, I could pretty well tuck you in a cupboard."

I've done it, in my time. "A room with a view?" I ask.

"My best room." She taps the tablet. "For one night? Just put your name on the card here"—she slides a piece of paper toward me—"and your address if you want. You can pay me in the morning, after you make sure the experience lives up to your expectations."

Since I have no money, that's fortunate. "You're so kind, Mayor Hayley," I say and leave the address on the card blank. I had a home, once, but have none now.

"Call me Martha. Being mayor's not all that big a deal around here, to be honest. Though of course it's nice being elected. All right, now, let me show you around down here, then I'll take you up to your room. Fair warning, there's not much to do here at night except watch TV or sit by the fire and read. I can leave some things out for you, tea and coffee and cookies in the kitchen, in case you get hungry before breakfast. The kitchen is over here, see."

She leads me through the shadowy dining parlor toward a pair of swinging saloon doors.

"Had these doors moved from the front over here to the kitchen entry. Antique."

"Very nice."

"We try our best to keep things original."

The kitchen is a large white and blue one with black pots hanging overhead and gold-bordered china leaning inside cupboards. Knives with well-rubbed handles are sorted into a butcher's block.

"Take anything you need from the fridge," she tells me. "Our season is basically over, like I say, and I prefer things to get eaten up before they go bad. Breakfast is at eight. If you do breakfast?"

"I don't really, Martha."

"I'm the same way. I don't like to start the day all stuffed and heavy. Now let's hoof it up to the gallery. You'll have the whole second floor to yourself. Well, the whole place, aside from me."

We climb the carpeted stair, each step with its fine brass rod holding the deep-napped rug in place. It makes a runner difficult to sweep, I know.

"Do you have anyone here to help you, Martha?"

"How sweet of you to ask. Not really. Mostly I take care of everything myself, now that I'm on my own. My ex left and moved to Sacramento, so . . ." She gives herself a little shake, as though some lint needs brushing away. "Doing all the work myself saves on costs, at least. We tend to think bottom-line around here, because we don't have a year-round season. And when the snow hits, the passes can close; then we're really on our own. So it's best to know how to be self-sufficient."

"And when does the snow come?" I ask, my mood turning eager. The cold that burns like hellfire, Miss Camber said, that can be so deep it buries a man.

"We've got a little system coming in tonight, matter of fact. Might get us our first flurries of the year. I have to say again"—she turns to look back at me at the top of the stairs—"what I said earlier about your clothes: not up to the weather. You don't have anything else with you?"

"I didn't plan to stop here."

"So you said, but you have to be careful this high, okay? People die from cold at this altitude. A front can sweep in out of nowhere and get really serious really fast. And then where will you be?"

As dead as I am now. "Thank you for your concern, Martha."

"It's just so you know. So, here we are on the guest floor. You like it? We preserved everything we could from the era." She beams, admiring her own landing. "All these sconces are rose glass, which is what the madams and the miners thought of as pure elegance back in the 1850s." We pass through a hallway of closed doors illuminated by crystal shades. "It's a little bawdy, I know. Of course we're a family-friendly establishment now. With a bit of spunk. The Corner Room is at the end of the hall. It has the nicest view of the square, or will in the morning." She takes a key from her quilted vest.

Inside, I see first bright satin curtains in sapphire blue drawn tightly together. A bright blue canopy hangs over the bed, dressed with fine blue pillows and a lace coverlet. A darker blue carpet covers the floor.

What a royal room to touch and stroke, I think. And all mine. For the night.

"All right." The mayor looks around. "See if you have everything you need. I want you to be comfortable. Bathroom there. Coffee and tea maker here. Extra blankets. If you happen to want to get up in the night, I'll leave the lights on in the hallway, and a few downstairs. And I'll put an extra shawl out for you, too, by the fire. If you need me, for any reason, I'm up on the third floor. It was the door we passed right at the top of the landing. Don't hesitate to knock or even come on up if you want or need anything. I'm here to attend to your needs. Think you'll be all right, alone here?"

"I will be. It's perfect." It is.

"Glad to hear it. Here's your key, then. Have a good evening, Rose. See you in the morning."

She gives me an innkeeper's nod, then closes the door behind her.

I turn. Delighted. Here's such a fine crystal water pitcher—and for the night, it belongs to me. And these sharp-cut glasses. *Mine.* And the dainty white linens folded beside them. *Mine.* The carved white dresser. The framed picture on the wall above it. A ghost, if she's left her haunt, has no possessions. I didn't think I would miss having things, linens and furniture to hover over and claim. But at the moment, oh, I do. The heavy-framed photo above the dresser is darkened in the way of old tintypes, like the pictures that used to hang in my last home. The photographer has pointed his camera at a local celebration, the town turned out in their finery on the square, bundled in furs and shawls on a snowy day, with flags hanging frozen from the balconies all around. Men stand shoulder to shoulder in deep coats and slouch hats, their boots crusted, while a few women lift their chins under heavy black bonnets. Every eye stares in one direction, as if at something just over my shoulder. In a low corner, a date is written in pale ink: *1852.*

A number to put with the faces of the dead. But no names. Looking at them, I wonder: *what would we say to each other if you weren't lost and gone, but were granted a wild stubbornness, as I was?*

A faint tinkling comes from outside the curtained windows. I go and peer out. It's only the chimes I heard earlier, lilting across the square.

I let the draperies fall. All around this little village, I suppose, the living are putting themselves to bed, to sleep. Something I can't do. I can't sleep. I don't dream. I imagine others, settling onto their plump pillows, pulling their blankets up to their chins, closing their eyes inside the darkness.

It's then, when the living think themselves safe in sleep, that a door might creak, like this one, and a light break open, and a ghost walk out into the night.

Those who can't sleep, haunt.

We use the night to learn what only the night can teach: how to face loneliness.

I walk down the crystal-lit hall, between the row of closed rooms. Near the landing, outside the innkeeper's door, I stop, and listen. Through the keyhole I hear Martha softly snoring. In. Out. In. Out. Her living breath, I haven't forgotten, is one that praised the murder of ghosts. She said we ghosts are *poor, lost things* that need to be *blasted*. I reach my hand toward her door. I'm wide awake. I could take vengeance if I cared to.

Still, this woman gave me a home for the night. It's more than I've had in a while.

I move away, leaving her to the drift of dreams. I make my way down the stairs, with no sound. There's a talent to being a spirit, with or without a borrowed body, that the living will never know unless they die and linger long enough to make their own soul's acquaintance.

In the dark parlors below, the spindle-backed chairs sit empty, and the wood in the fireplace lies split and unlit. The mayor, as promised, has left a shawl for me, and a light on in the kitchen. In the shimmering porcelain and blue room a tea cup and spoon wait for me, beside small sweets I can lift and smell but not swallow.

It turns out there's a price for moving through the world as something new.

It means old longings must find some fresh way to be fed.

Still, I'll never say, as the hunter Philip Pratt does, that a ghost should give up her longings because longing is all she ever feels. *Isn't it*—I think as I put the sweets down—*longing, hope, desire, that the living most feel, too?* And even though it's feeling—wanting and pain and anger, rage—that most risks giving a ghost away in this world, still I'll never say that what the soul must do is stop feeling altogether; or that a soul who might have to control her feelings just to survive is any less than a man, like Philip Pratt, who's free to howl his pain far and wide.

"The ghost of a feeling is still a feeling," I say out loud, simply to hear my own voice come from inside this body I've claimed. "I'll never say a haunt shouldn't feel what she feels."

A whispering, agreeing sound comes from the wall beside me.

Coming from a hidden place.

An answering hiss.

Low.

4

"Who's there?" I call, my soul racing.

From where—*there?*—behind the oven glass—the gentle scratching comes.

It's a phantom's tap. A knocking.

Tap. Tap. Tap.

Our greetings aren't like those of the living. Our sounds must come across space and time. We're echoes careful not to say where we started.

My soul waits. Breathless.

We dead know the dead. We feel, we hear the same echoes. We've passed the same way. I was told there were no ghosts in White Bar. Yet someone, plainly, is here. Someone who knows how to last, and so knows it's best not to show ourselves to any but kin and kind.

Still . . .

Be careful, I urge myself. For I've learned there is no certain friendship in the meeting of spirits. Passed souls are no different than living ones. Some good. Some cruel. As easily as the living, some betray the others. I've seen it done. Perhaps I've even done it myself.

29

All the saints are dead, so the Irish saying goes, but not all who die are saints.

Again I call, "Who's there?"

Two hands, smooth, young, appear at the greasy window. Palms facing me, pressed against the glass.

I come nearer, excited, and see sleeves ruched tight at the wrists, printed with tiny, faded flowers.

Careful, I think. *Still, be careful.*

"I can see you. Who are you? Can you tell me? Can you come out?"

The hands don't move. Or can't.

They quiver.

With a faint click-click, the oven is lit. It begins to glow.

Now the hands slap, pound.

"*I burn!*" the hissing cry comes, frantic.

Pain. Such terrible pain.

"I hear you! I can see you! Can you get out? You must try!"

The young hands writhe against the glass. They scorch and twist.

Terror. At every moment we carry in us what killed us. "It was something terrible that happened to you, I know, I know! But I'm here. I'm Emma. Can you come out? Can you see me?"

No answer. Only those hands, writhing, beckoning in the heat. Fingers outstretched. Are they asking to be freed? Or luring me in to follow them?

Careful. Careful.

"Can you come out to me? Come out, if you can, so I can see you."

"*I burn.*" The hiss begins to fade. "*I burn. I burn.*"

"I know, but you must come out and—"

With a click, the hands disappear. The oven is cold again.

"Wait!"

No, she's gone.

Back into death's silence.

My soul beats, wildly. What's just happened? Did I speak the wrong words? Did I ask too much?

A soul, living or dead, doesn't always know the right thing to say to a stranger.

But I'm not alone, I think. *I'm not alone . . .*

I feel it. Not only the certainty. But what it is I want. I race through the hotel with this new hunger, haunting, hunting, searching with it, down every hall, hoping she might be able to see me, from wherever it is she hides.

I show her my desire. *I want to know you.* It's a beginning, at least. And a beginning is all you can ever ask, after you've ended . . .

I haunt with a leaping hope, all night long.

5

"Well, look who's up early!" Mayor Martha says cheerfully, coming down the stairs in the morning and seeing me standing alone in the dining room. "You're a quiet riser. And way ahead of me!"

She notices I haven't touched the shawl she left for me. She's wearing a fresh quilted vest. Her steely hair is combed and smells newly soaped and dried. She's so alive. She bends to light the kindling under the logs in the hearth, pokes at the fire, then rubs the ash and soot from her hands and smiles, unknowing, at me.

"Did you have a peaceful night's rest, Rose? Did you find the goodies I left for you in the kitchen?"

I did find something, I remind myself. The spirit, she never showed herself to me again—*but then*, I think, *she might have been confused and not understood that my ghost, like hers, is hidden inside something else.*

Or perhaps she knows her way too well around death and around this place, and knows she has cause to be careful in this town where other ghosts have been blasted to dust. No ghost will let herself be seen unless she wants to be seen—or unless she's goaded by a hunter to anger or pain. But by what means might I, or should I, provoke a ghost?

The mayor is still smiling at me. "I remember you don't want any breakfast. Do you want coffee, though? Or are you heading"—she glances at my straight shoulders—"straight out the door already?"

"No," I answer, coming toward her and the smoking fire. "I was just doing a bit of thinking, here in your pretty parlor. I've been feeling, all night—I hope this doesn't sound strange—that White Bar might be the perfect place for me to stop, for a little while. I'm wondering"—I smile back at her—"how it might be if I stayed on for a few days? If you can spare the room?"

I don't say: *I will be staying here, one way or the other.*

She turns slowly, considering, toward the hotel desk. "A few more days, Rose?"

"If you can manage it. I wouldn't want to be any trouble."

She tilts her head, surprised, watchful. "Even though you don't have what you need, luggage-wise, for these mountains?"

"I could get some things."

"Sure, but you should know we're pretty much a one-night town, in November. Not much left open now except the café and the museum and the general store, maybe one art gallery. Not much to do except look at the falls, and that takes maybe half an hour. If you stay, I'm just worried I'd be taking advantage of you, you know. And I don't like to do that, not if—not when you feel like you've been running and searching for something, as you put it," she says cautiously.

"But that's just it, Martha." For the soul can be nimble when it needs to be. "I really *have* been running and searching. There's something I haven't told you that . . . that I've suffered through, not so long ago . . . and there's something, now, here, that feels so good and right for me, after what I've been through. I think, for some reason, White Bar might be a magical place. I think I knew it as soon as I came. It makes me never want to leave at all. It feels"—I put a little plea into my voice—"so *different*. A place a body can trust."

She gives me a long look—and then some steel seems to soften inside her.

I see it. Plain as day. I can't claim to be able to read every soul I meet. Yet I've lasted so long, now, in life and in death, I've come across nearly every card a living face can show.

Mayor Martha Hayley is flush with happiness.

"Rose, gal, you see more than most people usually do." She stares at me. "White Bar really *is* a special place. It's not just old-timey trinkets and postcards and relics, like most people think." She blushes, proudly, excited. "It *is* a place of trust, like you say. We're entrusted with so *much* here. With each other . . . and making our little town work . . . caring for our little corner of history . . . But most people don't ever see that. They just use us for a rest stop, and go on. But Rose, hon . . . are you really sure it's the right thing for you to stay here right now? A place you don't even know, with so few . . . resources?"

"Martha, would it help if I told you I'm starting my life over after someone told me I don't deserve a life at all?"

As if a bolt from heaven has struck her, Martha's shoulders stiffen. She seems to grow taller in front of me.

"I *knew* it!" She pounds her fist on her desk, from her fresh height. "I just knew it! I called Mary Berringer last night, and I told her, I think there's some story here with this young Rose coming out of nowhere with almost nothing in her hands. You've *escaped* someone. I knew it! Well, whoever they are"—she raises her voice—"God damn them to hell! Did they—no, no, you don't want to go into the details, I can see that and I understand and respect it. But this changes everything. You poor girl!" She reaches out—too shy, I see, to take my hand, so she strokes my sleeve instead. "Now, you listen to me. You don't need to go anywhere, right now. Just lie low with us for a while, and get strong again. The Bar is such a *good* place for that. A fine place. You know, White Bar took me and Dale in after we lost everything? In the mortgage crash when nobody got punished but us little fish. We were literally on our way to the casinos to try to turn the almost nothing we had left into something, and we felt so worthless, just worthless, and we happened to stop here just to take a breath and ask ourselves what on earth we were doing . . . and we sat down in the café, just like you did, and the next thing we knew we met people, and found out the hotel was sitting empty and run down, and the *next* thing we knew John and Mary were loaning us money to buy it . . . and now look at where I am. Mayor! And then, even when Dale left me flat"—her voice breaks and goes flat, too, but not weak—"the Bar lifted me up again. That's just how it is here. We stick together. Now, you come back into the dining room with me." She takes my elbow and tugs on it. "I know you don't do breakfast, but how about some tea to warm you, while we talk a few things through, and see what we can come up with in terms of clothes and things for you. You sit down right here," she says, pointing to a table, "and we'll get something hot into you and *onto* you."

She disappears into the kitchen and comes back with a pot and cups and saucers and sugar and milk, and bends and serves me, as I used to serve others. Oh, such a lovely feeling it is, to be waited on hand and foot! It makes you feel like you're someone important just by sitting down, and makes someone else seem less so, bending their back toward you.

And that's the trick and trouble of it.

"Martha," I say, "you sit down now, too."

"I will, I will. I do want to know more about you." She drops into the creaking chair across from me. "Like, what you do for a living? So we can see what there might be for you to do around here. How to fit you in."

"I was a housekeeper."

"Now *that* could work out! But"—she chews her lip and nods—"what you mostly want is independence. That's what we work for here. A sense of control. I know, and a lot of us do, what it feels like to lose that sense of being in charge. I know what it means to have found out you were mistaken in someone . . ." Her brash voice falters again. "But the thing is, with the help of others, you pick yourself up, you find your center again, and you go on. And it's in the going on that you see how *any* misfortune, no matter how big it is, can be made into something small. It's the wonderful thing about time, right? It's like doing the laundry. It shrinks the past."

I don't tell her what I'm thinking: *Time isn't like that at all. It doesn't shrink the past. It stretches it.*

"You are so right, Martha," I say and stir my tea. When she isn't looking, I tip my cup over the side, slopping some of it into my saucer. "And surely we deserve some reward, after all we've been through."

"Damn straight!"

"And thank you so much for letting me stay. I'm so happy I came here, even if it was only by accident I did. Because what I say is, why should it matter how you get somewhere you need to be, just so long as you do?"

Her eyes shine at me. Philip Pratt, he says I'm evil and a curse to everything I touch. When all I do is speak truth to the living, even if they don't always know what I mean by it.

"That's exactly right, Rose! And I tell you what: I believe things always happen for a reason. Like, sometimes you need help, and boom! Help arrives. Which brings me to something else. I have an idea. Why don't you take today to just look around our little paradise, and see if you like it, and maybe meet a few more people, and if you like what you see, why don't you stay on, not just for a few days but for the whole winter? I could sure use your skills and help getting everything shut down

36

for the season. And so could the Berringers. They're getting on in years, you could probably tell. Every season gets a little tougher for them . . . And maybe Bill at the café could use some help, or Harold over at the store, or Ruth at the museum . . . We'll see. But in the meantime, I can give you the room, though you'll need to get a better coat and some boots. I can maybe get you started with some things, and Harry can, too—and most important, you can recover from whoever that scumbag was who didn't do right by you, and let us help save you. Because that's what we do here, Rose. We *save*. We *preserve*. It's what we're especially good at."

I'm being taken in so easily. Now why is that?

"What are you thinking, Rose?"

"Only how lucky I am." For no matter what the reason is for all this kindness and flattery, it will give me time to find the ghost with the flowered sleeves. And that's what I want to do now. More than anything else. I want to find someone who knows time, long, long time, the way I do. "Now, what would you say is the best way for me to get started?"

"I'd say with Ruthie, Ruth Huellet. She'll be over at the museum, organizing things before she shuts down for the season. I'll just give her a call and let her know you're coming." She stands. "She can tell you all about us. A museum, history, is always a good place to start, and so important, don't you think?"

"I do."

"Are you sure you don't want anything to eat before you get out and about?"

"I'm only hungry to find out everything I can."

"Well then, I say *we're* the lucky ones! We can sure use your youthful energy around here. Okay. I'm telling Ruth that Christmas has come early, and not just weather-wise, but because we just got the sweetest little gift. That's how I want you to see yourself, Rose, you got that? Not as somebody down on her luck, hiding out. But as our Rose in winter."

And she looks down so kindly at me, I can almost forget she'd want me blasted to nothingness, if she could see underneath this pale skin.

6

A bright, sparkling veil lies at my feet.

I step from the hotel's tall porch. My shoes sink in with a gentle rubbing sound. I bend to touch the whiteness.

Snow. So this is snow?

Not a veil, but a thousand tiny crystals clinging to the gloves the mayor has lent me.

The stones on the square are twinkling. The town's metal statue wears a jaunty shawl across his shoulders, and the balconies all around him flash, coated in light.

It's only a few inches, the mayor's just said, opening the door.

Not so deep it could bury a man, I think.

But wonderful. Oh, such a thing it is, to be able to see and touch the world!

The mayor is laughing behind me, on her porch. "Can't believe you've never seen snow before! Nothing compared to what we sometimes get. But watch your step, okay? That stone building over there at the far end of the square, that's the museum. Ruth's expecting you. Have fun."

I go, carefully. Not only the streets glisten. The sky gleams like marble. The trees are trimmed in a bright, drooping glaze. I walk with Martha's borrowed coat wrapped around me and the knitted scarf I took quickly from her, so she wouldn't see the dried wound gouging this body's neck. The smell of the mayor's clean hair rises from the muffler's wool. Of course I'm used to wearing a stranger's clothing by now, and walking inside another. Still, it's different when the warmth is handed kindly and intentionally to you.

I cross the square. I'm balancing on the snow in my flat shoes, walking evenly as I pass the brooding statue, a man carrying a great pack and a pick and shovel on his back, his slouch hat sharply brimmed. Beyond him the wind chimes dangle in flutes from their porches, and a sign hangs motionless on the low stone building Martha pointed out to me. It reads, in curled letters, WHITE BAR JAILHOUSE MUSEUM.

Deep-set, iron-barred windows greet me, queerly livened with calico curtains. The museum was once the town keep, Martha told me, but really, she said, there was no need for anything of that kind now, since there was no crime to speak of in the Bar—"unless you count being trapped when the passes close with only whatever Harry in the general store has in the way of coffee."

I pull at a bell rope beside an iron door, and a deep chime sounds. A voice inside calls to come in. More bells jingle over my head as I push the door open on its heavy hinges. The people of White Bar, I notice, like their visitors announced.

A round woman with blue eyes comes toward me from between bookshelves and mounted trinkets cluttering paneled walls, her face smiling and soft. She's middle-aged, younger than the mayor, and much more so than John and Mary Berringer. She's been doing some kind of work, I see—cleaning, maybe, since she wears an apron. Her neck is shiny and her eyes are puffed with sweat and labor.

"Rose!" She smiles and holds out a damp hand. "Martha said you were coming over!"

I take the hand, keeping my gloves on so she won't feel the ice of me. "And you're Ruth," I say. "It's so very nice to meet you."

"Come on in! Welcome to the Jailhouse Museum. Where the past meets the present and the law meets the lawbreaker." She laughs, then coughs, half choking, patting her chest as though the heated air is too close for her.

It is a close, crowded place. I stand at the front of a narrow, beamed room made narrower by stacks of metal pans, folded horse blankets, rusting post boxes, butter churns, a wicker baby carriage strung from the ceiling above, worn saddles and frayed harnesses, sawblades nailed to posts, wooden chests opened and spilling unsorted clothes, crates filled with polished stones, photographs in every size, and baskets filled with ribboned soaps. The air smells sickly sweet and cloying. Cobwebs swing loose from the dark ceiling. Low glass cases are spotted with fingers and dust, some half polished away.

"Sorry everything's a bit of a mess," Ruth Huellet says. "I'm just getting started on winter cleaning."

"Have I come at too busy a time?" For there's nothing more grating than being slowed down when you want the drudgery finished.

"No, I don't mind taking a break." She pulls off her apron and with a sigh wipes back her bangs. "Plus, it's nice getting a visitor this late in the season. It's your first time in the Bar, Martha says."

"It is."

"How do you like us so far?"

"I love the quiet and the snow."

"That's nice!" She beams and seems happy. "Martha says you might even stay for a while. She says for me to get you introduced to the Bar and some of our history. I don't know how much of a gold rush buff you are, or how interested . . . there is a *lot* of stuff in here." She waves her damp, soapy hands. "It can seem a bit much, at first."

"I'm very interested, Ruth," I say. *I've come,* I don't yet say, *to know who here might have died in a fire.*

The fire that burned her pleading hands. A ghost speaks from the pain that haunts her. But I must be careful not to give her, or myself, away with too eager questions. Not with Pratt prowling the countryside.

"You'll notice not all of this, strictly speaking, is museum quality," Ruth apologizes, leading me past a row of opened boxes. "Every time someone leaves the Bar, they dump all their old stuff on me, like this. Like I'm a Goodwill donation site."

So, White Bar is a place people are leaving, then. If it's such a happy town, as the mayor says, why would that be?

"Is this your museum then, Ruth?" I ask, skirting a stack of chipped china plate.

She tells me that no, the collection, all the artifacts, belong to the town—but the building had always belonged to her family. "My last name is Huellet. We Huellets go way back to when this was a gold rush camp. We weren't the first non-indigenous people to arrive here—that would have been Mexican traders passing through—they found the first nuggets here and then got chased off by the whites—but we came not long after that. When this was a camp called Eno. First tent went up 1850. Here's a sketch of what the camp looked like then."

She takes me to a wall covered in maps and sketches. In their center is a small drawing of a group of pitched tents ringed by ugly, stumped trees.

"A lot of these buildings, including this jail, didn't go up until 1852." She taps the far edge of the drawing. "This building stayed a jail until it got converted to a museum this last century, by my great-grandmother, Cora Huellet. She started this collection. Now it's my responsibility. My

calling. Along with making my handmade Huellet's Healing Soaps."
She points, proudly, at the baskets filled with ribboned squares. "All
organic, all natural. Now, over here"—she turns—"there's a photo of
two of my ancestors. The Huellet brothers were doctors. This handsome
one here, in the white hat, Caleb Huellet, was also our first mayor. His
brother, Huston, was more of a behind-the-scenes guy. I hope you don't
mind me talking about my family." She lingers, then turns away from the
portraits of the serious-looking men. "I'm sort of proud of them. I try
not to get carried away."

"I don't mind at all," I tell her. Sometimes you long to speak of your
family, and can't.

She nods, grateful. "What I'll do now is give you a bit of the talk I
give most of the tourists. Sound all right to you?"

I agree, and she goes on chattering as we wind through more clutter.
We stop beside a glass case filled with arrowheads. "The Miwok. They
were here first. They're all gone now." Then beside another, filled with
piles of gold stone. "These aren't real nuggets. Only painted. It wouldn't be
safe to keep real gold out like this. Plus, if it was the real thing, White Bar
would be as rich as Midas—and we all wouldn't have to work so hard."

"But," she says, and her face turns proud again as she walks back-
ward, facing me, "it's the gold that put us on the map. At first there was
so much of the yellow stuff lying around, the men could pick it up right
off the ground, or pluck it out of the river. By 1851, though, all the easy
pickings were gone, and the digging really started. It was a hard life for
the men here. The prospectors, they mucked for pay dirt every day, even
Sunday, except for the few who tried to keep to their religions. The winters were so cold, their hands froze black, and the summers baked their
eyes. Still the camp kept growing."

By 1852 there were three hotels, she says—"to call them by their
polite name"—two undertakers, a stable, Chinese laundries, and goods

stores, and also six saloons, and brawls, and accidents, and sickness, and disease.

Accidents, I think. *Fires.*

"What made us different from other towns," Ruth Huellet goes on, coming back to the faded maps, "is that pretty quickly we tried to get civilized. You can see here the camp was laid out around a square. Not at all what you normally saw in a boomtown. Some of the men who came from the East, like my ancestors Caleb and Huston, wanted something that looked more like home. They also brought in law and order. If you'll look here"—she leads me sideways to a small, doorless, stony room— "you can see the original jail cell. The bars are gone, and we've made it a nice display area; but you can still get a sense of how tight it was, with these granite walls. Nobody got away."

"Tight as a coffin," I say aloud.

"You bet."

A hanging lantern throws a shadow on the wall, above a table with a brass scale and a standing medicine cabinet filled with blue bottles. Beside this, a photograph of miners with long, drooping beards and hollow eyes, leaning over a wooden trough belching mud and water. They look dazed and weary.

"These medicine bottles, here, belonged to my ancestors. They were part of the movement to get the camp healthy and civilized. They got help from Lionel Berringer, the first sheriff. Have you met the Berringers, John and Mary? They're from old blood, too, like me. The Huellets and the Berringers got things in order and renamed the town, but unfortunately it was for a sad reason. The name White Bar refers to this white ridge of falls outside of town, over here in this picture. It's not a natural formation. It's what's left from a dynamite disaster. In 1852, some miners were trying to change the course of the river, which was something they did back then, to get at the gold they thought was underneath it. But the blast went wrong and four men died. There's a little marker out by the river in memory of them."

A blast. Flames. Fire. "Tell me, Ruth," I say, looking more closely at the photograph of the falls and the foam, "did any fire spread?"

"You would think it would have. Wildfire was always a big hazard here. That's why this building is all stone and iron, when others were wood. Some even—I know it sounds stupid—had canvas roofs. But apparently, the blast didn't hurt the town. Since it was at the river, maybe it was far enough away."

"And who died in the explosion?"

"Only the four men. It was a day of mourning for the camp. We don't have a picture of that, but we do have this one taken not long after, the same year."

She points into another corner of the cell, and here I see the familiar photograph, the same one that hangs in my hotel room. The hatted and bonneted townspeople standing on the snow-draped square, their faces lifted.

"I know this one," I say, looking up. "It's at Martha's."

"Right, you'll see it all over town. It's on our postcards, too." She leads me out of the cell and to a little rack of mementos beside a brass cash register. "It's our signature image," she says, showing me. "It really captures the look and the spirit of the times. You can tell from the flags it was some kind of winter celebration or thanksgiving. What you can really see are all the details, the clothes people were wearing, what the buildings and the square looked like, how so many of the trees were cut down, now all grown back. Notice even a few women"—she points them out—"though they were rare around that time, outside of the bordellos. I just love this image. All those people. Full of . . . ambition."

I search among them for a glimpse of ruched, flowered sleeves. There are only women draped in black, in black coats and bonnets. A strange color for a celebration.

I ask, "Is there a graveyard around here?"

"No, we don't have any cemeteries. Or graves." She fusses with the card rack, rearranging it. "The ground here's too pocked with mines and holes, which is why we couldn't even get a tram built this past summer. Everyone gets buried over at Dutch Gap. It's the next town over." She turns to stand behind the register, formally. "That's where we go when we need a big supermarket, doctors, things like that. We're pretty isolated here. And our population tends to be older. My son lives with his father in Reno." She looks down at the money tray. "Some people think we're kind of a dead place now."

It's an opening. "You don't mean dead like ghosts, do you, Ruth?"

"Oh, no! You don't have to worry about anything like that here. Whenever we've had trouble, we've always had it taken care of, right away. Please don't think you have to be nervous, okay?" She looks up at me, hopefully. "Please know it's safe and peaceful here. Martha told me a little bit, the little she knows about your . . . your situation. And I promise you, Rose." Her blue eyes look into mine, directly. "We'll protect you here. We're just that kind of place."

The same words Martha used. "You're all so very kind. So you say there are no—"

"A lot of us know what it's like," she interrupts—then stops, and swallows, as if she's holding back something inside her. "What it's like to feel down and out. But don't you let anyone get to you, Rose. I was in a bad relationship a while back. With my son's father. We weren't married. He tried to get me to leave the Bar. I thought I might, for a while. But I left him flat when I found out what a leech he was." She holds her empty hands out to me, as if to beg. "Because we have to stand up for ourselves, right? Mary Berringer says life's too precious to live out someone else's idea of what we should be."

"Ruth," I say kindly, for though I'm dead and cold, I feel with every inch of my soul, and with this body, and I can see when a living woman has suffered and walks in skin that still aches. "You're right. We should be who we are, not who others say." Never can truer words be spoken. "Is there something more you want to tell me about your . . . trials?" For she seems about to burst, holding her life, her past, inside her.

She stiffens all at once and turns toward her soaps, rearranging them, too, before she reaches for a little pile of papers resting on a small table and shrugs firmly. "No. I'm fine. Just having one of those moments, you know. Would you like to take one of our walking-tour maps?" She clears her throat, smiles quickly, and holds out a sheet to me. "It's self-guided, and shows you our historic buildings and what the layout of the boomtown was like, and then it takes you to the falls."

She doesn't want to talk truth anymore.

"Will it tell me about the history of the buildings?" I ask easily, and to be kind again. "Any damage or repairs to them?"

"Yeah. Things break and then people fix them."

She walks me to the door, and with her shoulders turned away from her museum, she hangs her head and says, "I'm sorry about snapping like that. I'm feeling a little out of it today. Touchy. It's just life, you know. Work. Just trying to make enough room even to walk around in here."

"Ruth, did Martha tell you I might stay on and help?" I put my hand out. An old habit. My job was to tidy and clean.

"No!" She straightens, suddenly. "You shouldn't have to do that! You shouldn't be bothered with *anything* like that right now. I'm serious. Just take care of *yourself*, Rose. Let *us* help *you*. We want you to feel safe and happy here, and in control of things. Do you know," she says, sagging again, opening the door with the jangling bells, "I think it's just when you've been around for a long time, sometimes people think you'll go on and on and on, without any complaint or exhaustion. But you do get exhausted." She looks down at her boots. "You just don't have anyone to complain to. Thank you for being so nice, Rose. I like you. I hope you like it here." She holds the door open, wide. *I've cut too close to something*, I think. *She clearly wants me to go.* "I hope you'll stay with us here in the Bar for a while. Maybe longer. We could use some fresh blood around here. And you'll see we're a special little town. We just need a lot of keeping up. It's a responsibility. But then it gives you so much that's special and unique in return." She seems to be trying to console herself. "The specialness is why we all stay on here. You have a wonderful walk." She waves, and starts to close the door, shivering against the cold. "Be careful around the river. It can get icy along the bank, even with just a little bit of snow like this."

"Ruth, is there something more I can do for you?" I know a look of struggle when I see it, and how a soul feels when it wants to speak freely but can't.

"Not really." She pulls away. "Just keep your eyes open. There's so much here that's interesting to see."

7

There's no simple map to a stranger's soul. No arrow that will point out one heart's way to another.

All I can do is look down at the map Ruth Huellet has given to me.

If you want to know what truly haunts a place, I once heard Philip Pratt say, then you must seek out what a place is, and where the pain lodges in it.

Am I a hunter now?

No. Not that. No matter what, I must be careful not to become like him. Never a cold heart only interested in finding the pain, the haunt, and not what it means, or what you might do when you find it.

I once saw him blast a ghost to ashes and insist it wasn't human suffering crying out as the soul broke, because his victim was already dead.

As though *when* you cry matters more than *why*.

The thin snow is stiffer, louder now under my shoes. The buildings around the square are gray, not brightly lit, though the hour's creeping toward midday. It's gotten colder, not warmer. The sun's face is missing behind the marble of the clouds.

No one else walks with me in the cold and stillness. I go slowly, marking on the guide what I see around me. That building, there, with the fringe of wind chimes, that was once the livery stables. And that tidy, shingled building there would be the general store, with its fresh-scrubbed windows. A muscular man works inside, I see, wiping them with a cloth. Several closed shops come next. Now here is the Berringer Inn, dressed with window boxes tilted forward under its sills. Across from it is another mansion, marked on the map as Huellet House, its gingerbread needing paint, its porch sagging, though a metal plaque marks it like a general's tomb.

The mayor's hotel is still the best-looking house in town, I decide, along with the White Bar Café. After the restaurant, at the top of the square, I pass more shuttered shops as a bit of wind whips past, tossing up fits of snow against their dangling signs.

PHOTOGRAPHY STUDIO!
GET IN COSTUME, TRAVEL THROUGH TIME,
SEE HOW YOU WOULD HAVE LOOKED IN THE
GOLD RUSH DAYS!

At the corner, another chiseled wooden announcement, with a painted direction below it.

WHITE BAR FALLS AHEAD
⟶

No one stirs on the somber road leading away from the square. The townspeople of White Bar, it seems, are staying indoors, quiet and at home, on this day of the first snow. Nothing but the fresh wind mutters as I leave the village and pass again under piney woods, laced in green and white, with cabins tucked in here and there, some shuttered, others with chimneys smoking and porches swept clean of scruff.

As a clearing opens, rimmed with gold trees and white-tipped pines, the wind skitters away into a shallow meadow filled with deeper snow and scattered leaves and limbs, as though everything loose has been tossed into it. At its edge a whitened hill rises.

The map in these gloved hands reads, *Future Home of Viewscape! Enjoy a Panorama of the High Range!*

So this must be where the summer tram was meant to rise, a chance for the living to enjoy the feeling of flight—who, when ghosts fly, call us lawless, for not keeping to the dirt we're buried under.

I follow the sound of water tumbling close at hand. *You'll come next*, I read, *to the Eno River.* A wide stream flashes between the trees, a blue-gray course jumbled with iced rocks, the largest jutting into the current, churning the surface into a white ridge that foams and tumbles down into a blue hole beneath. The falls sound strangely soft, as though the pool below them is deep and welcoming. The path ends at a fence of crossed logs and at the marker Ruth Huellet spoke of:

WHITE BAR FALLS
IN MEMORY OF FOUR BRAVE MEN WHO DIED HERE IN 1852
BRINKS, TANHEUSER, COLLUM, SMITH
IN ALL THEIR HOPES THEY PERISHED

No other prayer left above the falling water. Only the rush of the froth tumbling. I put the map away and lift my chin and say aloud to the dead:

"I stand here and honor you—Brinks, Tanheuser, Collum, and Smith. My name is Emma Rose Finnis. My soul was once laid low, like yours. I know what it means to lie at the bottom of a pit. I've been where you are. Accident is the name we give to a fate we didn't ask to meet. I know how hard it is to crawl ashore, afterward, and how few of us manage it. Take heart, if you can hear me. There is at least one here who still walks, who has the will to walk, who the hunters haven't found yet and sunk. The water hasn't taken us all. Not yet. It never will, if I can help it. I'll stay true. Though it's a lonely walk, here, by the river. Unless you'll join me?"

I wait. But no one rises.

Not all who die linger.

I turn away and look for signs of a fire. There are none. It was too long ago, certainly. The trees are fresh and young, some green with a bright moss. A tall dressed cedar to my left shakes and sways, quivering as though something heavy rests on top of it. A bit of light comes rippling through its webbed branches. The light turns into a shadow, then into spotted black pads on the ground, breaking into footsteps, feet coming for my own, as my back presses to the fence and the falls churn behind.

The shadow steps keep padding toward me.

"Who is it?" I whisper, alert. "Is it you?"

I feel no answer. Only the rising breeze.

This moving shadow. It's not the same presence as the ghost of the flowered sleeves.

The shadow doesn't burn. It hovers, it sways from side to side. It swings, circling me.

"Who are you?" I say. "I'm one of you. I'm no hunter."

My back is pressing hard into the fence, with the falls below.

"Hey!" a voice calls. "Hey there! Watch out!"

The shadow halts. Then, as silently as it climbed down from the tree, it climbs up again, and vanishes.

"Hey!" I hear a woman's voice calling out again. "Watch out, that fence behind you isn't all that strong!"

I turn, calmly—to convince the living and the dead, and myself, I wasn't frightened.

Yet even a ghost can shake.

A rusting truck with an empty bed has stopped at the edge of the road. A woman's head leans from its lowered window. Her bright, jacketed sleeve stretches out and waves to me.

"That log fence! Behind you!"

I move away from it.

The door of the truck opens. The woman leaps down from it, her black hair swinging to one side—long and straight locks. The way mine once hung.

"Whoa, you had me worried there for a minute," she calls, her words clear as a chime. "Seemed like you weren't exactly aware of what you were doing. You okay? You look okay. Hi. I'm Su Kwon. I live in town. You must be Rose."

The living person standing in front of me is tall and sharp-boned. Her smiling face is friendly, even with that bit of a frown in it. Around her is a dashing scarf, woven around her neck.

I say, "I was just startled. I didn't expect anyone."

"Didn't mean to sneak up on you. Martha told me you were staying in town and Ruth said you were out and about and I should keep an eye out for you. Not that I'm stalking you or anything!" She makes another friendly grimace while pulling her thick gloves tighter on her long fingers. "I'm just out on my rounds. Saw you between the trees, and wanted to be sure you were okay. Because I heard, I know about—listen, people talk here, you might as well know. It's a small town, so you have to get used to that, and people finding out that . . . that, well, you've had a rough time, recently, Rose. I just wanted to be sure you weren't, you know, contemplating anything rash, or feeling *too* sorry for yourself?"

No. A ghost only feels sorry for herself till she remembers there are others who should feel sorrier still. *Are you there, ghost?*

"Am I being too forward?" she asks when I don't answer. "Sorry. You stay up here long enough, you sort of forget all the protocols of the rest of the world." She smiles, her teeth very white. "Sometimes I even start talking to myself, out loud, and don't even know it. You're feeling all right, though, I can see that now. Good! I guess you must have walked over here from Ruth's. Doing the walking tour? I can give you a ride back if you like. My pickup is warm. Or warm-ish, anyways."

I look back toward the shadowy, swaying cedar. No name, yet, for what crawled out of it and stalked me. Though its shadow might still be watching. Able to give us both away.

"A ride would be wonderful, Miss Kwon. And it's so nice to meet you." I smile brightly back at her, as I've smiled at others I've ridden with. "I'm just out today learning about White Bar."

"Cool. You can call me Su. And I'll bet you're looking for more than what's on that map, am I right? Yeah, it's pretty bare-bones. Come on. I can give you more of the real lowdown. Oops, my truck here is a bit of a mess." She opens the door and slides papers and scraps of metal from the wagon seat so I can climb aboard.

I glance back to see if we're being followed.

"I'm a bit of a scavenger," she says. "A hoarder, really. I was about to hit Miner's Basin when I saw you. That was the meadow you passed on the way in. I've been digging out"—she starts the rasping engine—"all the scrap left there from the screwed-up tram-build. I'm a metal artist." She jerks the wheel. "I have a gallery on the square. The one with all the chimes out front."

We seem to be alone now. For the time being.

"Yes, I've heard them," I say.

"They're mostly for the tourist trade. Inside, and in my studio, is my large-scale work. Lots of inspiration around here for starting fresh, for thinking big." She nods at me, encouragingly. "The Bar is small, but the mountains aren't. Lots of material here for reinventing what's been broken. Rock, old glass, copper, metal. In fact, you mind if I still stop for just a minute at the Basin? It's what I was on my way to do when I saw you. I've had my eye on a scrap of steel buried over there. And honestly, your timing is perfect. I could use the help—the piece is too long and unwieldy for me to carry by myself. Now you're here, do you mind giving me a hand and getting it into the truck bed? If you can stand a few more minutes of cold?"

If this Su Kwon digs for buried things, well, perhaps she might be useful to me.

"Of course," I say.

"Great. We call this Miner's Basin because"—she stops at the clearing filled with snow and branches—"it was where a lot of the prospectors used to camp, back in the day. Sometimes we just call it the Basin. Or the Meadow. Right now, it's a sort of boondoggle. A failed experiment, you could say. This was the spot where they were going to put in the lift. The town had an investor all lined up, and the investor called in a contractor, but turns out the ground is a mess and the contractor didn't ameliorate the site and one of the workers fell into a hole and nearly died, so then the investor goes bankrupt, and presto, we're left with all the cleanup. I told the town council I'd be happy to haul the metal away, and use it—so that's what I've been doing since the summer. I'm just getting to some of the good stuff now. You be careful." She opens the door again. "Those shoes you have on look like they belong to someone working in a nice office building."

"It's salvage you're doing?" I say as I get out. I remember what Martha said. *We save things here.*

"Yep. Exactly. Okay, just step where I step, keep your shoes more or less dry."

In the wake of living footprints I tread now, on the light snow. I match Su Kwon, step for step, to the center of the scrap-cluttered meadow. And for a moment I feel more alive than dead, because I don't walk alone, among shadows.

She stops at what looks like a buried fin. Then lifts out the end of a long gleaming sawblade, tugging it from its white drift.

"This was going to be some kind of metal stripping in the wheel-house. If you could grab onto this end"—she hands the blade's smooth edge to me—"I'll go to the other end and dig it out. It'll be heavy and wobbly. But I think together we can get it to my truck. Ready?"

I am. We lift and carry it like a body. I step carefully, leading the way to the road.

"Rose, you're stronger than you look! Swing it around, will you, so I can drop the tailgate down. Okay. Now we coil it in as best we can. There! Perfect."

She steps back and takes a deep breath, licking her lips. How easily the living take in the world, in that way, taste it, blow it out, and then breathe it in again. And they don't even think about the luck of having life's bright candle in your chest, lit over and over again.

"What are you thinking?" She tilts her head at me and swings her hair back. "You're looking serious."

"I was thinking, if I'm strong, it must be because of where I've come from."

"You're Irish, Martha told me. I wouldn't have guessed it from your coloring."

"Irish American."

"Cool. Let's get back in the truck before our noses freeze off."

We do, and as she sits back she says, "My family's Korean American. With all the trimmings. Hard workers. Family comes first. Succeed or die trying."

"Same here." We died trying. We Finnises.

"But I'm a serious disappointment to my elders." She shrugs and stares out the windshield. "You?"

I don't know and never will. "My mother died bringing me into this world," I say. "All my brothers died as babies. My father died when I was young. I was alone after that, except for the work I had to go out and do, housekeeping. I was sixteen."

Her sharp face turns sad and kind. "That's awful, Rose. You had to work to support yourself when you were that young? I'm so sorry to hear that. I don't know if it helps you at all to hear this," she says, turning her wheel, "but hard stories aren't uncommon around here. Broken hearts. Disasters. Failures. Rebellions. Just so you're aware, you've come to a place that's beautiful and peaceful, but it's mostly because the people who live here didn't find peace anywhere else. They've come here and built it. Or rebuilt it. Look around. See all the pines?" I've been watching them for shadows, yes. "They look old, but they aren't. None of this is old-growth. Everything here, except the buildings on the square, has been cut down and built up again. Controlled, reshaped. I like that. I bend metal for a living, so I feel right at home. But some people are surprised when they come here. They think everything around here is original. It isn't; how could it be? I'll take you down some of our back lanes and show you what I mean."

She takes me past modern cabins hidden from the road, with slate porches and slanted metal roofs. "Waiting for newcomers, like me. I've been here just a little less than a year. The Berringers and Ruth are old stock, but the rest of us are all outsiders. But what's wonderful is, the

Bar totally welcomes that. If the fit is good, I mean." She looks to the right. "Those are all empty houses. Some people have moved out. The Bar doesn't have easy access to medical care. And you have to like the solitude when the tourists leave. On the upside, if you become a citizen of the Bar you're greeted with open arms and have dozens of friends overnight. I've never felt more at home—and I'm a weird arty chick escaped from Silicon Valley. And look at Martha. Not from here at all, but now she's mayor, and everyone loves and trusts her. I guess what I'm saying is, sometimes you find treasure just lying on the ground, you know? I want you to know you can feel good about where you've landed, Rose. No matter what's happened to you in the past."

So anxious all the good people of White Bar are for a new body to join their village . . . while they have shapes unseen walking among them.

"I do wonder, Su," I say smoothly, "what it might be like to stay here. I don't mind lonely places, myself. But old ones do have their quirks." I pretend to shiver, and go on. "Ghosts, for example. They're all gone from the cities, they say, but I hear they still linger in the countryside." It's why I've been traveling through it, since I left the coast. "They can be so frightening. I hope these woods are clean."

"They *totally* are. We have no trouble here at all. And I don't think ghosts are what we need to be afraid of, in any case. I think what we need to be afraid of is not being attended to, Rose. Of not being listened to and heard and accepted as we are."

"What?" I ask, surprised.

"Well, if you want to know, I could tell you a *real* ghost story."

But . . . aren't all our stories real?

When she was a girl, this Su Kwon tells me, she lived with her family in a large, airy house, and with them, in the traditional way, lived a bachelor uncle, her mother's brother, named Uncle Bao. He was a loving and patient man, the perfect relative, and a perfect guest, though he had one fear: tight spaces.

"Claustrophobic," she explains as she slows her truck through an icy ditch. "Ever since he was a kid. But it got worse when he was diagnosed with his heart condition. Our uncle got to where he was absolutely terrified of being smothered. He told us, if he died, to be sure not to let anyone cover up his face with a sheet. He said he couldn't bear the thought of it. We all knew that about Uncle Bao. Never let him feel suffocated. Then one year he went into the hospital for heart surgery, and he was perfectly fine afterwards when we came to visit him, but then when we came back, later in the day, he had a sheet over his face. We all wailed. We were so horrified. We had failed him. The hospital had failed him. Everything had failed him."

The morning after the funeral, her family awoke and found every knife from the kitchen cupboard laid out on the dining room table. Her mother tried putting the knives away. The next day, they came back. Her father tried throwing them away. Again they returned. They tried throwing them in the bay. Again they returned.

"Everyone said we needed to hire a cleaner. They said we had no choice, Uncle had become a ghost, and he had to be put down. But my mother kept insisting, no. She said Bao didn't deserve to be treated like a mad dog, that that isn't what we do in our tradition. So she volunteered to stay up all night in the dining room to see if she could speak with him. The rest of my family were afraid, but agreed. We were all supposed to go to our rooms that night, stay asleep, stay away. But me? I didn't. I crept out and crouched in the hallway. I saw my mother sitting in the dining room in a chair flat against the wall. There was only this one light on, hanging over the dinner table. She stayed still. Waiting. Nothing happened. Nothing happened for so long, I finally fell asleep on the hallway rug. I only woke when I heard a tinkling sound. The knives were all out on the tablecloth. And I could hear someone sobbing.

"My mother, she's a small person, but tough. She wasn't the one crying. She was staring at the knives. All the blades were pointing not at her, but away from her. I saw her look down at the hem of the tablecloth. It was shivering, trembling near the floor. She told me later on she didn't know how she knew what she had to do. She just got up, walked over to that table, faced the knife handles, picked up the biggest, sharpest blade, bent down, and slid it under the cloth at the floor. Something took it from her, and she ran back to her chair. I rushed over to her, afraid. She held me, both of us shaking. Then we saw the tip of the knife. Slicing right up the side of the tablecloth. Cutting it."

Two hands appeared, and parted the ripped fabric. A bald head came through. Then Uncle Bao's body. Still wearing his gray hospital gown. The half-naked man blinked, then stood, then bowed to where the two of them were sitting. Then he turned his naked back on them and climbed onto the dining table, reaching for the hanging lamp above it, pulling himself up, feet first, until he walked upside down on the ceiling, and disappeared through a grate.

"Everyone told us he'd haunt the attic next—but nope. Uncle Bao never did. The next night everything was calm. We never saw Uncle again. He was at peace. My mother says that the *gwisin*—our word for ghosts—are just like anyone else. We all need to be attended to, and respected. It would have been the most terrible thing in the world to call a cleaner in, my mother believed, and I agree. God knows we have plenty of things to be afraid of and worried about these days"—she looks up at the gray sky through her window—"but souls wanting peace and happiness? Who are just like us? They aren't one of them. I've always thought we should leave our fears for better—or rather worse—things."

I turn to stare at this long-haired woman driving beside me—for I've never seen her like in all my days. I've never, not once, heard such words uttered by a living human being.

"A wonder," I say, in a whisper.

She laughs. "Glad you're not shocked. I wasn't trying to shock you. I'm just trying to explain what I mean. About honoring what people need. Everyone wants peace. Why make a crime out of it?"

"But not everyone," I say quickly, to correct her. The living aren't all the same. Not all want only peace and rest. So why would all the dead?

She slows the truck, turning to look at me, interested. We come to a stop in an alley behind the square.

"You don't think we're all Uncle Bao, in the end?" she asks.

"Some are, maybe. Others, no. Maybe some want the farthest thing from rest."

"And what would be the farthest thing from rest, do you think?"

Adventure, I tell her. Love. Whatever you were denied in life. Justice. Freedom.

"Adventure. Freedom." She nods, and her thin brows pull together. "I wonder if you're right." She goes on looking at me, weighing, then breaks into a wide, happy smile. "Rose! You are so cool! We need to have more time to talk. I have to get back to my studio and get to work—but let's make some time to get to know each other better, when you can? Right now, I want you to tell me where you want to go. Don't worry about the metal in the back, you've helped enough, I'll get Bill or Harold to finish the job. Let me get you oriented real quick now we're back in town." She points out the window. "That up there on the right is the back entrance to my gallery, next to the back door to Harold's General Store. Across the alley is my workshop—that barn door. You can come on over and knock whenever you want to find me. Right now, I can take you to where the rest of the tour is, if you want. Up from Ruth's museum it's a nice walk to what we call the Knob, near the bridge, if you think you can do it in those shoes. We need to talk to Harold about getting you some better ones. Or I could take you back over to Martha's place. What's your mood? Where to?"

My mood is still wonder, but I ask, "What's the Knob?"

"Where the schoolhouse is. The second historic one in town. The first one burned down."

I open the door quickly. "I'll go there."

"Wait, I could drive you up."

"No, thank you," I say, forgetting everything else but this: *I burn. I burn.*

"I hope all my talking didn't wear you out." Su Kwon bends anxiously. "I know I can be a bit of a gabber."

"Not at all." *I burn.*

"I'm here if you need anything, okay? Just let me know. I mean it." She waves as I leave the alley. I soon lose sight of her.

I hurry past the barred and closed Jailhouse Museum. I hurry away from the empty white square. All seems more still now, after her chattering. And lonelier, too.

Best keep your thoughts, Emma Rose, I tell myself, *on the ones that matter. You're not here to jaw with the living.*

I climb, hurrying, hurrying—I won't slow, I don't tire, I never tire, even if sometimes I feel every inch of this skin, tight against me—keeping my eye on the building that when I first came I took for a church.

When a wrong thought comes to you, you change it.

8

I take the map again from my pocket, the pocket of the mayor's coat, to read:

Your tour of White Bar comes to an end as you walk up for a view from Schoolhouse Knob. Named for the one-room school that still stands above town, its viewpoint will reward you with a panorama of the High Sierras, the Eno River Valley, and a glimpse into a nearly forgotten aspect of Gold Rush life. The White Bar Schoolhouse was built in 1852. It was in continuous use until the start of the Great Depression. Though children were rare in the mining camps of the late 1840s, by the 1850s families were beginning to settle in the region. Walk the yard and imagine the voices of children and adults ringing out in play. Though the schoolroom is closed to visitors to preserve its artifacts for future generations, feel free to look through the antique-paned windows, where you'll see the teacher's and pupils' desks, the pegged, wide-planked floor, and the potbellied stove necessary for warmth during the harsh winters. Thank you for visiting Historic White Bar, where we welcome you with a Heart of Gold!

I reach the peeling white clapboard at last. The door to the steepled building is chained and locked, but through tall, rippled-glass windows, rimed with cold, I see into a room and a past as familiar to me as if I've traveled so far only to land right where I began.

It's much the same one-room schoolhouse as the one where long ago I was put in a corner and made to count to five hundred. Plank walls. Seats hard as nails. Sloping desks, each desk nailed to the seat in front of it. The American flag tasseled in one corner. An hourglass on a bench to mark the time. I had to leave school each day at noon and carry lunch pails from the boardinghouses to the lumberjacks cutting down trees. Yet I made sure to do all the lessons I missed, my father's voice ringing in my ears: *Never let anyone tell you we Irish are poor and uneducated, Emma Rose. It's a thousand years of blood and knowledge we've got running through our veins, and it's all come with us here to America, as much as our backs and necks have, and you must always remember and know that. You'll always remember and know that, now, won't you?*

After he died, it was no more school for me, and no more learning about mountains, or how to write in a fair hand, or how to be more than a scullery maid.

But after I died and rose again I became more than I was. I've learned a thousand things in many thousands of days. A ghost has ages to study the world, a chance to teach herself whatever it is she needs to know. I'm no longer just a poor girl who scrubbed floors. Philip Pratt doesn't believe a ghost can grow wiser. Yet I have, so that I know, for instance, that I'm looking into a room only pretending to be empty. Its faded books might be shelved, its black stove dark and cold, that finger of white chalk sitting motionless beside its slate. But the light in this room doesn't fall the way it should, so late in the afternoon, from these tall windows. It wavers, slithering across the wooden floor like a river slipping from its banks.

The flickering, waving light climbs the desk with the slate. The blank tablet rocks a little, as though the wind were shivering it—though there can be no wind inside a locked room.

"Who's there?" I ask from the window. "What do you want me to see? Should I come in?"

A soul is always learning what she can and can't do. This body that lets me touch and walk the world—it can't easily fly, and it can't slip through a keyhole, as my bare soul can. But my soul is strong. I look down the road. No one's coming from town. I circle to the back of the schoolhouse, where a grove of pines has grown up next to it. What I must do is push the root of my will against the earth, loosing myself from the ground, lifting this cold body with me. It feels like carrying the weight of shoulders on my shoulders. On the roof, I can relax again, keeping low on these hands and knees, bellying my way to the short steeple. It's an empty belfry, with a trapdoor unlocked. I suppose White Bar never imagined a visitor might invite herself in this way.

I'm careful to drop where the pegged floor is empty in front of the iron stove. A little puff of dust whirls under these shoes and this coat. The stovepipe at my side is cold to the touch. The pupils' seats are dusty. On the chalkboard behind the teacher's platform, the letters of the alphabet curl, *A, B, C.* I move, carefully, careful now, to the back of the classroom, where the schoolchild's slate still trembles on the last row, on a desk worn and scratched.

On it, written in chalk, in blockish letters, there is now a single, vibrating word.

Broken.

I nod. "Something has broken."

The desk shakes underneath it.

My soul shakes, too. We're speaking at last. Across time, fear, danger. It's no easy thing, to meet where you aren't supposed to.

"Will you show me more? I'm as dead as you. You can trust me."
And with that, I'm shown.

The sun turns high and bright and hot, coming in through the windows. The desks are filled with living children. Nine squirming bodies. The girls' hair is short and bobbed, the boys' parted in the center and greased.

On the platform, at a wiped chalkboard, a teacher stands. She wears wire spectacles. Her hair is short and pin-curled, her dark dress falling just below the knees.

But there are more in the room. Not like the others. Fewer. Not nine. Six.

The nine living children sitting in their seats raise their hands and call out excited answers to their teacher's queries. The ghostly children stand beside them, dead and pale, and say not a word. Their collars are limp. Their faces unsmiling. Their eyes, unblinking, stare forward. Their hair is roughly cut, long or braided. The girls' dresses are long-sleeved gray sheaths of dotted or flowered calico. The dead boys wear rough gray pants and short-seamed coats.

They stare at the head of the classroom, where, too, a ghostly schoolmaster stands, in his frayed black coat over a frayed collar. His hair is tucked behind his ears. His string tie twists at his long neck. Wordlessly, he glares at the standing children, his eyes fixed on them. A mesmerizing gaze.

The oldest pupils are at the back, as they were in my day. The last one standing is a tall girl in flowered calico. Her dress is ruched at the wrists. Her hair is russet brown, too thick for the childish braids she wears. She stares in front of her, her ghostly face like stone.

The ghost of the flowered sleeves.

I feel my face light, my soul soar. We've done it. We've found each other.

She shows no answering light. She's frozen. In torment. She and her fellow spirits are so much older than the children they hover beside. Older, even, than I am, their clumsy boots laced high, their shirt buttons made of wood, their hair tied with twine. For how long, I wonder, has this schoolhouse been haunted?

The girl turns to look at me. Her eyes burning.

I feel you, I burn back at her. *I see you. What happened to you?*

She turns and stares, accusing, at the teacher.

I reach out toward her, but at a noise the vision she's made for me crumbles.

I swear like a lumberjack. *Shite.* What's happened? I look out the schoolhouse windows. Someone is coming up the Knob.

We, I, can't be found in this locked room. There's nothing for it but to go up and out again. I will this small body free from earth's pull and strain up through the trapdoor, keeping low on the roof again, and edge down the back of the schoolhouse, coming to rest on the snow, walking out just in time to meet a heavy-booted man tramping over the icy schoolyard, carrying something in his arms.

"There you are, Rose!" He waves as though he knows me and I should know him. "Thought I saw you a while ago heading up here. I'm Harold Dubois, from the General Store? Su alerted me you had some immediate needs. I've got"—he holds out a pair of boots made of stiff, black rubber—"something I think you're after." His bright eyes over his stubbled chin look down at me, kindly. "You really can't go around in flimsy flats, you know, especially this time of year. You'll slip and crack your head on a rock. If you don't lose your toes first."

Harold. From the General Store. I nod, still cursing inside. I don't *need* any more kindness from the living. Why must everyone come when they're not wanted? Su Kwon sent him, and now he's here to find me, and so I must smile sweetly, I suppose, in thanks. In the slanted light, I see he's the muscled man who was busy earlier cleaning his store windows. Harold Dubois wears a knit cap, and under his stubble his neck is deeply tanned, like a man who's been to sea.

"Mr. Dubois, thank you, you're so kind."

He grins, pleased. "Sure thing! Want to see if they fit? Come on over to the stoop here, try them on. They're overshoes. They'll do for now till we can get you something more suited."

I take the rubber in my hands. It feels heavy, plodding. It'll weigh me down even more.

"And don't you worry about the price, now." He stands beside the stoop, leaning over me. "We can't have a guest like you wandering around and hurting yourself. You've been through enough already. Or so I hear." His dark neck flushes, embarrassed. "Anyway. You just slip 'em over what you got on now. That's how these work. Then later, like I say, we can get you some proper things."

He's so eager. Like all of them.

He looks away as I dress my feet. He brushes a bit of snow from the chain on the locked door, craning his head up toward the steeple, then down at the ground.

"Good on your feet?"

"Like they're my own," I say.

"Sized right, then. Good. Now you can make your way safely down the hill. Coming up the Knob is one thing, see, but going down is another. It can be awkward." He scratches under his cap. "You need good tread, especially this late in the day. You always have to be more careful when the melt re-freezes. That's when people get hurt." He backs away from the stoop as I stand up from it, patiently. "Did you have enough time to peek into our schoolhouse, Rose? Isn't she a peach? Needs a bit of paint, maybe a few fresh shingles. Other than that, she's shipshape. Ruth handles the inside, me and Bill take care of the exterior. Come spring, she'll get a fresh coat."

You don't know, I think, *what's still fresh inside.*

He coughs when I say nothing. "Well, we should probably be getting going. Gets dark here quicker than you might think. And it's getting colder, isn't it? We really do need to get you something better than Martha's last year's coat." He holds out his hand, like a gentleman clearing the way for me.

I turn back once to look at the schoolhouse. Its tall frosted windows are blank. They glint like empty mirrors. I know better. *I've seen you,* I think, nodding. *I'll be back.*

He leads the way down the hill. "It really is a view from up here, isn't it, Rose? You get the best sense of the layout of the valley." He breathes in, a deep, happy suck. "I always like to imagine how it looked when we were a camp. All the miners' tents and cabins, and the wooden buildings all new. Of course, that part of our history died out and we went into a terrible slump for a long time, until the 1970s, when the gold rush became interesting to people again. Then things picked up. Sometimes you have to go through a low period"—he looks at me confidingly—"to lead you to a better place. But I guess I'm not telling you anything you don't already know."

"I'd say I learn more every minute I'm here, Mr. Dubois."

He smiles and adds, encouraged, "The prospectors even had a saying for it: 'Sweet are the uses of adversity.'"

Spoken like a man who never drowned.

"I'm from the city," he says all at once, as though remembering it. "After I got out of the marines I worked as a trucker. I had the same route, year after year, from Oakland to Tahoe and back. Day in, day out. Five hours up, five hours down. Delivering toilet supplies to the hotels

69

and casinos. 'Sweet are the uses of adversity'? It was killing me, honestly. Nobody tells you how some work, it takes every last bit of joy out of you until you end up feeling like . . . like nothing. Like there's no meaning to you, like you're just some insignificant metal ball being rolled back and forth on a board someone else is tipping. I hope you don't know and will never know what that feels like, young as you are." He stares straight ahead of him, pained.

"I'm sorry," I say, and mean it. Sometimes being dead makes me short-tempered, I know.

"Thanks." He scratches under his cap again. "But then it got worse. My wife, she died of cancer. And"—he clears his throat, looking down toward the lit square—"and, and I just, I couldn't take it, you know. One day it got so bad I drove off my route, I don't know what I thought I was going to do, I think maybe I was just going to crash all the toilet paper into a lake and drown myself . . . And then, lo and behold, I see this sign, for a place called White Bar. I can't explain it. I just knew I had to come here. The words sounded so high, so clean. And I pulled in, and it was like, I don't know, like this storybook America. You know, the Old Wild West, like it used to be? Where in other places, you can't even see it anymore, because it's either gone or else it's like some theme park with casinos and fast food. Here, you look out, and most of the old buildings are still the way they were. I came back as soon as I could, without my truck, and everyone here was so warm and welcoming, and they heard my story, and it turned out the couple who owned the General Store were retiring and moving to Palm Springs, so I took a chance, I emptied everything out of my retirement savings and I moved to the Bar and I never looked back. And you must be thinking, why is he telling me all this? It's because there's *meaning* here. There's purpose. I don't know if anyone's talked to you about that yet, if you've felt it yet. But there's something unique here. And the longer you're here, the more you realize it."

He stops now that we've reached the edge of the square and looks at me as though he very much wants to help. "When something is beautiful"—his skin flushes again—"it's worth protecting. And you don't even have to have big bucks to make your stake here, Rose. We need all kinds of help to make the Bar a go. You've met Bill? He's a cook, he works for the mayor. He's a great guy. Other folks have businesses, or work for people who do. It's such a peaceful way of life. And the longer you're here, the more you become a part of it. I guess that's how it is in other places, too, but in the Bar, it really *feels* like something. We feel like we're all in something together. Committed to keeping this little slice of heaven going. I guess I'm just trying to tell you it's a good place adversity has brought you to, just like me."

"And do you tell everyone this, Mr. Dubois?"

What I mean is: does the Bar always shoe strangers, unasked?

"Call me Harry, please. Oops! Sorry. My phone is buzzing."

He taps his device. He reads it. His steaming breath hitches.

"It's a message. From Martha." He blinks down. "Something's happened in the museum." He wheels to face in the direction of the jail, and slips a little on the ice.

He's surprised when I steady him with a gloved hand. But I don't like to see anyone fall.

"We have to go," he says. "Quick."

Behind the iron door, Martha, pale-faced, is sitting on the floor. Ruth Huellet's head rests on her lap, her soft cheeks stiff, her hair finely threaded with blood. Her blue eyes stare wide.

"Jesus." Harold drops to his knees. "Ruth! Ruthie! What's happened to her?"

"I don't know," Martha bends over her, rocking.

71

I know, I think. *I know that look.*

I'm brushed to one side as others come hurrying in—Bill, and others unknown to me.

"Came as fast as I could," Bill pants. "Have you called the ambulance from Dutch Gap?"

The mayor's voice is tear-filled as she holds Ruth's round head. "They're on their way. Thirty minutes they said. That was ten minutes ago. The roads are bad."

"But what happened?"

"I was calling Ruthie to check on Ro—" Martha glances up at me, then away again. "I called and she didn't answer, and I called again and again, and you *know* she always answers. I knew something had to be wrong."

"Is she breathing?" a woman hovering nearby calls out, afraid.

"Yes. There's that."

A man cries, "I wonder if it's a stroke! It could be a stroke!"

Mary Berringer comes next through the door, her elderly, white face puckered. John Berringer comes behind her. The small museum is filling now with people, pressed against the cases. I move deeper into the back, toward the old jail cell, a good place to call out from, without being noticed, "She needs a blanket!"

There is such a coldness, I know, as you draw near death. You feel it, your soul struggling to keep hold of the stiff glove of your hand.

Bill pulls an old saddle blanket from the pile beside him and tucks it carefully around Ruth's sides.

"Listen to me," he whispers to her, "you're going to be all right, Ruthie."

"Maybe she fell." Harold Dubois crouches and whispers, too. "There's blood on the back of her head. She could have fallen, hurt herself. Or maybe the stroke came, and she fell. I don't know, I don't know."

If I were close, I'd say to Ruth Huellet, *Hold fast, hold fast, now. Hold on to living, as long as you can, for death will tug hard at your feet. Fight. Try.*

"Where's the goddamn ambulance?" a man shouts. "It should be here by now!"

I watch them all, the tense citizens of White Bar. They're afraid, clutching each other in their coats and mufflers. All around them, the museum's cases and pictures glisten like a hall of twisted mirrors. In the glare, I see what the others don't. In the corner, by the case with the Indian arrowheads inside it, a box has tumbled to the floor, with papers spilling out of it. Just above it, on the edge of the glass, is a dark streak of blood.

"The ambulance! Listen! It's coming!"

Martha holds Ruth tighter and says, "You're going to be all right, Ruthie, you hear me?" She turns to the men. "Now. You. Bill. Harry. You listen to me. I'll be the one to follow Ruth. I'll take my truck. You all watch over the hotel, please, and . . . our guest. All right, they're here. Make room, get out of the way, they're coming."

The men in hooded jackets arrive, carrying with them a bright orange gurney. They set its shell on the crowded floor and tell everyone to please step back, go outside. All hasten out into the dusk but for Martha, who keeps close, and Bill, who's backed into the jail cell with me.

He looks as if he needs some comfort. I remember how he stared at me, that first day, so hopefully in the café. With his lonely eyes.

"It'll be all right, Bill," I say, though I can't say it's true.

"She's breathing, right? She's not paralyzed that way. She's going to be all right."

She might be. Then again, you might fight as hard as you can, kicking against the waves, and still be dragged down to the bottom.

"Bill," I say to be kind—for what else is there to do? Pain is the same, pain is all the same, in every place and time—"Why don't you tell Ruth's friends you're going to the café to make some coffee for them? That could be a good thing."

"I could do that!"

The men in jackets have bound Ruth's head with a tight strap and buckled more across her body. They lift and carry her out now through the iron door. The mayor follows close behind. Bill goes along with her, saying, "I'm going to get everyone to the café, Martha. We have coffee and rolls, and we'll all wait together there."

"Do that. And I'll call with news as soon as I know."

When he turns, I've already flown up into the rafters and into a dark cobwebbed eave. To wait and watch and learn more. Because I know that look on Ruth Huellet's disappearing face. I know what felled her.

She saw a ghost.

9

When I was a little girl, I was afraid of the dead. Not only of the ghosts that hid under my bed; I heard the howls in the waves at night. My father tried to tell me, *Emma Rose, those aren't the cries of the dead. Those are only the ships creaking at anchor beyond the shoals. Or the creatures of the deep breaching and calling to each other in their own language. It might be the straining of the horns at the lighthouse.*

He said all this to comfort me. And I listened. And believed not a word. For I knew with a child's certainty there were movements that circled and watched me. Sometimes they crawled into the bed of my ear, sometimes only tugged at the blanket of air above me. I was afraid, because I knew some souls could sometimes slip that blanket, and appear.

It's only when you become what you fear that you hover in the rafters and understand how hard it is to balance between light and dark.

"Rose?"

Bill has come back into the jailhouse looking for me. He searches every corner. All the others have gone out under the square's hooded lamps.

He turns this way and that, but doesn't think to look up to where I hide. Why should he?

Harold hurries in. "Bill. The ambulance and Martha are gone. What are you doing?"

"I was just looking for Rose. I thought she was in here."

"She's probably gone back to the hotel."

"I just hope all this hasn't put her off."

"She seems steady enough. A good girl, in a pinch."

"But tonight wasn't pretty, Harry."

"No, it wasn't."

"Shouldn't we go and look for her?"

"No." The old marine shakes his knit cap underneath me. "We don't want to hound her. Let's give her some space. We need to take a breath, all of us, and focus on Ruthie, first. Come on, old friend." He squeezes Bill's shoulder. "You said you were going to open up the café. And we need to phone anyone who hasn't heard yet what's happened."

"Harry," Bill asks as they go, "did you see poor Ruth's eyes?"

"Pitiful. I know."

"She won't die, though."

"That's right. We won't let her. Besides, there're so few of us left. She'll know to fight and pull through, you watch. Let's go take care of the others."

They turn off the lights. The museum falls dim, but not dark. I uncurl these feet from the beam and let them hang down, like a child's. I'm perched just above the spot of drying blood on the glass case filled with Indian arrowheads. Below me lies the tumbled box with papers spilling out of it. *Every time someone leaves the Bar*, Ruth had said, *they dump all their old stuff on me.* I leap down and bend over it.

She would have been holding this in her hands, I imagine, when something frightened her to the bone.

I sit on the floor, feeling the hardness of it. In the gloomy light, there's a note spilled out of the box, handwritten.

Ruthie,
I guess you've heard by now we're shutting down the photo shop. We're putting it on the market in the spring. We just want a different life now, is all. Here's something for you before we go. We were getting things ready ahead of the sale and pulled up a rotted floorboard and found all these underneath. Must be from the original place, when it was the undertaker's. You'll see it's important. Part of the history and the duty. The Bar will want to know and have it. We'll be off. Take care of yourself. We'll miss you. We keep the faith. Always.

No signature—as if the writer and Ruth knew each other well, so none was needed. Underneath the note, a collection of spotted yellow sheets, thinner, older. The first sheet, in a faded brown hand, reads:

Wood planks, forty
Nails, two hundred
Ten yards velvet
Spirits of alcohol
Ten yards black ribbon
Oil of lavender
Pomade, two tins
Tortoiseshell brush and comb
Needles and thread
Signed in receipt, D. L. Kiersten

I know such a list. It's everything you'd need to bury a body. Below this, another sheet, of the same age and in the same hand:

Attached a letter found among the possessions of and in the hand belonging to Landon Albert Longhurst, the deceased. Likely meant to be posted in the last year but never was. No address to post to deceased's family. Keep for reference.

Then in a different, steeply slanted hand.

September 5, 1852
Sierra Nevada, California
Dearest Sister,
It's been many months since I last wrote, I know. Be assured I'm alive and well, and convey the news to Mother and Father. I'm happy to inform you all of my situation here. I've been for some months now the owner of a modestly paying claim in a place called Eno. I've recovered from the hardships of my first efforts at mining, and have settled for the moment in one of the more northerly camps. Much has changed in the two years since we last saw each other. Father's penchant for calling me ungrateful notwithstanding, I can say I'm truly thankful I came West. You will know better than anyone it would never have suited me to take over his school—not with the Rush on and all its chances for success and adventure. You would be amazed by this place, Beth. It's half wild and half civilized, hotels being thrown up overnight along with billiard halls and prospectors' shanties (including my own) and even a few genteel, two-story manses that wouldn't seem out of place in the most staid town in Connecticut. Men from all corners of the world are here, tramping in the mud, from Boston lawyers and English mill hands to French and Spanish farmers and shopkeepers; all of us picking and blasting and swearing at rock, chasing the thinnest vein. Lately there are also a few families that

have come to town which might add something in the way of better manners. We have a canvas church now, a stone jail, and a schoolhouse being cobbled together in a meadow. As it happens, it is regarding the latter improvement that I write, for it seems after much correspondence and waiting, a schoolmistress hired by mail has failed to arrive, and since there has been no sign of her, though half a dozen pupils are waiting, and with my claim of late paying only fitfully, I went and made myself known to the informal leaders of the camp, a pair of Wisconsin physicians (brothers), offering myself for the position. I must have performed my mental gymnastics well enough because I am now appointed the first schoolmaster of Eno, which means a regular salary, lodgings attached to the post office, and the task of doing something with the backward children of the town. I am writing to convey my address to you, which I'll append below, and also, please request Father to send my books to me forthwith so that I may no no no no no no no <u>NO NO NO NO NO NO NO NO NO NO NO NO NO NO NO NO</u>

The strange, lanky ink turns wild, blotched, flinging across the sheet.

NO and a thousand more times NO. I'll never send a word of this goddamned letter. I'll never come a-pleading to that man, writing him by hiding behind Beth. Let him think I've died. I'll answer his cruelty with . . . nothing. I've crossed an entire continent with the nothing he gave me; let him see how he likes the taste of it. I'll say nothing about crossing mountains and desert, the thrill and the thirst, the exhaustion, then the dysentery, the graves of the dead lining the trail, the first joyful glimpse of California, the mad-eyed men already there, the busy whores, the rush of finding my first nugget, the despair as the vein played out, the toughening of the body, the hardening of the soul. Because if this isn't going to be a letter, but a confession, well, then let it be an honest one, at least, some scribble that records: I escaped from a man who beat me into submission all my life, or who tried to. But whose are the stronger fists now? Let that be a lesson to the students I'll soon have. A lesson to all!

The maddened scribble had been ended, in some former time, with a gash of ink.

I fold the sheets back into the shoebox. I close it, carefully.

Philip Pratt says names call out ghosts.

Landon Albert Longhurst, I think, but don't say.

Someone might be watching.

I stand, slowly, where Ruth Huellet must have stood before she was cut down. She must have been reading, just here, and perhaps read the letter aloud, not knowing that she might be recalling a ghost's life and hatreds to him, and calling it down on her own head.

I don't ask the air: *Are you still here?*

Better to act as though I'm sober and sad.

I nod toward the letter, as though I understand it. Then I leave it where I found it, turning away, as if sadly, taking a book from the museum's shelves and clasping it to me, as though for comfort.

"Such terrible history in this place," I whisper.

Though the girl with flowered sleeves had not looked with sadness at her schoolmaster. Her eyes had blazed at him. Accusing.

I feel my eyes burn, too.

I know what it means when a man asks whose fists are stronger.

10

What strange colors snow turns to under lamplight. Mealy grays, like unwashed laundry.

It's now nightfall, and across the square the citizens of White Bar have gathered with Bill at the café to wait for news about Ruth. At the windows, he hurries back and forth. I see him darting between the tables, his face anxious.

I cross to the mayor's hotel and find Su Kwon sitting behind Martha's desk under the rose-pink lamps.

"Rose!" She leaps up. "There you are! I'm so glad to see you! We were all getting worried, with it so cold out. Are you all right? I know you saw poor Ruth. Bill said you were there."

"I didn't mean to worry anyone." I haven't been thinking of them at all, in fact. "How is Ruth?"

"In intensive care. Martha called. I'm holding down the fort till she gets back. I see Harry got you some boots." She looks down, half distracted. "Come on, you'll want to take them off and set them by the fire to dry. I brought in more wood. Hauling things at least makes me feel

81

like I'm doing something." She shakes her head, her long, sweeping hair, clearly upset. "I was in my shop welding all afternoon. I never caught what was going on till I saw the ambulance leave. Ruth isn't very old. It's such a shock." She busily arranges my boots on one side of the hearth. "Martha said to be sure to keep you comfortable. It's been a hard day for her. Especially since more visitors have shown up." She points up to the ceiling. "They keep pounding around up there. It's driving me nuts. I think they're finally settling down. Did you get something for dinner?"

"I'm fine."

"What do you have there with you?"

"A book. From Ruth's."

"Oh." She smiles, again distracted. "*Hunters of Gold.* That's a good one. I read that one, too, when I first came here. I'm glad you've got something to keep you occupied tonight." She adjusts her colored scarf. "I hate that you've just arrived and then this terrible thing happens. I hope at least it shows you how folks respond to a crisis here. We really do watch out for each another. Martha knew right away Ruth was in trouble. I've been thinking maybe Ruth's been overworking herself between the museum and her soap business and the schoolhouse. Oh, come *on!*" she interrupts herself, raising her eyes to the ceiling again. "Why so much stomping around up there? They must be dumping out their backpacks. They're through-hikers, doing the Pacific Crest Trail, showed up right when the ambulance did. They're staying only one night. They said they might be coming down for a nightcap." Frowning, she throws another log on the fire, then peers through the lace-curtained window. "I came here so fast I didn't tend to my own fire. Should've closed the damper."

That's given me the chance I need.

"Su, why don't you let me take care of the hotel and the guests, and you go back over to your place? I've lots of experience tending to people and houses. It's what I used to do all day long, remember."

"No. I couldn't ask you to do that," she says, certainly.

"Why not?"

"Because . . . because you're a guest here."

"Is that all I am?" I say, as though hurt. "Truly? A guest?"

A clever choice. Her sharp face lightens.

"I've begun to think you're much more than that, Rose. Truly."

"What you need to do," I say, bustling her forward, "is get back to your shop. I can see you want to."

"I *was* working on something," she admits.

"And you were still thinking about it, looking out the window, weren't you? It's something important you were . . . bending . . . wasn't it?"

If I can just bend her the way I want . . .

"Wow. Rose. You remember me saying that? You're exactly right. When I got the news about Ruth I was right in the middle of something really, really *pulling* on me—a new piece—out of the salvage you helped me with today. When I get going on a new idea that way," she says, her eyes open but not seeing me, "I need to follow it with all my attention. I don't mean to say I stop caring about anything else, that I'm not thinking about Ruth. I am. It's hard to explain. Inspiration, insight, it grabs you. Anyway." Her eyes come back to me. "It's hard to let go, when it gets a hold of you like that. Thanks for picking up on it. I'm seriously starting to adore you. You sense what's going on. How do you do that?"

Haunting is listening.

I go to the door and open it for her. "Go on, now, take your coat. All will be well here."

She takes my cold hands, startling us both, then pulls away. "Okay. But you know where I am if you need anything. And you'll be okay with the college kids?" She grimaces toward the stairs. "They're noisy but might be nice enough. I can come back and make breakfast for them in the morning, if Martha isn't back yet."

"No need for that."

"You are gold, Rose. Something really special. You're going to stay here, with us. I have totally decided it. I *want* you to stay here. I want to get to know you. There's something about you, something . . . I don't care what awful thing it was that brought you here." She looks into my eyes. "Wait, that didn't come out right. You know what I mean. Of course I care. I just want you to know I'm glad you're here. No matter how it happened. See you soon."

She goes, her colorful clothing flying across the square.

I feel lighter and darker at the same time.

There's nothing for it, for the moment, but to do as I've said I'll do. Yet it feels like some part of me isn't in the room, has gone out with—

Not with a friend, surely. Among the living, the dead have no friends.

I turn to the fireplace and poke the unruly logs to give them more air. The bumping overhead has stopped. It's the padding of footsteps I hear now, coming down the stairs.

A red-cheeked young couple wanders into the parlor. They wear baggy clothes stretched at the arms and knees, and brown stockings on their shoeless feet. They each slide toward the fire and into one of the parlor chairs, the boy hefting his heels onto the stone hearth, the girl crossing her socks underneath her.

"Man," she sighs. "This is almost too perfect."

"Delish," the boy says.

She grins and gives me a little wave. "Hi. I'm Brin. Nice to meet you . . . ?"

"Rose."

"Nice to meet you, Rose. You don't look like a Rose. You look more like a . . . Lily."

The boy rolls his eyes at me. "Brin's, um, at altitude, if you know what I mean. Hi. I'm Kyle."

84

"Hello, Kyle."

The girl stretches out, reaching her fingers toward the fire. "It just feels so good to sit and be *dry*."

"Everything we own is wet," the boy explains, stretching his toes out, too. "We've been doing the PCT. Snow's coming in harder over the next few days, so we thought we'd better hoof it on down a few feet and consider our options."

"We were totally *crushing* it, though, Ky," the girl yawns.

"Totally, babe."

"Twenty miles a day. *Killin'* it."

"We got kind of a late start," the boy says to me, "but we thought we'd knock out as much of the trail as we could before things got too brutal. We're glad you're open." He yawns. "We've been out for weeks."

My old servant's voice comes out of me. "Do you have everything you need in your rooms?"

"One room." The girl swoons toward the boy. "We're engaged, yo!"

She pulls a device out of her pocket and holds it up for me to see. In its glow the two of them pose on a jutting slab of mountain granite, she hoisted in his arms, balanced over nothing but thin air.

That's just how I looked, before I fell off the edge of a lighthouse. So trusting we are, when we're young.

"Congratulations," is all I tell them.

She takes the photo back. "This is sort of our pre-honeymoon in the mountains. We love it here. You from around here, Rose?"

"From the coast," I answer and wonder how long it will it be before they go back to their room and I can go back to untangling this town. "I'm only helping out here, for a little while."

"Sweet. So what's it like here? It's like a really antique place, right? Gold Rush town, we read. Any gold still here?"

The boy sniffs. "We'd all be better off if no gold had been found anywhere at all."

The girl makes a face at him. "Ugh. Ky. Please?"

"The whole monetary system is whack. I say we go back to a barter economy. And no hoarding of resources. Equal shares for all!"

I blink, and in my mind's eye I'm young again, and alive, and the boy I love is dancing with me and whispering much the same thing in my ear: *It's a modern world we live in now, and there'll be plenty for all. Come with me. Come with me, Emma.*

But then I died, and I lost him, and he died far away from me. And if I think on these things too long, I'll grow hot inside, and grab that iron poker from the grate, and gut someone's stomach with it.

It's Brin's turn to roll her eyes. "Just ignore Ky. He's an impractical idealist. So, Rose, like, there's not much on the internet about this place except that it's one of the Best-Kept Secret Getaways. I read that the Donner Party came through here, or close by, or a Donner ghost, or something, which I think is so totally sad, I mean I think that whole story is so sad, but not ghosts. I don't think they're sad."

"Why not, babe?" The boy strokes her knee.

She strokes him back. "I know it's not politically correct, but I love the whole *idea* of staying on as a ghost. I think it would be *amazing*. I mean, I know it's not really sustainable, and if you see a ghost, I know, I know it's illegal not to report it and all that—but still I'd like to go on forever, if it were up to me. Think about everything you'd *see*. How far you could go."

"Babe, it's unnatural," the boy says. So young. So certain death is far from him. "And seriously, you'd have to watch everyone you love die. Wouldn't that suck?"

"That can happen even if you're *alive*, my dude. Rose, what do you think?"

I like her. She's the smarter one of the pair, I decide. So I give her a bit of the truth. "I think the dead go on forever, everywhere, whether they're ghosts or not. Every piece of earth is a grave, isn't it? One way or another. When you're living, you walk around, even if you don't know it, on ground first traveled by the dead." *The graves*, the schoolmaster Landon Albert Longhurst wrote in his letter, *lined the trail*. "Even in places where the ground looks freshly broken, it's lined with bones. Human and animal both. No matter where you put your feet, no matter how high or low, you're still walking the trail of death. Always."

They stare at me. Awkward. Uncomfortable.

"Yeah, um, I guess we've never thought of it that way before?" the boy says, and looks at his girl, jerking his chin in a signal for them both to go back up the stairs. "Um, sweetie, I'm feeling pretty tired now. You know, I think we should probably go upstairs and . . . and, um, prepare for the morning."

"Right." The girl stands. "Need to get organized for tomorrow. Back to pounding the trail of the dead again," she jokes.

Foolish girl. She doesn't see, behind her, roused by her teasing, a hand reaching out from the fire. An unburned sleeve.

"Let's get you upstairs," I say, quickly. "I'll go with you and make sure everything is all ready."

"No, no." The boy takes his girl's hand. "We can manage. Have to get an early start in the morning. Need to get to sleep as soon as we can."

"I'm going up to make sure everything's all right," I insist as the ghostly arm stretches behind them, grasping for them.

Their stockinged feet, unknowing, slide ahead of me, up the stairs.

On the landing, the sconces are glowing red, not pink.

They don't notice. "Our room's right here." The girl unlocks it.

I ask, "Do you have enough blankets?"

"I'm sure we do, thanks."

"And will you be wanting breakfast in the morning?"

"Thanks, but we'll be getting going, like, super early, before sunrise, so I don't think so. Thanks again for the room." She shuts the door. I hear groaning laughter on the other side.

The red light flickers softly.

I turn toward a crackling sound.

A little girl, with the same arm that stretched out from the fire, is standing on the landing.

She looks sweet. All of eight or nine. Her blond, wan braids rest against her handsewn dress with baize-green sleeves. Not flowered sleeves. A small boy appears beside her, in a short, uneven coat, holding her hand, his skin darker than hers, his black hair crookedly cut.

I recognize them. Two of the ghost children from the schoolhouse. My stilled heart goes out to them.

"Good evening. I'm Emma. It's so lovely to see you here."

Their little bodies waver, translucent, bristling. They're half angry, exposed. Uncertain.

"What might your names be?" I ask. "I know they say we shouldn't say our real names out loud. The hunters, they often use them to call us out and finish us. But I like my own name. And we have a right to them."

The children shake their heads at me.

"There are more of you, yes?"

They say nothing. They back away.

I heard Philip Pratt say, once, something about the ghosts of children. He said those who die so young aren't yet finished souls, so their actions are harder to predict after death.

"I'm a friend," I say. "I'm like you. You must feel it."

They keep watching, cold and glistening.

"Why are you here, little ones?" I ask.

"He's looking for us," the girl whispers. "He'll find us."

"Who'll find you?"

"Teacher," she says simply.

I try the name from the mad letter. "Longhurst. Is that your teacher?"

"Addy!" The boy tugs at her hand, afraid.

"We're going." The girl grips him tighter. "Someone else is coming."

"Wait," I say, "wait, please. Where can I find you? At the school-house?"

"Not anymore. It's broken. It's all broken."

They brush past me, flying down the stairs, fading. I go after them. The door of the hotel opens.

Martha has returned. She leans exhausted against her desk.

"Rose," she says with a weak shake of her head.

I say, calmly, because I must act as though nothing marvelous has happened, "Martha. Are you all right?"

"I'm so glad to be home." She rubs a hand over her steely brow. "It's been such a night. With Ruth. She still can't speak. She can't tell us what happened. It's terrible."

I still have time, then. Time before Ruth says that she saw a ghost. Before the hunters come. *But how much time?* I worry.

"The doctors can't even give us a prognosis. We just have to wait." Martha raises her head. She looks to the staircase. "My other guests?"

"Gone to their beds."

"What do they want to eat? In the morning?"

"They're leaving early and don't want anything, they said."

"A small blessing. Oh, Rose. Rose, I'm so tired." She closes her eyes. "So very, very tired of losing people."

"You must go to sleep, then." I guide her toward the staircase. Above, on the landing, the light is an innocent pink again. "Put down your worry, for a while."

"Was Su here?"

"She was, but I sent her away. I know how to manage."

"You're too good, Rose." She shakes her head again. "Aren't you tired, too? Have you been waiting up for me?"

"I have." The kindest thing to say.

A flicker of a smile under the steeliness. "I haven't had anyone wait up for me in a long, long time."

"I know. Let's get you to bed now."

"Things are the way they are," she sighs. "Whatever happens is going to happen. You make your bed, and you have to lie in it."

I help her to the landing. Even into her room. Her quarters are neatly made, and so spare they might as well be a monk's cell. As though Martha Hayley were a guest in her own home.

"Rose, thank you. I can manage now. I'll see you in the morning."

"Till morning, then."

No children return to the hallway, although I open the door of my room to shine a light from it, and wait and turn over possibilities and clues, the bits of gold that have fallen into my hand.

Haunting is waiting.

11

In the morning I hear Martha's voice floating up from the front desk as I walk down the stairs.

". . . coming along . . . Yes, a really nice girl . . . I wish Ruth could weigh in . . . I'm checking in every hour or so . . . The hospital said they'd call if there was any change . . . Yes, I'll ask . . . I understand, of course, of course . . . And there's Su as well, if you think it's time for her to . . . I agree. We'll be all right. Yes. As soon as she's up. All right. Don't strain yourself. I don't think we can handle any more upset, right now."

She sees me and hangs up.

"Rose! Did I disturb you?"

"No, I've been awake and reading a book. Are you feeling better this morning?"

She looks well rested around the eyes.

"Much better." She nods in thanks. "It's amazing what a few hours of sleep can do, isn't it? And the hikers left without any trouble. They changed their minds, decided to get off the trail and go home, said they'd pick it up again someday. Probably for the best." She looks out her window. "Weather's still holding, but another system is on its way. Heavier

91

snow. I'm going to head back to the hospital ahead of the storm to see if there's anything I can do for Ruth. I was just telling Mary Berringer . . ."

She looks at me as though she hopes for an invitation to say more.

"And how are Mr. and Mrs. Berringer this morning?" I oblige. There's nothing easier, or more useful, than giving a soul what it wants.

"Oh, they're cut up to pieces by all this. They've known Ruthie for longer than any of us, ever since she was born. I told them I know they care about her, but they need to be at home. At their age, it's best they stay put and conserve their strength for the winter. In fact, Rose, they—we—were just wondering . . . if you might be able to go over to their place today, and help them? They're shutting their inn down for the season, and now that they're both in their eighties it's getting harder on them. They need to get some silver and linens put up . . . a couple of final chores . . . Normally I go over and help out, but do you think you might be able to?"

It's the elders in a town who know the most about its buried bones. "Of course," I oblige again. "I'd be happy to. I'd like to get to know them better."

"Wonderful. I'd be so grateful. And if you can get them talking while you're helping, keep their mind off things . . . that would be terrific. You'll like chatting with them, Rose. They've been here forever. A Berringer was the first lawman in White Bar. I think sometimes John likes to pretend we still have a sheriff, the way he barks at us all. But of course, don't tell them I said that," she says quickly, brushing the dust from her desk. "Good people, the Berringers, of course. The fact there's a town here at all is pretty much because of Berringers and Huellets. Without them we probably just would have ended up a pile of sticks and rubble. It's how most gold rush towns ended up."

The gold rush, I'd read in the book I'd taken from the museum, *was short-lived. Five years or less for most of the boomtowns. As the early days of gold fever waned, hardships set in. Competition, assaults, and claim-jumping soared. Matters of justice were often settled by mob rule, including whippings and hangings. Disease reared its head and raged through the camps, often undoctored. Partnerships, marriages, families collapsed under the pressure. For those communities that managed to survive the collapse of the boom—and most didn't, their ruins still clinging to the slopes of the high ranges—there was some recourse to be found in farming or ranching. The rest, the Great Ghost Towns of the West, were for many years remote and unwelcoming. In some places hauntings kept development at bay for decades, until the advances of the late twentieth century afforded technologies to bring peace back to the mountains. Today, Gold Country is best known as a pleasant and storied place to visit, with its resorts, cabins, and quaint restaurants.*

"I told the Berringers I'd send you over right after coffee." Martha hurries toward the dining room. "Let's not keep them cooling their heels. You don't like to keep them, I mean old folks, waiting."

Mary Berringer opens the door to her inn. Her entryway is crowded with flowered wreaths, painted vases, and a hall tree covered in shawls and warm caps.

"Rose." She presses her hands, sweetly, to my cheeks. "You're so quick! Come inside and get warm."

I wipe my new boots on the doormat and step inside, asking, "How are you and Mr. Berringer bearing up?"

"I would say we're managing, dear." She closes the door gently behind me. "Martha has told us Ruth is stable. For that, we are grateful. We know it's best to go on with our chins up. So that's what we're going to do. Ruth would want us to keep moving forward. Come this way, my dear. We've been polishing and ironing in the back."

I follow her shawled shoulders through the parlors of the first floor, thick with heavy, dark furniture and more urns and vases. We pass a fine wooden staircase, with a bannister rubbed smooth from years of comings and goings, and a dining room full of tall, carved pieces.

"Such nice things you have, Mrs. Berringer," I say, truthfully.

"Thank you, dear. We try to hold on to the charms of yesteryear, live up to what visitors expect of an inn in this area."

"And you and Mr. Berringer run it all alone?"

"We do. It can be"—she looks over her fringed shoulder at me, smiling—"quite a job in high season. We had hoped our grown children would have come back and taken over from us. But of course, the innkeeper's life isn't for everyone. Here's the sitting room, and John!" She leads me in to a cozy parlor, shuttered and warm. "He's been at the polishing and I've been getting the linens ready for storage. John, look who's here, all ready to help us."

The old man peers up from a round table castled with silver servers and urns.

"She doesn't look ready to me."

"Rose," the old woman gasps, "my goodness, he's right, I haven't even taken your coat! Now you give me that and go sit with John. We've made a good start, but we're just so tuckered, doing so much, especially with all the plate."

I go to sit across from the man and his polishing rags, and see right away that most of the work is, curiously, finished. Knives lie glistening like silver ribs in an open velvet box. A few small chafing dishes are left, tarnished. The linen's neatly folded on a deal table.

"You've made more than a start," I point out.

Mrs. Berringer sits down beside me. "Yes, but every bit of help is welcome, no matter when or how it comes! John, Rose has been admiring our things, our house. It was built in 1852," she says, turning to me, "though we don't have a plaque, like Ruth's does. We've done too much updating."

"Jetted tubs," John Berringer grumbles.

"But it was *worth* it, John! You have to know when it's time to improve. Speaking of which"—she pats one of my wrists, seeming to have forgotten I was meant to come and housekeep for them—"what do *you* think of, dear, when you hear talk of improvement, and doing better, however you can? Is that something you aspire to?"

So perhaps I'm the one to be rubbed up? I pick up the polish and the chafing dish and say, "I don't know if I understand you, Mrs. Berringer."

"You can call me Mary, dear. Well, all I mean is that I know—John and I *both* know—that you've recently been through . . . troubles. We won't speak of them if you don't want to, of course." She pats my sleeve again, sober now and serious. "We're here to guard your privacy. You are safe with us. What I mean is"—she leans kindly toward me, as the old man watches from across the table—"with what you've just suffered, what might be the *antidote*, do you think? What might be the *good* life, now? I don't mean only a life of comfort and safety, though everyone deserves that, if they can find it. John and I"—she sighs and sits back—"have lived long lives, and what we've learned is that while comfort is important, far more important is living a life of meaning. What we're saying, dear, is that we're *concerned* for you. What will you do now, with your life at a crossroads?" She looks tenderly at me, like a preacher hoping for my salvation. "What might you do to restore your dignity and self-respect, and your sense of purpose? Do you believe you have a right to good things? No matter how badly life has treated you? Do you see yourself as the kind of person who will take a good chance, if it comes your way? And become part of a community, a special community that nowadays needs young people, like you?"

They can't know I'm far older than they are, and needy, too.

"Maybe she's not ready," the old man humphs and shrugs.

"It's more that I don't know what to say," I answer him. "I think," I say, turning to his wife, "you're asking me to stay in White Bar?"

"Exactly!" she says, beaming. "To consider it, dear! To consider becoming part of a way of life that was here to comfort you when you needed it."

"Maybe the girl wants to know more about us," John says, watching me.

Not a dull man. I nod in reply. "I've been trying to learn as much as I can, Mr. Berringer. I do feel so drawn to the ... the history here. You're right, it seems so full of meaning." I need to get them to say more.

"It is, it is!" The old woman presses her hands together excitedly. "John and I know the history better than anyone else! We're the oldest residents, you see, from one of the oldest families—along with Ruth's. Ruth's forebears were a pair of doctors. John and I—we're cousins—are descended from the first sheriff in town. Together, the Huellets and the Berringers—"

"Yes," I say, "I know, they brought order to the town. Ruth told me. They built the jail. And the school," I add, smoothly. "The school, too."

The old man barks, "Which school's she talking about?"

"There was more than one?" I ask, my ears pricking.

"Yes, dear, there were two," Mary Berringer answers. "But we don't talk about it publicly, dear, I mean, not in the museum ... not with all the *families*, you see, that come here during the season. It wouldn't set the right *tone*. We don't want to sell ourselves as an unhappy place. We're not"—she wrinkles her nose—"Donner Lake, here. People don't come here to feel *morose*. They come because they want to feel the excitement of the pioneering days of the gold rush, the spirit of our Old Prospector, our statue out there on the square, and what it took to pull riches straight out of the ground with nothing but your own muscle. But I guess"—she looks at her husband—"we should speak the truth to dear Rose, don't you think, John? If we're hoping she'll stay, and help us?"

"She looks ready now, I guess."

"You see, Rose ..." The old woman looks anxiously into my eyes, seems satisfied by what she finds there, and goes on. "The sad story is that the first school in White Bar, down in what we call the Basin, burned and had to be destroyed. A teacher went mad there. His gold claim didn't pan out, and he got what they called back then the panic. He locked his pupils in the schoolhouse and killed them. Justice being what it was in those days, they strung him up on a tree. And then they tore the school down, and built the new one you see on the Knob. It's something we don't stress in the town's history. Though worse things have happened in these mountains—" She falters.

"Cannibalism," the old man puts in.

"We don't," she goes on, "want visitors to think we're that kind of place, the kind of place where people go insane. We're all about peace and serenity here, as Martha says. Not failure. We're about success. We're one of the few boomtowns in this part of the Sierra to last. And now that we've told you all this"—she smiles, almost tearfully—"you can see how much we *trust* you, Rose. This isn't a story we tell to just anyone. Only those we know, in our hearts, are the most worthy of our trust. In fact—" She stands all at once. "We'll trust you with even more. John. John! I'm going to go get the letter."

"If you think it's best," he says. "And just what are we supposed to do while you're at it?"

"Why don't you show Rose where to put the linens away? We're so lucky to have her help"—she nods eagerly—"we should use it."

She disappears, hurrying through a side door. The old man fidgets in his chair, arching as though his bones ache.

"So." He points. "Can you carry that much linen all in one go? Haul it to the hutch in the dining room? The big armoire, in there? Just go put it on the top shelf inside. Hard for us to reach. Need to keep the material away from the moths and rats. And anything else that infests."

"Of course."

The pile of runners weighs little to me. *Every burden is lighter than death*, I think. I go quickly so I'll be able to return and learn more about the murderous schoolmaster Longhurst; so that my hunt might move quickly forward; so that . . . what?

I falter in front of the burled chest in the dining room, catching myself. *Admit it, Emma Rose. You've thought no farther than finding others like you—not what you'd do after you found them. And what about a whole schoolroom full of spirits?*

Uneasy, I reach one hand out to unlock the armoire. The creaking hinges swing wide open.

I fall back with a cry.

A human outline. Inside.

The burl's interior is streaked, painted with the ashy shadow of a body. A blasted spirit burned, frozen, arms wide, in its final scream.

A blasted soul.

Because a hunter was here. And did a hunter's work.

All faltering goes out of me.

We had one hiding in an armoire in the dining room, they said in the café. *The doors on it were forever sticking, and oiling the hinges didn't do the trick.*

This is what they do. This is how they "clean" us.

I feel nothing but pure anger. I will—

A voice behind me chimes, "Oops, forgot to tell you about that, kid."

The old man is apologizing, shrugging. "Gave you a surprise, I bet. Had a problem in there quite a few years ago. Professional took care of it for us, though. This antique is even more valuable now. More historical. Just put everything up on the high shelf, would you?"

Before I can answer his wife comes, with an envelope in her hand.

"I see you're getting a little more of our history!" Her wrinkled face is earnest. "Now, if you've never seen one of those before, that's called a flash cast. It was quite a while ago. We have no troubles now. We don't tolerate trouble. John, you finish putting those linens away. Now here, dear Rose, is the letter I was telling you about." She puts it in my hand before I can withdraw it. "We *trust* you with it, Rose. We want to show you that when we really care about someone, who says they feel drawn to us—and when we feel exactly the same way, oh my goodness, we feel it so much—we hold nothing back. Our lives, our fortunes, our truths. This will tell you more about our private history. And John, I've also had another idea. I think we should have a little get-together this evening at the café, to introduce Rose to everyone else."

I feel not a letter but ashes in my hand.

"A fine idea," her husband says approvingly. "It'll make everyone feel better, after Ruthie."

"We'll make it around six? Come, dear Rose." She's brought my coat as well, and begins walking me to the front door. "You take some time for yourself, now, before dinner, to read things over; and I'm sure you'll see how much we respect you and want to help you find a new place, new *meaning*, and everything you deserve. But don't thank us yet." She squeezes me, happily. "You don't know how much you help us, just by being here. Read the teacher's confession—this is an original, historical document, we know you'll be careful with it—and we'll see you at the café this evening. We'll let everyone know to come. It will be a joy to share with you who and what we love, and that we know you'll come to love, too. Goodbye, dear."

They shut the door of the inn behind me, abruptly. The last I see of them, behind the frozen window boxes, they're embracing, folding each other into relieved arms. And all the loneliness and anger inside me, it's so cold and fierce, the icicles stop their dripping on the porch at my feet, and the dried flowers shatter in their beds.

12

It's a hideous thing, to be wanted and not.

To know that, as a ghost, everywhere you look, you see what wants you found . . . only to finish you. Destroy you.

The only way you manage it is by pretending you don't feel what you feel, don't know what you know. You blend in and mix with those who want you dead, though they smile in your face, sweetly. You look back across the square at the curtained inn where they just fawned over you, and you know it's all a trick of the light. To survive in this world, you must wear a skin that isn't your own, borrow a coat that fits but will never warm, smile when you want to slash and burn.

You must go on. As best you can.

I sit at the base of the Old Prospector's statue, and in my hands are the sheets the Berringers want me to read, sheets that fill them with a thrill of secrecy; but it's not with them, with the living, I feel and take secret company, but with those in the armoires, hiding in the basements and attics and closets, in the chimneys and schoolrooms, in all the places I've hidden in, too, because I didn't die the way the world wanted me to die.

In the cold, gray, clear light, I open the letter of one dead.
It doesn't matter who the dead man is. It's my duty.

October 20, 1852

Dearest Sister,

For the second time, I try to write to you. An earlier letter, written
some weeks ago, I found myself for various reasons unable to send. I
have no wish to burden you with my strange fits. I am well. After two
seasons of prospecting, I've secured a toehold in the wilds of California
where, it might surprise you, I have found employment serving as a
schoolmaster to a group of ragtag children. They sit in front of me even
as I write this. I've given them a lesson to round out the final hour of
today's class. My first day as a schoolmaster was, I'll admit, difficult.
I never meant to follow in our father's footsteps. Also, I was faced, as
I entered, with the most rudimentary schoolhouse, its only window a
row of glass jars nestled between chinked logs, throwing strange light
on a passel of half-combed heads. A boy whose name turned out to
be Jack, eleven years of age, I spotted first for his wild red hair and
for a bruise that looked like a smudge across his wan face. Adelaide,
eight years old, I noticed next—the kind of blond apparition so rare
in a place like this I thought at first I had imagined her. Ola I saw
next, tall and unsmiling; a stout, dark girl of fifteen, with hair the
color of a rusted anvil, and a plain face. William, also dark, is a tot
of six years, in mended knickers, his boots unable to touch the ground
under his seat. Anton, the oldest boy, sits meekly at the back, a brother
I thought at first to Adelaide, but no; their fathers are partners in the
Tack and Hardware and they both live in the rough-hewn houses that

merchants, not miners, are beginning to build behind the square that anchors this place.

I am in a town lately renamed White Bar. The ground on which our schoolhouse is planted had been ordered cleared by the Messrs. Huellet, doctors and informal leaders and benefactors of this community, after four men set dynamite to the riverbank nearby and died collapsing a cavern beneath the surface. The miners' camp has now been moved well upriver, and after a sufficient interval the doctors declared the bad luck and "pestilence" of the former camp cleansed. The funds that built this school are generated by the sale of the brothers' Huellet's Healing Tonic, which is very popular here and also in the surrounding camps.

Thus, I find myself, each day, in this room in a fresh, muddy clearing, with the sound of a waterfall created by man's folly rushing not far from my ears.

I told my pupils that like them I am a newcomer, and hail from Connecticut.

"Where's that?" little William called.

"Where is that please, sir," I corrected him, for I will not have these children being ruffians, by God. They must learn.

Though we have neither map nor globe, only rough desks, some slates, and chalk.

"In the East," I said. "By the Atlantic Ocean. Have any of you ever seen an ocean?"

I wish I could describe for you how sadly the younger ones shook their heads. Ola and the older boys sat shamefaced, as though I had tested them and they'd missed the mark.

So I went on quickly, "We are at present many miles from the nearest ocean, the Pacific. But what is near to hand are all the puzzles *and wonders and mysteries locked inside what is already known to us, or may easily become known."*

I told them to take up their slates. I set them to copy an acrostic, the one we used to do when we were young, do you remember?

The bell tolls slowly
Over the empty pews
Lost are all the lonely
Lacking Heaven's news.

The children all bent uncertain to their tasks. I was anxious for them as I walked up and down the room, studying their work, but saw, with relief, that while some of them might be unmannered, they at least do have their letters. The youngest, along with Jack, copy poorly, but Adelaide writes in a smooth hand, and Ola in a sturdy one.

I remember Anton asked looking at his slate, "Mr. Longhurst, sir, does this word, toll, have more than one meaning?"

I told him it could mean a charge or fare, as well as the ringing of a bell.

The children had looked to the chinked wall beside the door, where the bell rope—our school bell being a heavy iron kettle adapted to this purpose—is hooked. Ola tends to raise her hand into the air, slowly, as though she's hefting a weight that troubles her.

"There's another meaning to toll, I think, sir," she said.

I asked her what.

"A burden. A claim takes its toll on you, my father says."

I believe she's quicker than her motions might suggest.

We make slow progress on numbers—addition, subtraction. I smile as best I can, even through general confusion. Because I am trying not to be like Father, a teacher who strikes students for their errors, so that they cringe and gape at the door hoping the bell might toll and release them from hell.

I remember well that feeling. You?

The students are fidgeting, fish trying to lose the hook. I will write more as I can.

October 26

Today Will and Addy are sitting side by side, their childish frowns knotted over unfamiliar spellings. Anton and Ola bend over their desks, shoulders forward, pushing against ignorance's wheel. Jack makes a pretense of reading, his eyes sliding toward our glass-jarred window as though measuring its height for his escape.

They are coming, at least, each day. A different kind of escape. This school, I believe, is their only flight from the harshness of camp life. Anton and Addy are somewhat fortunate; their families make a living selling picks and shovels to wide-eyed miners who still believe there is gold to be found in this valley. Young Will walks a hard road. Willie's father was a Spaniard who fell drunk and drowned last year in the Eno. His mother was a whore, who now however is a baker of French pies.

Ola's family has come to near ruin on a bad claim. She works every day before and after school, picking through silt. Jack is a boy at the mercy of his whiskey-loving father, and tries to conceal the bruises on his arm by pulling at the sleeves of his shirt.

Yet I insist they all do well at school. We all must rise above our miseries.

I am, apart from my regular misgivings that I've fallen into the very sort of life I came West to avoid, accepting of my fate. If there have been difficulties, thus far, they haven't come from inside this crude schoolhouse but rather from the town itself. There is suspicion in the camp that the White Bar schoolmistress is instead a schoolmaster. It's been made clear to me, by looks and signs and jokes, that I'm engaged in a womanly profession. Perhaps this was to be expected. There are many in this remote valley who come from rude places, and have no sense of the traditions of schoolteaching in the East. I hope, in time, to show them that a knowledge of books and numbers and letters should be welcomed with gratitude, not suspicion. And I must hope that, like ballast to a ship, I can be a counterweight to the stupid and small and dim and unimaginative people that can be found in every corner on earth.

In any case, I am pleased to write that we all go on very well here in Schoolhouse Meadow. I might even say we have made a little camp, a little country for ourselves. Each day we begin by saluting the flag and each other, then set ourselves to our tasks. I grow each day more interested in their work; I find it shows a seriousness I had not thought possible. Of course, I won't stay in this position beyond a season or two. It's merely a stopgap. I'd rather shoot myself than become Father.

November 3
Progress: Will has made some headway on his letters and spelling. Addy is a child of natural gifts, with a sweet, clear voice, a joy to hear singing now that the weather has turned to rain and it is too cold for us to exercise outdoors. Jack continues stubborn. Knowledge seems to come to him and then seep away again, as if through the holes in his sleeves. Anton and Ola are catching up to their counterparts in the East, and I begin to hope will be acceptable graduates. It is Ola among all of them, however, who makes the most rapid advance. She is a surprise to me. Her manner appears slow, even laborious, and her dark brow often comes down in a frown that is as much resistance as it

is concentration. Yet she's the one who strides through each lesson with purpose. She'll need more books, soon.

At the moment, we make do with what we've been able to glean from the townspeople—some soggy Dickens and The Arabian Nights. I've approached the Doctors Huellet, who I was sure would have something in their medical libraries that could entertain the minds of my older pupils. The doctors have been building a fine house on the square, in the place their medicinal stand first occupied. They're sending, I've heard, for their wives from the East. Yet when I asked if the school might have the loan of some of their medical volumes, Caleb Huellet, our new mayor, looked askance at me and said he had nothing suitable for my needs. I ventured to mention this to Mrs. Berringer, the sheriff's wife, since my lodging is near to her own home. I simply said it was disappointing the doctors had not brought more of their own library with them. Her response startled me. She huffed and stated that "traveling doctors couldn't be expected to carry more than any other prospector on their backs, and it was unfair to judge men who had done so much good in such a short time, for any lack of paper." Her speech struck me as strange, because indeed I hadn't asked for any form of medical credential or diploma; only for the sharing of any books they might, as others in the camp, and now the town, have brought with them.

November 4

I haven't been able to stop my mind from speculating on what I wrote above. The truth is I am beginning to wonder about the medical educations of the Brothers Huellet. I've been remembering their arrival in camp. It was in a covered wagon, filled with nothing but canvas-covered crates of elixirs bearing their name. It was late spring of this past year, and a torpor, a sickness had hung over the Basin.

I'd worked my claim to exhaustion and little more. I was consider-
ing abandoning the Eno River and moving on, like others who felt
the camp had become unlucky. I happened to be in town on a Satur-
day playing billiards, when the explosion tore the throat of the river
open and shook the saloon windows. As the smoke cleared, the Huellet
brothers were everywhere—caring for the four dying men—shout-
ing for an emergency meeting—sharing it as their medical opinion
that the illness that had been plaguing the camp was clouding men's
judgment—and that Huellet's Tonic was in plentiful supply to cure
the trouble.

Their elixir sold briskly. The complexion of the town at first
improved, it's true. The river camp was razed and the meadow cleared.
The Hardware and Tack doubled in size, and the jail was built. The
speed at which all of this was accomplished was celebrated as a miracle,
put down to the doctors' industry on all fronts.

But here in the privacy of my papers I will record I've become
suspicious as the doctors' mansion rises on the square. I ask myself if
this is mere jealousy on my part—since I have accomplished in two
years along this river nearly nothing, while these men in their beaver
hats succeeded in a matter of weeks. I ask myself why I don't feel more
grateful for the position I now hold, which allows me more comfort
than I've known since I said goodbye to you, sister, at the rail station.
Hadn't I started my journey, just as the Huellet brothers had, with
great ambition in my pocket? Is it that these men are simply better
than I am? Or are some men better at finding a slim vein, and goug-
ing it?

I have wondered, too, about the curious timing of the arrival of the
Huellet brothers along the river, right before the explosion that took
the lives of four miners who were no more or less clouded in judgment
than any of us.

But then I wonder if it is some deficit in my <u>own</u> character that
makes me so quick to mistrust. Is this envy raising its ugly flag? I ask
myself. Am I envious of the fine house the brothers are building on the
square, and of the no doubt fine wives they'll be bedding inside it? Am I
envious of their success not only in business but in love? But I can't think
too closely on my solitary state. If I dwell for too long on the truth that
I've been alone and unsuccessful amid fields of gold where others have
found luck . . . I become despondent, angry, almost ready to lash out at
anyone. Such passion I feel . . . remembering the passion that drove me
here. Yet somehow I have squandered that passion, spending it on a
tiny pile of yellow dust. Such rage I might feel, if ever I allowed myself
to. And here, now, I've written another letter that will never be sent,
because it speaks too much, goes too far. Hope fails me. I want only hope.
And perhaps to love and be loved. And failing hope and love . . . what?

I set the wrinkled sheets down on this cold lap.

Failing hope and love . . . what?

What's left, the dead man means, when the world moves on and
finds its companions, and you are left alone, at the end of words, holding
hunger and longing dry in your lap, and nowhere to put their kindling?

The Prospector's hulking shadow above me makes no answer.

But I can't think too closely on my solitary state.

There's nothing more to read or be said, so I fold the faded sheets,
quickly, with their envelope into the mayor's coat.

And stand and look back to face the empty windows of the inn.

If the Berringers had wanted not only to share with me White Bar's
hidden past but to show me what feeling alone and unlucky in the world
might drive a soul to, they needn't have gone to the trouble, I remind
myself. I've lived all my life and afterlife knowing what hurt, rage, and

the lack of love can do to the heart. I see the Prospector's bronze ax, strapped to his pack, and need no more letters from Longhurst to know the rest of the tale.

The schoolmaster broke.

Sometimes, a kind of pain runs so fiercely through this body I wish I had, too, some sharp weapon in my hands to cut it with, sharper than whatever power it is that slices these torn bits of lace falling from the sky.

Look, it's snowing again, I think. *But you can't let yourself feel lost in the cold, Emma Rose. You mustn't.*

A tinkling sound comes from across the square. It's Su Kwon, stepping out of her art gallery, hanging a fresh, gleaming wind chime from her porch roof. I straighten so she can see me and raise my hand in a salute. She waves back and beckons.

On the porch, she tucks my arm into hers, friendly, the soft shock of her beating life pressed close to my shoulder. The trouble with having a body that can be touched is that it makes you want to touch all the more.

She's wearing a thick sweater and fur-topped boots, and a necklace of stones in glinting colors.

"Rose, glad I've got you! Come on through the gallery. I need to show you something."

She leads me in. I have only a moment to glance at splintered wooden walls covered with rusted pieces of metal that fling and reach out in strange, twisting tongues. Farther into the room, wild, fantastic waves of iron balance on squares of stone. A woodstove glows in the corner. I see a desk scattered with paper drawings, a tiny, messy kitchen, and stairs running to a loft and bed above.

"It's this way to my studio. So have you just been over"—she pulls open an unlatched door at the back of the gallery—"at Mary and John's?

109

They're the movers and shakers around here, you know. Could you tell? Did they like you?" She breezes outdoors again, the snowfall clinging to her hair, and pulls open a barn door on the other side of the alley. "Because if they didn't, they're insane. Okay, get ready, I want to show you what I just finished."

I'm standing inside an old stable heated with glowing burners and filled with stacks and sheets of metal and piles of stone. We pass deep racks that hold pieces of iron pipe; hanging tools and strange, glinting machines; braces I have no name for. Her truck stands in front of a closed carriage door, and beside it something covered with a blue cloth.

"That's my snowmobile," she says as I stare at it. "Over that side is where I fire, and here's where I weld." She picks up a metal mask and jauntily hides her face behind it, showing me nothing but her eyes. She sets it down. "In this corner is what I want to show you. Do you recognize it, Rose?"

Rising from an open space littered with shavings of metal is a great shining piece of arched steel. It curves in a horseshoe—the shape of luck. Yet it's big enough to throw a shadow over my head.

The base is a slab of flecked gray stone, where the metal is footed.

She reaches up and touches the arch, excitedly. "Remember? The scrap you helped me haul? Bent steel, anchored in granite. It's all from the meadow. The rock, too. This is what I've been obsessing over. It's been quite a job, the calibration, the weight, getting it to balance just right, so it looks like this, like a floating door. I have *you* to thank for the idea." Her eyes dance, glowing. "It's because of our conversation yesterday. I'd been brooding over what you said in my truck—that some souls might want peace, and others not. I think you might be right, Rose. How can we assume we know what anyone else wants or needs, in the end? For me, this whole piece is that big question mark. Notice the arch. Like a question that turns on and touches itself. Like a door.

Because a question, it came to me, is always a door, and a door is always a question. And the question isn't just, *What's on the other side of this?* or even, *Should I go through this door?* It is"—she strokes the keen edge of it—"*what makes this a door?* Isn't this just a hunk of scrap pulled from an unlucky place and soldered to rock? What makes it a doorway? Is it because I say so? Is saying something is a certain thing enough to make it so? Maybe. Maybe there's always a door, room to move, an option, another way. Always the ghost of a door—that's what I'm thinking of calling it, the Ghost Door—waiting somewhere, even if you don't know it." She lets go of it. "I think it's my best piece. There's even a little natural vibration to it. If you listen, you can hear it. A hum. Or anyway, I can hear it when I'm not talking." She laughs. "Me and my motormouth. Talking to myself—all the time! Do you like it, though? I hope you do. I won't go fishing for compliments . . . but you really, really like it, right?"

I do. I don't know why. I stare at it, wonderingly, and listen, and hear the stillness of the meadow where we gathered it, and the throb of the nearby waterfall, and the soft crunch of snow under our footprints. It's what I said to the young couple at the hotel: even in places where the ground looks fresh, it's lined with passing.

"A door"— I nod—"with what you can't see behind it."

"Yes!" She balls her hands into fists and raises them. "I *knew* you'd get it! That's why I couldn't wait to show it to you. I'm so jazzed. It'll get a good price, too. If I can even bear to let go of it. But okay, all right, enough about me, my thing, how are *you*, what have you been up to, did you have a good visit with the Berringers, is everything moving along? I saw you go over there. What did they say? Any word on poor Ruth? I know Martha's on her way to the hospital again. Wait, you don't have to keep on standing." She pulls two wooden stools out from a work bench, and we sit. "What else did Mary and John say? Did they tell you anything about the Bar?"

They told me too much and too little, I don't say. "They said they told me things they wouldn't tell the tourists."

"Fantastic!" She draws her breath in. "You're really *in* around here once the Berringers let you in. What did they tell you, exactly?"

"About a teacher who killed his pupils."

"Good. Good. Well, no." She shakes her head. "I mean, of course it's not good, it's terrible. This guy named Longhurst, he went crazy and burned them down in a fire one winter in the meadow and got sentenced to hang . . . I mean it's good in the sense that I'm glad they told you. It's not something the town shares with visitors. But me, I want you to really know this place. Warts and all. I would've told you myself, but it's not my place to . . . and it's better if it comes from the community's leaders."

"They gave me a letter. From him. It explains about a school, in a meadow. Was it"—I point to the Ghost Door—"the same meadow?" No matter where we put our feet, no matter how high or low, we're always walking the trail of the dead.

She nods. "That is *so* great they lent it to you, Rose. It means the old-timers really trust you. They mean it for a compliment. I know it might seem a sort of strange welcome-to-the-neighborhood present, but they're honoring you, trying to show you how much the Bar likes you. Have you read it yet? When I did, a few weeks after I came, I felt terrible. You can see, actually feel the disaster coming in it. Then, after a while, I can't explain it, I also felt . . . at peace, somehow. With being shown the words. It's something, when someone shares a secret with you, and they don't say, 'Now don't tell anyone about this!'—because they already know you won't. Because they trust and *believe* in you. They feel about you the thing you've always known about yourself: that you can be trusted, you know what you're doing. That meant a lot to me when I first came here. Did I tell you my family did everything they could to stop me from being an artist?" She looks away, half laughing. "My father wanted me to stay in his tech firm, marry some guy who worked for him he'd already picked out for me, stay in the company, be one of his vice presidents. He said it was ridiculous and crazy for me to want to play with 'junk' all day long, and that if I did, I'd never amount to anything, plus he'd cut me off without a penny." She shrugs, twisting on her stool. "I left, and he did. Cut me dead. Still doesn't talk to me. My mother and I are the only ones who still speak. I say more, I share more with Martha and Bill and Mary and John, and Harry, than I do with my own family. You want to know what's crazy?" She laughs again, but not in a way that hurts. "*That* is. Being up here, in the middle of nowhere, and getting more love from the Bar than I can get from my own kin. And love is what matters. Believe me. Love, and getting to do some work that feels meaningful."

Yes. And failing love and hope, what?

She's brushing something from her face. I would comfort her, but she's already asking if I want anything to drink, how about some tea, hot, does that sound good?

She's showing me such kindness . . . but . . . I have my own work, I have to remember.

She jumps up from her stool. "Okay. You stay right where you are, enjoy my work. I'll go in the gallery and make you some *cha*. Be right back."

She leaves me with the Ghost Door and its whispering.

Haunting is listening.

I leave my stool and go to the arc of metal. There's a sound to it, inside its empty center. Hushed, but not soft. Wordless, but not silent.

I draw still closer, till I stand beside its opening. I hear what sounds like heavy breathing. In. Out. In. Out. I reach a hand toward it, into the empty space between the metal. And feel the damp exhale against my cold skin.

113

I pull away.

"Rose!" Su's come back suddenly, flinging the barn door open with a gust of snow, staring at her telephone. "I don't know what's going on, but we have to get moving."

"Where?"

"We need to get to the café. The Berringers have called a special meeting."

"I know, so I can meet more of you." But now—

"No. This isn't that. The town council and Martha have called some sort of emergency meeting. I hope it doesn't have to do with Ruth. I have to go. Please, Rose, come too? The Berringers asked that we both come. They want you to be part of us. *I* want you to be. And emergencies need calm voices, like yours. Will you come?" she asks, a look of friendship and eagerness in her face. "It would be so good if you could."

Here is a different breath, I think, a fresh gust of air, right in front of me. Her face so open I could walk through it.

Why do I want to go with her, I wonder? Is it this skin I wear, remembering other skin? Or the memory of old, dead friends, inside me, or inside this body . . . remembered lives . . . I don't know, I don't know. I know only here is some kind of hope, looking at me, and if you don't have that, what?

"I'm coming."

"Thank you, thank you, thank you, Rose!"

In the alley, the snow is whirling now, thick and wild.

"Big storm coming finally," she says as she takes my arm and we both race.

13

We slip through the back door of the White Bar Café, past an old butcher's block, boxed and canned supplies on shelves, a latched meat locker.

I hear the voices before I see the bundled bodies that go along with them. The townspeople have come alone or in pairs under the ringing bells of the front door, in snowy coats and caps, some finding their way shivering to booths and stools, others standing just inside the frost-tinged windows.

Su is greeted warmly, folded into kind embraces, and asked, does she know what's happening?

"No, not really, do you? I worry it's something about Ruth. Have you met Rose yet, our newcomer? She's so special, and we're so lucky to have her staying with us."

Welcoming faces smile at me, hopeful and worried at the same time.

Someone in a booth shouts, "Okay now, where's our mayor?"

"She's on her way," Bill calls from his red counter. "Driving back from the hospital right now."

Su whispers to me, "We should stand here at the back, and let the older folks have the seats."

"Bill, is this about Ruth?" another calls.

"That's what we're all waiting to find out. Her son's been with her, I know. Martha will tell us more."

John Berringer holds the ringing door open for his wife and they both come in, shaking the snow from their fur-lined hoods. Bill comes forward and takes their coats.

"Everyone's here?" Mary Berringer asks.

"Just about, Mary."

"Well then!" She looks around at the gathered town before taking an empty booth. Her husband sits down beside her. "So. Martha is on her way. She said to come and be prepared to hear news regarding Ruth that we all need to hear."

A ripple of nerves flutters through the room.

"What news is that?"

"Has poor Ruth passed on?"

Mary shakes her head. "I know it's not that."

Someone points at the wall where Su and I lean. "Should *they* be here?"

"Who?" the old woman says sharply.

"Su and the new one, Mrs. B."

"Of course they should!" she says, impatient. "Exactly how many people do you see in this room, Pete Collier? How many of us are left to carry on the responsibilities and duties of the Bar? With Ruth not here, there are fewer than thirty of us. Of course everyone should be here. Everyone who was invited is welcome."

"You got it?" John Berringer snaps.

Su looks a question at me. "Have no idea what that was, but I guess we're cool."

Another shout. "Here comes Martha's truck!"

The mayor pushes in now under the jangling bells, in a flurry of snow and mud. She pulls her hood back from her head, her hair standing on end. She seems upset and uncertain.

"What is it, Martha? What's happened to Ruth?"

She drops on a stool by the counter. "We have only a few minutes, friends." She deflates, out of breath. "I'm only just ahead of Ruth's son, Seth. He's on his way from the hospital. He'll be here any second."

"But why does it matter? What about Ruth?"

"Ruth is fine."

"Then tell us what's happened," Mary Berringer commands.

"Ruth's doing much better. She's speaking again. That's the problem. She's told her son everything. So get ready, everyone. He's already called someone."

"We are perfectly ready." Mary puts her chin up. "We always have been."

Martha straightens. "All right then. He's here."

A fresh motor halts outside the frosted windows. A young man, his head bent against the wind and snow, bursts through the door and rings into the quieted room.

He's out of breath, too, and it takes a moment for him to find his balance. I see he has his mother's soft face, but his shoulders are hunched and narrow.

He glares at Martha and the rest of the room.

"Seth, dear!" Mary Berringer sends a little wave up from her table. "How nice to see you again. It's been so long! Since you were a tween, I think."

He turns to her, angrily. "Who are you?"

"Mary Berringer. A good friend of your mother's."

"Right. Mama told me. The queen bee. So. This is the rest of the hive?"

Su bristles beside me. "What the hell?"

I say nothing. I have no eyes except for the young, angry man. I know rage ready to strike when I see it. And I know what Ruth Huellet saw. As does he. Soon everyone will know. Hunters, cleaners will be called. There won't be much time, now. I'll have to—

Su grabs me as I start to go.

"It's all right," she says. "Stay here."

Bill steps out from behind his counter, a fist curled at each side of his apron.

"It's all right, Bill," Mary Berringer says, without turning toward him. "It's all right, everyone. Seth, dear. You look like you have something you want to say to us?"

"I do! And I think you all know what. Mama's got her voice back, and she says it's all your fault she's lost the use of half her body. She says you have a whole pack of them here. She says one of them attacked her!"

"Excuse me? A whole pack of what, dear?"

"You know very well what!" he sputters. "She says everyone here is in on it, that you have some kind of arrangement with them. But she's done, she's tired of all of it, pretending like you're some kind of gods, like you have everything under control. When obviously you don't, not if one is on the loose. I'm here to tell you all your sick little party is over. I've reported you. I've called it in, said you've been aiding and assisting and protecting ghosts illegally, and you've been doing it for forever, it sounds like."

Aiding and protecting . . . us?

"Holy shit." Su whistles.

White Bar knows its ghosts. *What does that mean?* My soul beats, unbelieving.

Mayor Martha stands up from her stool. "I'm afraid we don't know what you're talking about," she says.

Mary Berringer, still seated comfortably, says, "Martha's right, dear. We can't imagine what on earth your poor mother must be thinking. All we know is she hit her head. Very badly. The doctors say there's been a great deal of neurological damage. I'm so sorry to have to break this to you, dear, but it sounds as though your mama's been having some trouble with . . . reality. She's been in and out of consciousness. Isn't that right?"

Bill and Harry are inching closer to Seth.

And I'm nearer now than I've ever been to embracing—cheering— the living.

Ruth's son cries, "She still knows what she's saying when she's awake! She was lucid enough with me! She said ghouls have always been here, and you all know it, you keep them, you protect them, and you make her be the front woman in that museum even though it's against the law what you're doing, and she's exhausted, she's plain exhausted with all of it and all of you. You dump everything on her because that's the way it's always been. The Huellets are always the ones left to make things work, right? Well *I'm* a Huellet"—he wheels and faces all of them—"and I'm telling you, this ends now! I say we've had enough hiding and lies. I'm putting a stop to it. You know I could have you all put in jail for harboring fugitives? But Mama said that would make her unhappy, so fine, I've called in a private cleaner instead, and he's on his way, and *you're* going to pay his fee, and *you're* going to get this place straightened out, and then, and only then, when you've taken care of what should have been taken care of a long time ago, only then will we call it even, and Mama and me will be gone."

A private cleaner. My thoughts freeze. *Which cleaner?*

"Gone?" Bill stares him down. "How do you figure that?"

119

"I'll have Mama sell the mansion and then we, she'll take the money and clear out to Palm Springs. Just like any others around here with any decent sense should do."

"You say *we*." Mary Berringer stands up from her booth. "But you never gave your mother the time of day before now. I wonder why that is?"

I begin moving away, toward the back door. *Which cleaner?*

"Your mother," Mary goes on, "always did say both you and your father were nothing but leeches and not to be trusted. If she's exhausted, it's because of you. Draining and draining her. Keeping poor Ruth poor, keeping her working two jobs, not even able to put a coat of paint on that mansion, as you call it, while you lazed around Reno with your worthless father and played blackjack. Why, you're not a Huellet! You're not even worthy of the name. But I'll tell you what: if your dear mother did see a ghost, then fine, we'll do as we've always done. We welcome cleaners, we tolerate no trouble here, we—"

"Not one ghost. My mother said you keep a pack, like pets. And you can't fool me."

"Bill." Mary makes a signal with her hand. "Harold."

"And—and—"The boy stammers, looking afraid. "You won't be able to fool this cleaner when he comes later on tonight, because I've called in the best, the one who's been all over the news lately. He says we have to be more vigilant now than ever because the lawbreakers are getting more creative, more powerful, they're going rogue, they're turning into—hey—what are you doing—take your hands off me!—hey—hey!"

Pratt. Philip Pratt, he means.

Su steps forward. "Wait a minute, what are you—?"

"Bill and Harold are just going to give Seth some time to think things over," Mary says, nodding.

"Are you with us, everyone?" John Berringer shouts to the room.

"We're with you!" comes the shrill answer.

"He needs a little time to come to his senses." The old woman waves a spotted hand as Seth Huellet is dragged away. "It can be so easy to become confused and make mistakes, when you're under stress, as poor Ruth and Seth have been. Bill and Harold, take him to the freezer to cool off a bit . . ."

". . . while we get serious and get ahead of this," Martha finishes.

"But a hunter's already been called!" someone cries.

"We can manage that."

Philip Pratt. Pratt is coming here.

As I reach the back door, Su marches forward to confront them. "Stop. You need to explain what is going on. Right now!"

Mary takes her by the hand. "Of course, dear, of course. We didn't mean to spring things on you this way. So hectic and bewildering this all must seem to you. Although we've certainly given you enough hints and clues, over the past months. We have a special duty and responsibility here in the Bar. We, yes, keep watch over the dead. We have done so for nearly two hundred years. We know how to keep the frightening from being frightening. We control it. Corral it. We have tamed it. And we'll show you how. We have a tradition that requires much strength and imagination and creativity to carry out—just like your own work. You have power over the elements—fire and metal. Now imagine having power over the souls of others. It takes a special strength, I can tell you. A strength you already have—you just don't know everything you can do with it yet. But you *will* know, I promise, and come to cherish it as we do, and help us to preserve it. Along with young Rose, who also has more strength than she knows."

"Where is that gal, anyway?" John Berringer looks around.

I'm behind the butcher's block, at the door to the alley. I could turn back. Attack them. But how, in this body, without giving myself away?

How, how could I have thought I could trust the living?

"What are you saying?" Su is asking. "Are you saying you're . . . masters of the dead?"

"Yes, dear. That's exactly what we're saying."

Su sucks in her breath, awed.

How long do you walk the earth before you give up all hope?

I hear the cries of the young man being dragged into the meat locker. I see Mary and Martha and the others eagerly drawing near an eager Su. I want to terrify and scatter every one of them, yet I have no time, no time, for it's the dead I must find my way to, before Pratt comes and finishes us all.

Failing love and hope, what?

The only hope of a ghost is other ghosts.

I'm a ghost.

PART TWO

THE DOOR

14

A rubbish bin stands in the alley behind the White Bar Café, an icy metal box, dark in the whirling snow. I leap onto it, push against it, fly up to the false-fronted building's roof, high in the night above the town.

I look down at my borrowed rubber boots.

There's only one thing I can do now. So I'll do it.

I slip from the dead woman's soft, gashed body and leave it tucked in the ice behind the town's deceitful gables.

Wait here, I whisper. *The cold will keep you.*

Without a body, I'm unframed, loose, naked. Yet also light and free.

I race, weightless, over all the false faces of the Bar, dropping into the alley at Su Kwon's barn.

I glide between the barn's cracks. I stand before the whispering, breathing steel that I know, that every inch of my bared soul knows, is more than just a piece of metal bent into the shape of luck.

Here's what being dead teaches you:

When one door closes, imagine another.

I step through the Ghost Door.

Something tickles my hand. Not my invisible, ghostly hand. When I look down, it's a strong and muscled fist. The fist of Emma Rose Finnis.

Horseflesh nudges against it, steaming.

The mare's harness shakes.

Her soft muzzle breathes heavily against me. In. Out.

I look to my right. A man in a stiff, furred coat with a kerchief tied around his neck mucks stall hay out into a dirty alley.

Outside, through the open doors of the barn, a weak sun bounces over the backs of moving men and open wagons.

The man stops his work to look me up and down, surprised.

"Can I help you, Miss? Need a mount?"

So I can be seen. I look down again. I'm in my old shirtwaist, the long skirt, the boots I died in, in 1915. My black hair coils over my shoulder, red ribbons knotted in it.

I won't look out of place here, perhaps.

I stroke the mare's mane. "I'm looking for a way through," I say, truthful.

"To where?"

"This is the town of White Bar, yes?"

"Is now. Was Eno Camp." He points between the stalls. "If you want through to the center of town, there's the square. Mind you're not kicked."

I thank him and leave behind steaming muzzles and twitching rumps.

Here before me lies the familiar town—though new as a Monday. The square is filled with stacked planks and muddy troughs and fresh piles of rubble. The day is snowless but must be cold, judging by the fur coats and slouch hats the men wear pulled down low over their eyes, and the red faces of the women standing shawled on the balcony of the hotel above me, calling down to me across the creak of wheels and complaints of the mules.

"Ho there! You won't last out there, sweetie, in that airy getup! Come on up here!" They laugh. "We'll teach you how to earn what's warm with that muslin!"

I smile and lift my hand to them, but say nothing, picking my way across the ruts. Painted canvas banners hang from fresh balconies, announcing the names of the billiard halls. A feed store has gone up beside the Berringers' brand-new house, along with a French bakery, a sundries, and a laundry. The jailhouse sits at the corner, newly mortared. There, across, is Ruth's mansion, Huellet House, its dormers and chimneys unfinished over a porch tricked out with fine scrolled posts and fancy bull's-eyed windows. The window glass is splattered with specks of mud. Two coated men are taking their ease in high-backed rocking chairs under the gingerbreaded filigree. One wears a white Panama hat, the other sports a beaver. Other caps are tipped respectfully their way by the gruff drivers of the wagons and the soggy-bearded men with kerchiefs tied around their necks. The reclining Huellets nod back.

I recognize them from their pictures in the museum. I find a corner in the mud, and watch as a woman in a black skirt with a silver timepiece pinned to her chest and a thick cape over her shoulders comes hurrying toward them. The men on the porch nod at her, as if to give her permission to come up. She climbs the porch stairs.

She bows to the white hat. "Dr. Huellet. Mayor Huellet," she says to the brown beaver.

The leaders of the town.

"Good day to you, Mrs. Garrison," they both say.

"A moment of your time, please, sirs? I'm afraid I've come to spill a mother's heart to you both. We've heard news that there's fever creeping once again along the river. And you know"—her voice grows low, anxious—"how the miners have been coming upstream from the diggings into town on Sundays. We have our boy Anton to think of. He's a good boy, but his constitution isn't as strong as we'd like, and I think we ought to do something to keep the rougher element from undoing all the good work you've done emptying out the near camp and building the school."

The beaver hat tilts to one side. "But the men need to come on Sunday to conduct their business, Mrs. Garrison." The mayor's voice is deep and certain. "The economic health of our little community depends on it. You know that as well as anyone."

"Of course, of course, I understand, Mr. Mayor, of course. My husband and I both do. We need the daily commerce at the Hardware and Tack as much as anyone. But when it comes to our children . . ."

The doctor in his white hat leans forward, smiling quickly, as if to overrule his brother. "Naturally we share your concern. And I'll say this: a true mother can never be overzealous in her ministrations! Why don't you come inside, Mrs. Garrison, and I'll mix a special tonic for your son."

"If you think it wise, Doctor? A necessary precaution?"

"I do, Mrs. Garrison, I do." His voice is higher than his brother's, and musical. "Good health is the armature of the soul. And the presence of wisdom *ensures* the absence of infection. Step inside, if you please."

The woman puts her hands around her waist, gasping a little, as though she's not well herself, and lifts her long skirt as she enters the unfinished house.

No sooner has she gone in than a man comes forward, in his turn, his ragged coat collar turned up against the cold. He calls to the mayor sitting alone on the porch, raising his hat politely to him.

I recognize him, too. The mesmerizing gaze from the schoolhouse.

The teacher the younger children whispered of, *He'll find us*. Landon Albert Longhurst.

"Mr. Mayor," Longhurst says.

"How fare you this fine sundown, schoolmaster?"

"Well. And you?"

"In excellent spirits and health, thank the Lord."

"How fortunate. If I might have a word with you, please?"

The mayor doesn't invite the schoolmaster to sit, though the chair where his brother rocked gleams like an empty saddle.

The teacher clears his throat and sets his long, whiskered jaw.

"I've come about a pupil of mine."

"Oh? One of those whippersnappers giving you trouble?"

"Not at all. In fact, it's the trouble that comes *to* him I want to speak to you about."

"Sickness?" The mayor tilts his head. "Lethargy? A lack of vigor? A weakness of the blood?"

"No. At least"—the mad teacher looks to his left and to his right, and as he does so notices me watching him, and blinks, surprised—"at least not, to be blunt, in the ordinary sense of the term 'sickness.' It's young Jack Granger. He comes to school daily with bruises around his head."

"A pity. My brother will mix a tonic for his—"

"I don't consider it a matter for elixirs, sir. Jack suffers at his father's hand."

The mayor lowers his voice and narrows his eyes. "Has the boy said as much?"

"He hasn't had to. You know what Granger is like. We all do."

"Well." The man rocks back in his chair. "Perhaps the boy has been derelict in his chores. Slow to obey. Far be it from any of us to tell a father how to school his son."

"Sir, allow me to say—and I speak from experience—that beating is not schooling. It's a degradation, and more often results in a hardening of the spirit, as well as unwarranted suspicion of any instance of kindness. Young Jack *looks* for harsh treatment. He expects, he all but asks for insult and injury. It's pitiful, watching a boy of his eager years curl his shoulders against a lesson, for fear he'll miss the mark, fear he'll be hit. I presume it's strong men we want to raise for this town and for this territory? Then you ought to have a word with Granger, in your capacity as head of the School Board."

"Why haven't you done so yourself?"

"The last time I saw him he was drunk, and called me a nellie."

The mayor laughs. "And you had earned this insult, in his eyes, by—?"

"Being a schoolteacher."

"And now you're here returning fire, is that it? Seeking a little vengeance?"

"Not at all," Longhurst says stiffly. "My worry is solely on Jack's behalf."

"Then I'll have my brother send them both a tonic."

"I think the cure lies in plain speaking, not more alcohol."

"You're a doctor, suddenly?"

"I am not, sir." The schoolmaster clenches a fist. Anger keeping itself in check.

"Then I'd be more careful"—the wooden rocker stills—"using the word 'cure.' That's far outside your ken, boy."

"And if I were you, Huellet, I'd be careful in dosing people where there is no need. Especially young children."

The mayor snaps, "You think you can tell us our business, do you?"

"Of course not. Why would I? When business is so good, I see." He gestures at the house.

The mayor laughs again, relaxing. "You've wandered far from your purpose, boy, which I don't suppose is appraising architecture. Your job is only to put book learning into empty heads. Well! Thank you for your visit. You'll want to get indoors, now, before Granger and other ruffians stir at night," he says, meaningly.

"I'm not afraid of ruffians. I'm used to them."

The schoolmaster turns on his boot heel and goes down the steps and into the mud.

I know at once: I must follow him.

I hang back among the men and mules as he makes his way over the rutted square. He passes the undertaker's parlor, heading toward a lane between hacked trees. I quicken my pace so as not to lose him and what this ghostly vision is meant to show me.

It's quieter in the dusky meadow. There are fewer people milling about. At its edge stands a log schoolhouse, with chinked sides and a peaked roof and short, square belfry.

Longhurst quickly wipes his worn boots on the crate that serves as the school's stoop before going inside. I stop, ready to do the same. But there's no muck on my boots, nor on my skirt, when I look down. I'm not of this time. Yet Longhurst is. The time knows it, somehow.

This isn't a ghostly vision, I understand, amazed. This is the true past I've traveled to. I'm haunting a world before I was born.

I push open the schoolhouse door. Longhurst is sitting at a small rough desk with a book in front of him, an inkwell at his patched elbow. The wood stove in the corner of the room flickers.

He looks at me, blinking again.

"I'm sorry . . . can I help you?"

"I'm not sure."

"Who are you?"

"I'm visiting."

"I see. And your business here, Miss, is—?"

His face is courteous. Not yet the face of the murderer of children. *How is it,* I think, *we're all innocent before we break?*

"I'm Emma Rose Finnis," I say evenly. "And you are Mr. Longhurst."

"Landon Longhurst, I am."

"You have five pupils in this school."

"I do." He blinks again. "Are you—are you the schoolmistress who was supposed to—?" He looks suddenly upset. Or is that a flash of relief crossing his face?

"I'm not here to teach. I want to learn, Mr. Longhurst. I want to know—why would you hurt them?"

"I'm sorry?"

"I want to know why a teacher would harm his pupils." The past holds all the answers to the present, I'm certain of it. If I ask the right questions, will I be able I stop him from hurting the others? "You must stop yourself before you—"

He frowns at me, without understanding.

Then his brow clears.

"Oh! You must have come by when we were at recess playing hide and seek in the trees! The children scream a bit when they're excited. The little ones, especially. They didn't mean to disturb. I apologize if they startled you. Are you new to our outpost? Where is it you've come from, Miss Finnis?"

It's a terrible thing to stand in front of a man long dead who doesn't know yet what he'll do, or how he'll die. He looks at me so intently, smiling. Pleasantly. As if he wants to know me. We look at each other, from different sides of the door of time. I see him staring at my thin clothes, and wondering. But he says nothing. Polite. Unknowing.

"Where are your pupils now?" I ask quickly. I need to see them. I must warn them.

"They've all gone home for their suppers. Excuse me." He rises from his desk. "I must close the stove for the night. I need to save the fuel."

I let him pass me and kneel to turn the dampers.

He straightens. "Are you from the East?" he asks, smiling. "I hear a touch of the Irish."

"The west coast."

"How pleasant the sea is. I miss it. All corners meet in this place, don't they?" He sighs. "The whole world has come to California, everyone and their brother and . . ." His jaw hardens. "Including the parasites." He looks toward the empty blue jars cradled between the logs for a window. He looks down at his tattered coat.

"What is it, Mr. Longhurst? What are you planning?"

"A well-timed question. Sometimes I'm filled with such . . . ideas. Such heat. It can be invigorating. Reflection, I mean." He stares emptily in front of him. "When it isn't completely futile."

"I must go," I say, for fear I might in some way be hastening the children's deaths. If this isn't a vision, can I change the course of time itself?

"Can I walk you somewhere, Miss Finnis?" So polite and well-spoken he is.

But then, so many cruel men use fine, elegant words.

"No thank you. I prefer to walk alone."

"Then good evening to you, Miss Finnis."

The schoolmaster's log house, when I take one look back at it, trails a last bit of smoke into the trees. Then it goes dark. He must have good eyes, Longhurst, to see his way through the gloam. There's just enough light left for me to hurry over a path toward the river, where I hear the sounds of people gathering in for the evening, the clamor of fire-building, cooking, washing. I reach the familiar rocky bank, where the falls churn. The whirling below is filled with pinned logs and rubble, not yet tidied after the men who died there trying to change its course.

From the other side of the water I smell the cooking of the Chinese. I remember it, from when I was a girl, as well as the murmur of their voices, and the outlines of the men in their long coats and braids. The camp seems to be all men, speaking to each other in shouts and coughs. A wooden bridge I don't recognize spans the rushing stream. I move toward it, as others seem to be using it to cross to town.

When I'm closer to it, I see someone coming across, a shape somehow familiar to me.

It's her. The girl with the flowered sleeves. Her thick braids, her slow, deliberate movements. The pupil who must be the one Longhurst in his letters called Ola. She's walking, her head down, with a thick shawl around her, carrying something in a flour sack in her arms crossed in front of her. Close behind two others walk with something of her gait about them, a man and a woman, hard on her heels, as if they're spurring a mule.

I reach them just as they leave the wooden bridge and start toward the square, now lit with lanterns and torches. The girl named Ola stops. I halt, too, and hope for some chance.

She turns to face the woman behind her. "I can't, Mama."

"You must, daughter."

The man, who must be her father, says with more kindness, "Ola. We have need. Let me do it."

She pulls the flour sack more tightly to her chest.

Her mother says slowly, "He'd want us to do what we can to get by."

"Papa. Please! It's all we have to remember him by."

"It's past time for toys, now. Let me—"

She flinches. "You won't get enough for it."

"Then you must go, Ola," he apologizes. "To the smithy's or the sundries."

"Sundries," the mother says firmly. "Other children in town may have good use of it."

The girl opens the sack and takes something from it. A hobbyhorse made of red tin.

"Go in now, girl," her mother urges, her voice hard, "alone. If all of us go, they'll see we have no coats and pay us less, such are the sins against charity."

The girl hunches and steps slowly onto the porch of the building that will one day be the White Bar Café. The painted sign in the window reads GOODS, TRADES, AND CLAIMS EXCHANGED. She opens the door.

The mother says, "Don't know as she'll be able to do it."

"She's a strong girl," her husband answers. "Drives a good bargain."

"She's worn down. She's too much at the diggins. She wants only to be at school."

"She doesn't need any more schooling."

"She'll sicken."

"She's hale. When we hit pay dirt—"

"Yes, when we hit pay dirt. We'll make it up to her. Yes."

"She's worn but still full of grit. We all are. And diggin' season ain't done."

"It's nearly done though, Tom."

"No one's leaving yet. Look."

He points at the men walking slumped in front of their mounts, and others wending and weaving, mufflered, into the saloons. The women are gone now from the cold balconies above. Prospectors hurry past the undertaker's coffins leaning against the clapboard parlor.

Death is near. Always.

I must speak to the girl of the flowered sleeves. She's gone alone into the shop. This will be my chance, I decide. I climb onto the porch, pushing against the door, but it's wrenched from my hand and I'm jerked, flung forward into bright white electric light.

"No one's here." Bill closes the café door, confused.

Harold is talking to Su Kwon. "You must be thinking we're a bunch of liars, Su."

I'm back in the present, I think, reeling. *Why? Why?*

Su is sitting in a booth with the Berringers. No one notices me.

I'm a wraith again, invisible.

"But that's not what we're about," Harold goes on. "We're not liars. Not one of us. How can something sacred be a lie? That's how I see it. You have to protect what's sacred. What's special. Isn't that right, Mary?"

I've been flung back across time. Time has schooled me, is that it, made this much plain: the past will not be changed, not even if you meet and know it.

I need to keep myself still and try to feel nothing. If I grow angry, with time, with fate, with truth, I'll show myself, and my own time will be up.

Stay calm and cold, Emma Rose, I steady myself. *Wait. Watch. Something will come to you.*

Mary Berringer is patting Su's hands. "Harold is right, dear. Now, Pete, you look like you'd like to add something?"

"I'd like to tell you my story, Su." A skinny man with a long face comes forward from the meeting. "When I first came to the Bar, I was horribly down on my luck. I'd just lost my job. My whole company went robot-automated. I found myself out on the street, after twenty years of labor, no offer of help, not even an apology, no severance, nothing. Taken out like the trash. God, I was so embarrassed to know it. I tried to drink myself to death and bankruptcy. I was headed to the casinos to do just that. But then I stopped here at the café, and I admitted to Bill, 'I'm hungry, I'm sad,' and Bill said, 'If you're sad and hungry, stay here and we'll feed you.' You made a big lunch for me, Bill, and you said, 'No charge, I can see you need it'—do you remember that? And Mary and John—I think you called them, didn't you, Bill?—they invited me to stay at their place, and all they asked in return was that I help them with a little cleaning and polishing. The mayor came by the next day, and she asked who I was and where I came from and what my story was, and I told her I was a groundskeeper, and she said to me, you know, there would be nothing nicer than having a maintenance and plowing service right here, and not over at Dutch Gap. Martha said the old gold might be gone from this place, but there's new gold here, and we'll help you find it. And the next thing I knew, I was made so welcome you wouldn't believe—although maybe you would, now you've been here a while. Then, after I'd been here a bit, I got the sense, I don't know, I just *knew*, there was something more going on. I could see it in everyone's faces, that there was something deeper giving them, everyone you see here, something special, a real sense of purpose and reason and easiness, like they were connected to something that kept them going even when everything else was going to hell. They had something I didn't. I could just *taste* it. And I know you've felt that too, Su. Well, I wanted it, whatever it was. I told Martha I wanted to be part of the Bar in every way there was to be a part of it, and she took it to the town council and everybody you see here, and she made my case, and I was finally introduced to the bargain. And the bargain changed my life. To know that I'm a guardian of life and death. Me, Pete Collier. Who nobody ever heard of. Me, I have a sacred responsibility, more powerful than the whole world would ever guess."

"Imagine that, Su," Mary says beside him. "That's what the bargain is. It goes back to the 1850s. Our town fathers agreed to give the schoolhouse ghosts a place to bide in, if they agreed to make no trouble and let us keep our town peaceful and happy. The bargain is that we will keep them all safe and hidden from the world, as long as they do as they're told. We won't be afraid of them as long as they don't make us afraid; and they don't have to be afraid of us as long as they don't make any trouble. All they have to do is keep inside the place that was built for them after they died. The schoolhouse on the Knob will never be torn down. It's their home, since, you see, every ghost needs a home. But they can't allow themselves to be seen by anyone. If they do, if they get out of line, then they're finished. Then the schoolhouse is razed. There have to be parameters, as with any arrangement. If they get out of line, there must be consequences. Am I leaving anything out, John?"

"You hit it all," the old man barks, satisfied.

Walk the earth a hundred years, I think, *and you'll never see the end of how pleased with itself cruelty can be.*

"Any of us who are let into the bargain," Harold says proudly, "is a privileged member, and has to keep the responsibility sacred and protected and hidden, or else be haunted and hounded and punished. And then of course these days if you know about and don't report a ghost, you also go to jail. So that's why even when people have left the Bar, they've respected the bargain and don't say anything. And neither will you, now—am I right, Su?"

Su nods, quickly.

"Of course," Mary adds, "not everyone can manage such responsibility, or should. So we're careful. And we've never had any trouble at all until now. Certainly not with the schoolhouse ghosts. Only a few

138

others, strays. It will be a hundred and seventy-three anniversaries of the bargain next week. Think of that. We've kept it going no matter what kind of problems there have ever been in this town. Because a promise is a bargain, and a bargain is a promise. Isn't that right, everyone?" she calls to the room. "And here we are, and here you are, Su, all these years later, let into the special trust of it."

"Only now the bargain's in danger," Mayor Martha says, leaning in, "and we have to respond as one. So we're having this meeting, and sharing all this with you. We're terribly sorry about poor Ruth and her son . . . but we have to do something about this, though it's breaking our hearts. And yours, too, I'm certain, now that we've shared everything with you."

I'm watching Su. Su, who was strong enough to bend metal.

She turns to the room.

"I want to thank you all for your honesty," she says, in her clear voice. "I understand what you've said to me. And I'll add just one more thing, if it's all right. If the spirits are out of line now, it might be because of the tram in the meadow. The Bar tried to build something on the very site of their suffering, didn't it? I'm thinking maybe that wasn't a good idea?"

A woman calls from the back, angrily, "Well *we* have to eat. *They* don't."

"Understood." Su nods her long hair. "But they do need respect. I know that from personal experience, with a dead uncle I had." I think and want to scream: *Uncle Bao, she's using you now, forgetting everything she said to me about you.* "You have to give them respect, if you want to keep them in line."

So quickly can a heart turn. It takes all my soul has, sometimes, not to despair.

"But you're the one who's been digging things up around there!" the same woman objects.

139

Su stares at her. "And how could I know any better? If you didn't tell me there were ghosts here?"

Bill jumps in. "It's all right, Su's right. All the digging and disruption out there might have done it. And maybe one of them took it out on our poor Ruth."

"If that's so," Mary Berringer says, rising, "I think we can give one of them up to this hunter, this—what is his name? What did you get out of that miserable Seth?" She turns to Bill.

"Philip Pratt."

"Philip Pratt. One ghost should satisfy him, and send him away, while at the same time teaching a lesson to the others, to keep order."

"But what about Ruth?" Martha says. "She's going to tell anyone who asks that there's more than one."

"Well, we'll have to explain to the cleaner she isn't in her right mind. She's hallucinating. That will be our first step. We have to protect what's ours."

"And Ruth's boy?"

"We'll take care of him."

"What about Rose?" Bill asks. "We've probably frightened her. But we shouldn't let her get away . . . should we?"

As if you could keep me.

Mary commands, "Martha, go check your place for her. Harold, do a little search of town. And Su, if she comes to you—we know she trusts you—you bring her to us."

"All right, but don't count her out yet, okay?" Su urges. "Rose is really cool. She's been through a lot of the same things we have, and worse, I think. I think she'll want to stay on and serve the future of this place. I really do feel that."

Oh, you can be sure, Su, Mary, Bill, all of you, that I will find a way to serve this place.

"In any case"—Mary buttons her coat—"Rose doesn't have a car, so she won't have gotten very far, not with this storm beating down. Bill, you stay here to deal with Seth. John and I will prepare to manage the cleaner when he arrives. Everyone else, just go about your business. Act normally. Are you all right, Su, dear?"

"I'm just amazed, that's all. This has been so . . . amazing."

"Everything's going to be easy now," the old woman says warmly. "We're very resourceful here, and always have been so. Call when you find Rose. I'm sure she's close by."

I am. *So close, old woman, that I brush you and your hood falls and seems to squeeze your neck, tightening for an instant. Yet you don't notice, or cry out. Because a cry comes from deep inside where feelings, a decent conscience, should be. Instead, you walk out the door, silent, with all the others.*

But it's Su I'll deal with first, and who I follow.

15

She tucks her long hair under her colorful scarf and tightens her coat. She walks around the edge of the lamplit square with her shoulders lifted against the howling wind and snow. She looks neither to her right nor to her left. The wind chimes at her gallery door batter madly. She imagines it's only the wind raking its nails across them.

With me invisible at her shoulder, Su Kwon lets herself inside and throws off her coat. She takes her glowing telephone from her pocket and presses it, quickly.

"Mama. It's me."

Her voice is small and tight.

"I know, I know. It's been a while. How's Dad? No, don't ask him. I need to talk to you. I miss you, Mom. I miss you so, so, so much."

She leans her cheek against the screen as though it might soothe her.

But nothing will save you now.

"No, I don't think it'll all work out eventually, somehow. That's not why I'm calling. Something's . . . happened here. No, work is fine. It's something else. Nothing I can talk about, really, without . . . I don't want to drag you into anything, is the thing. So let's just call it a local problem.

142

Something I have to decide how I'm going to handle, and decide quick. I need your help with one small piece of it. I'm going to text you a phone number to a little restaurant, a café, and I want you to call it and ask for someone named Seth. On the other end, someone's either going to say Seth's not there, or they have no idea who Seth is. I want you to say you're his boss and you can't reach him on his cell and you know he's there, at the White Bar Café. Then hang up. That's all you have to do. Why? Because you're letting someone know that someone knows and cares about this Seth guy. No, I can't tell you any more. Just stay light on your feet like you always do. No, you're not getting this Seth in trouble, the reverse, in fact. No, Jesus, I don't like him and he's not good-looking, Ma. What I like—and you can tell Dad this—is doing the right thing when you know it's the right thing. You and me, Ma, we listen to our guts, right? I know I sound serious. I am serious. But you'll do what I asked you? Thanks. The rest I have to try to handle on my own. It's delicate. Okay. You are amazing. I love you. I'm sending the number now. Bye."

She taps and sets the telephone down, and covers her sharp face with both hands. She doesn't know I'm standing right beside her.

I'm judging you.

She drops her hands. "Well." She looks at the twisted metal tongues on the walls around her. "So I guess this little piece of paradise turned out to be, yeah, not so much."

Around her eyes is the amazed look a face wears when it can't quite believe a thing. The look Pratt's face wore when I managed to escape him. The way my eyes must have started and stared when I knew I was going to sink to the bottom of the sea. *Surely*, the amazed look says, *I didn't make so grave a mistake.*

This time I want to have been wrong. But am I?

Su says aloud, "Rose, wherever you've gone, I hope you are far, far away from here and all this shit." She paces her gallery.

Then stops.

"I could tell them," she frets to herself, "that I've looked for Rose and can't find her anywhere. But she could still come back, before I get a chance to tell her about . . . And shit, what do they do to people who say no? Put them in the freezer?"

She stops, frightened. She understands.

There aren't just ghosts in this town. There are the dangerous living.

"All right." She gives herself a little shake. "I'll manage this. Figure it out. And keep Rose out of it—if she hasn't already cleared out. She doesn't need this. What do I need?" She lifts up her device again. "A lawyer, probably. Say nothing about all this, and I'm involved in crimes. Say something, and the ghosts are offed by the hunter that's coming. Okay. Concentrate. What needs doing first?"

She closes her eyes.

"Trust. Get them to trust you." She keeps them shut. "Who? Everyone. Keep the town trusting me. Get the hunter to trust me, too. That nets me the most options, the most time. Anything difficult takes finesse. If you can't get rid of the knives, then it's who you hand them to that matters, right, Ma? What?"

She turns, jumping.

I just tried to reach out and touch her. It's not the same without a body, a hand that can stroke. I need to feel her, to be sure.

Is she too good to be true? Is this, at last, real goodness? Or am I making another mistake?

She goes to the snow-filled windows.

"It's really blowing, now. Maybe the passes will close. Just enough to stop the cleaner, whoever he is."

I want to fold her in my arms.

Which arms?

I have none. They're in the bitter cold, where I left them.

So unexpected and confusing it is, trying to be free and flesh, both.

Hurry. Hurry, now, Emma Rose.

I fly from Su's gallery. On the café's false roof from under the thick snow I lift up the body I left and cloak myself in it. Here are muscles, crevices, arms, fingers, real bone. In the pocket of the mayor's coat I find Longhurst's letter. I take out the sheets, and the snowflakes fall across these palms and the letter both, brushing, touching.

Yes. It's just as I remembered. Ola is as Longhurst described, slow and sturdy. Anton was the son of the woman who came pleading to the Huellet brothers for help. Jack was the bruised boy Longhurst spoke to Caleb Huellet about. Addy and Will would be the ghosts that appeared to me at the hotel, holding hands. It's not just one ghost that's left the schoolhouse. It might be all of them, loose, disturbed, angry. Rightfully so. But dangerous to each other, I worry. To all of us.

I come to the end of the letter and also find, strangely, more sheets than there were. In the same hand, the same faded, wild, blotted ink, I discover words that are new yet somehow already old.

Something strange and unexpected, diary . . . as a diary this now clearly is.

I had a visitor at the schoolhouse this evening. A rather pleasant one. I was just sitting down to my desk when she appeared at the schoolhouse door, a strange woman in strange clothing. We have so many foreigners here who hail from all corners of the earth, I first thought she might be a Chilean, and that this would account for her dark cast and strange dress. But when she spoke it was in a brusque,

Gaelic manner. She asked about the school. She seemed interested to know about my pupils. I had the impression, while we spoke, that she was taking my measure (even as I was taking hers). Since we were strangers to each other, man and woman, I maintained a good distance and decorum. In fact, after a short span of minutes I hinted she should go, not because I wanted her to—I didn't—but because her staying much longer might give rise to talk among the people in town—though no doubt such talk would have done me good in the eyes of men like Jack Granger.

She went. I was sorry to see her go, and to be left to my cold walk back to my lodging. I have no idea where she might be lodging or what her business might be in town. It occurred to me she might be the schoolmistress that had been sent for months ago and failed to arrive—perhaps she was only now arriving, and came to assess whether she could still have her place?—but for some reason I feel this is unlikely. By no sign or word did she indicate she wanted to stand in my shoes. She seemed curious about the future and well-being of my pupils. When the truth is, by God, I know as little about anyone's future as I do my own. The children sometimes frighten me, when I look at them. They are by turns helpless and stern. They sometimes— Ola, especially—stare at me as though I am insufficient to their needs, as though they see through my ragged coat, my scholarly pretenses, and find me wanting.

I felt, I feel, unutterably lonely now. And yet not entirely alone. I saw in the stranger's eyes, too, the eyes of a wanderer come to a rough place. But that might simply be my fancy speaking. It's late, and the lantern sputters. I'm going to bed.

I don't understand.

What if you can't change the past, I wonder, *only be more tightly bound to it?*

As if in answer, below me a car engine announces itself with a rough hum under the wind. It wends its way slowly toward the square, through the storm. It shines its yellow lights, crawling, inching around the statue of the Prospector. Snow has crusted over its windshield, leaving only two wiped half circles, dark, like black eyes.

My soul knows what's arrived.

It's Philip Pratt.

The car edges up to a buried curb and stops. Pratt's bulk squeezes out of the door. Even in his long coat, I know him. He's grown heavier. He leans, then straightens, with a small bag in his hand, and starts with a slight limp toward the hotel.

It matters not at all to me that he was wounded when he tried to put me down. There are those who deserve compassion, and those who deserve understanding, and those who deserve no space in the heart at all, because their hearts are missing the door that would open into another's.

There are so many reasons I have to rage at this man, yet I must keep calm and invisible, or be discovered.

Yet such a sharp, hot pain I feel, knowing I'll have to hide from him this body, these arms, this precious skin that I've claimed and felt the world through and lived in all these months since I last faced him. Because he'll recognize it.

The mayor is coming out to greet him, beckoning him inside. He nods and follows her.

I must leave this body again, on another, higher roof now. The snow will keep it safe, even as my spirit throws itself toward danger.

16

Awaiting Mary Berringer says, from her chair beside the mayor's flickering fireplace, "Well, you must be Mr. Pratt."

"I am."

Close in, he looks as I remember. The same salt-and-pepper beard. The strong chin, thick hair. The same stylish clothing. That bit of swagger. Slowed by the limp.

The mayor is taking his luggage upstairs. I've curled, invisible, cold, in a smoky corner above them, to study this meeting.

"I'm Mrs. Berringer," Mary says, smiling at him. "And this is my husband, John. We add our welcome to Martha's."

"Thank you very much. May I?" He points to an empty chair.

"Please do."

"You made good time," John Berringer says, unusually polite.

"I was in the valley exploring another lead, as it happens. So I wasn't too far away."

I know that easy smile—though his eyes look deeper and wetter than they used to, as though they've been hoisted from the bottom of a well.

"What do you mean by another lead, Mr. Pratt?"

"Lately, I've been on the hunt for a specific phantom, Mrs. Berringer. You may have heard about it on the news. There was a sighting, not too far from here, a few days ago. A man in a car was attacked at Lake Berry, frightened, but allowed to survive. Tortured, in other words. You might have heard about some trouble we had up north, with a new strain of haunt?"

She shakes her white head. "I can't say that we have. But then we stay deliberately remote here and a little out of touch."

"Part of the charm of being in the mountains, ma'am?" He's flattering her. His way of getting what he wants.

"Exactly. Are you tired, Mr. Pratt? Should we let you rest, and begin all this in the morning?"

She wants to delay and distract him.

"Not at all, I generally keep late hours. Hazard of the profession. It's kind of you all to have waited up for me."

"We were anxious to make sure you arrived safely. Have you, dear?" She points to his knee.

"An old injury. Well, somewhat recent. Healing well."

"What happened? Are you in much pain?"

"A cracked pelvis, a broken knee. In the line of duty."

"Goodness!"

"Looks worse than it feels. It's nothing, comparatively."

"Compared to *what*?" John Berringer snorts.

"Compared, I suppose, to breaks that can't be mended." Pratt stares into the fire.

"You know, that's what we have to worry about, too, at our age," Mary says brightly. "Broken limbs are something we're quite careful about, my John and I. Now here is Martha, coming down to us again. She's a spring chicken!"

149

"A chicken, anyway." The mayor lets out a tight laugh. "Can I get you a hot coffee or tea?" she says to Pratt. "Or maybe something stronger?"

"Coffee would be wonderful. And thank you all again for this warm greeting. If you all feel comfortable with it, and since you're here, I can briefly get some information and clarification from you. That will give me a jump on our task in the morning." He takes out his notepad.

Mary stares at it. "Certainly. But if you don't mind, dear, we have some questions for you first. You come highly recommended, of course—but we do like to do a little vetting of our own, beforehand, you understand. Especially since it wasn't the town council that called you."

He seems surprised, but tips his shaggy head in agreement. "I perfectly understand, Mrs. Berringer. Fire away."

"We've read your profile, Mr. Pratt. But can you tell us a bit more about your experiences and guidelines as a cleaner? Or hunter—if that's the term you prefer?"

Pratt sets aside his notes and lifts his palms to the fire. "I don't mind either term—though hunting suggests a sporting activity, something done for pleasure, a certain kind of thrill. What I do is for the public good—and the private good, too, I believe. My guidelines are simple: the living deserve peace. They don't want to be hounded by the past. The dead, too, deserve peace, and rest. The work is not so much a hunt, a going after prey. I see cleaning, Mrs. Berringer, as closer to curating. Which to my mind means understanding and caring deeply about what belongs where, what's best for all. So my life has been devoted to curating spaces, in a way, to make sure the dead sleep peacefully in theirs, the earth, and the living can walk freely around their homes, their streets."

Ah, yes. I've heard all this before. The man warming his hands below me fancies himself a hero. He doesn't look down and see the blood under his fingernails.

150

Martha asks, bringing him his coffee, "How'd you get started in this line of work, Mr. Pratt? And any sugar with your coffee?"

"Thank you, no thank you. I had some natural proclivity, as a child. I was never afraid of the ghosts under my bed." I've heard this patter, too. He's like a music box that plays only the one ticking waltz. "Nor afraid to tell them they were under the wrong bed, and they needed to go. It's funny, but when you're a child, you have a very strong sense of black and white. It's only when we get older that we sometimes start to . . ." He pauses, blowing on his cup for a moment. "To . . . lose our certainties. I was doing non-technology-based cleanings when I was in my twenties and thirties, what we called séances back then. With the turn of the millennium and the development of the colliders, of course, everything changed. I became fascinated by the new hardware. And that's when things took off for me. When you combine—and I don't mean to sound grandiose here, only truthful—when you combine natural propensity with state-of-the-art weaponry, you yield good results. A lot of my competitors, particularly in the public sector, think the work is simply point and shoot. It isn't. It's so much more than that, friends." He nods at all of them. "There's an art to it, to getting the job done right. There's a passion you have to have for the work, a feeling. And that's what I bring to each assignment."

"It sounds like you enjoy your work, dear." Mary smiles.

"I do, Mrs. Berringer. I take pleasure in making the world a happier, more ordered place. Not in any hunt or hurt."

Liar. I've seen you wipe your boots, with satisfaction, on the dust of a blasted soul.

"Except you recently ran into a world of hurt, didn't you?" John Berringer leans toward him. "I've been doing a little research into you. And what happened this past summer. Along the coast. Deaths. An investigation?"

"I'm glad you've brought that up," Pratt says smoothly. "The state licensing board reviewed my work and cleared me of any negligence, Mr. Berringer. But yes, it was a painful summer. That particular haunting . . . was a complex one, and the dead that it involved . . ." He twitches, something I don't remember him doing before. "I don't like to ascribe emotions to the dead, you know—they don't feel in the same ways you or I do, it's a very narrow spectrum of feeling, primarily vengeance and anger and sadness . . . but in that case, an especially malicious and complicated range of ghostly behaviors and responses were involved, and they resulted in casualties. In tragedy. The deaths weren't my fault, but still, you feel . . . not responsible, but present. I was present for some very unhappy outcomes."

So, to your way of thinking, Mr. Pratt, the dead body I saved from being put six feet under was just an unhappy outcome.

"You poor man," Mary coos at him. "Didn't it shake your faith in your profession, dear? Don't you ever just want to quit, walk away from all these . . . *assignments?*"

"No. Not at all. If anything"—the certainty returns to his gruff voice—"it's sharpened my resolve, let me know I'm doing the right sort of work. When the living and the dead mix, Mrs. Berringer, nothing good comes out of it. And sometimes terrible things come. So that boundary must be preserved. I witnessed a particularly powerful and resourceful spirit there along the coast. I saw her steal the tissues of a freshly dead human being, take that body on as her own, and escape. I saw this happen, right in front of my eyes. Some of my colleagues believe I imagined the hybridization, under the stress of my injuries, or to avoid the outcomes of any trial or— But it's not in my nature to conjure chimeras, or deny culpability. I believe—in fact I know—there is now something out there the likes of which we have never before seen. And if we don't find it, and put it to rest, it will upend life as we know it, and everything that we agree *is* life. The resulting hybrid, it was . . . it looked like someone, something completely new . . . unrecognizable . . . an amalgam, a wedding of the dead and the living. Remarkable. Clever, I don't deny it. Our current weapons can't be shot at flesh, at human tissue, as a safety precaution. You understand that by taking over a fresh body, the spirit has insulated itself against further attack."

Well, a girl is entitled to a bit of Irish luck, isn't she?

"Good God! That's the ghost you were chasing at Lake Berry?" Martha gasps.

"And I'll chase her till I find her, Madam Mayor."

"But that sounds awful. Does the hunt become all you think about?"

"I won't deny I can be focused. Fixated on what's good and right and ordered and logical. But I'm not obsessed with one specific ghost, if that's what you mean."

Of course you aren't, dear.

"Don't you have a family, dear? Time for other passions and concerns?"

"I travel a great deal, Mrs. Berringer."

"But why stop for *our* problem, which, I hate to share with you, might in comparison to what you've just described seem like no problem at all?"

"Let us return to your situation, then. And no worries: I'm delighted to be here and to help. A cleaner still has to make a living, ma'am." He bows. "And I'll speak plainly: chasing something no one else as yet believes in is expensive. So I'm happy to assist. Tell me what it is you are dealing with in White Bar."

"Thank you, dear. That's exactly why we're here. John and Martha and I are part of the town council. Along with Ruth Huellet, our town archivist, who as you may know is in the hospital, and Bill Schoden and

Harold Dubois, who will be joining us shortly. They're just across the square, finishing up some business in the café, but now that they've seen your car they'll be bundling up to get over here."

Pratt takes up his pen. "And where is the young man who first made the report, Seth Huellet?"

"I believe he will be accompanying them. But Mr. Pratt, we may as well tell you that we're concerned you have been *misinformed*. Our dear Ruth has suffered a stroke, and hasn't been speaking plainly. The young man—her son—isn't really from this town, and hasn't seen his mother in many years, and we believe has jumped to conclusions that are not accurate. You'll likely want to go and see dear Ruth yourself, but what you hear may not jibe with reality, we're afraid."

"And what is that reality, Mrs. Berringer?"

"You'll be able to see for yourself in the morning. We preserve the past, here, Mr. Pratt; we are not, to our knowledge, haunted by it. We keep the past alive and well, in our buildings, customs, period details. People come here for the authentic gold rush experience. Perhaps this has created confusion for a young man who thinks he knows the Bar but who hasn't lived here and doesn't know us at all."

"He said"—Pratt looks at his notes—"according to his mother you were 'infested' with ghosts. He hasn't, he was clear, seen them himself."

Martha frowns. "Well, we certainly did have ghosts at one time. But now we're clean as a whistle. It's what the tourists demand, you know. Atmosphere, but clean."

"So you're saying, Mayor Hayley, you believe the report that brought me here is in error."

"That's our suspicion. Our hope. But of course, you're the expert, Mr. Pratt. You'll want to talk to—excuse me, I hear some stomping on my porch, I think they're here, Bill, Harry, and Seth. Just a moment, and you'll be able to ask Seth yourself."

The door blows open, and the three men, arms linked, stumble into the pink light of the sconces, their heads down, their necks painted with snow. The first to let go of Seth Huellet's narrow shoulder is Bill. Then Harold. They slap and shake the ice from their own backs and then, loudly, from the frail back of Ruth's son.

"Hey, sorry about your rug, Martha!" Harold calls and shivers. "Wild out there! First of a series of squalls, apparently."

"Don't worry about the carpet. Come sit by the fire, boys. This is Mr. Philip Pratt."

Harold turns first to Seth. "Let me take your coat, son, you're not from here, are you, so you don't know, but you don't want to stay in wet things, trust me. You'll freeze."

Seth Huellet lifts his head and chin, his iced hair falling back. He moves meekly to one side as Harold passes him with the gathered coats.

"Sit down, Seth," Martha invites. "Bill, can you get some more coffee for everyone?"

I stay curled in my corner. The snow blows in sheets across the windows.

"Good evening, everyone. I was just saying," Pratt continues, "that I'd like to get a few things a bit more in focus this evening, and then I'll hit this case hard and strong in the morning. If that's all right with the assembled council?"

"It is," Martha says.

"Now." Pratt returns, businesslike, to his notes. "You've made a claim—or one of you has"—he looks at Seth—"that this town is haunted, and you understand that once a claim has been made, it must be investigated."

"Of course." Mary nods at Seth. "We all understand entirely."

"You also understand that there are recent laws in this state that require you to report any haunting or any evidence or suggestion of a haunting, on pain of criminal penalty. This is to discourage the hiding of fugitives."

"My goodness, who would want to hide a ghost? They're such dreadful things!"

"Mrs. Berringer, it used to be everyone felt that way. Lately, however, misplaced sympathies have started to . . . arise. And the dead, or rather those who should be dead, have become more . . . adept. As we were discussing earlier. But let's see what we might be dealing with here, and assume it—or they—aren't part of the new strain. Son, you're the one who put in the call to me?"

"Sure," the young man mumbles.

"You visited your mother in the hospital. And she said she had been attacked."

"Well, um, no, she didn't say that, not exactly. She was sort of confused. Confusing. Her mouth's not working too well right now. Or her mind. Because of the accident. She hit her head." He looks around the room. "Stroke. She's half paralyzed."

"I'm so sorry to hear that. Then tell me again what she said, exactly."

"I don't remember, exactly. She hit her head."

"But"—Pratt smiles, encouragingly—"you didn't hit yours, did you?"

"No."

"Then please try to remember as much as you can. You reported that your mother had accused the town of White Bar of non-reportage of not one but several ghosts. That's quite an accusation."

"Poppycock!" John Berringer bursts out. "Poor Ruth's addled. We've reported every ghost who's ever troubled us here, as she would know better than anyone else, if she were in her right mind!"

"Would that mean you haven't reported ghosts who haven't troubled you?"

Even wounded, Pratt's still sharp. *Careful, everyone.*

"You can check our records," Martha offers. "Ghost after ghost was reported, especially when you hunters first came on the scene."

"Seth," Pratt tries again, not giving up, "your mother did or did not suggest several ghosts are in this vicinity?"

"No."

"No?"

"I mean, I, I think I misunderstood her. I think she doesn't even understand herself. Her mind is all garbled from the fall. I mean the accident."

"I thought you said it was a stroke. Have the doctors determined the cause of this—fall?"

"Not yet."

"You told me your mother was discovered wounded in a museum she runs."

"She was," Bill says, nodding. "It's just at the other end of the square, Mr. Pratt. She's very proud of it. We all are."

"I'm sure. I look forward to visiting it. Are you aware, councilmembers, that archival locations are where a significant portion of aggressive behaviors by the dead toward the living take place?"

They seem surprised.

"Why would that be?" Bill asks.

Well, we're not too fond of the past being gaped at as though it, and we, are freaks.

"Because museums are, in a way, cemeteries. Epitaphs. Places of final rest. Aggressive ghosts take exception to them. They don't want to be buried. Or they have been buried, and take exception to that fact."

"But our museum doesn't bury the past," Martha says. "It illuminates it."

"It's a question of perspective, I'm afraid. We, the living, we like to lift the past into the light. But the dead don't want to admit they're

157

a part of the past, don't want their being in the past illuminated. They don't want to accept the natural order of things. Seth, it sounds like you're uncertain, now, about what your mother told you? That's perfectly understandable. None of us"—he looks at all of them—"likes to think we might be walking with the dead swarming all around us. And it's true that it's rare, these days, to find more than a single entity in a given location that needs to be cleaned. Multiples are the exception now, not the rule. However, it's also true that those who have seen a ghost or ghosts tend *not* to be mistaken. We get very little false reporting, in my field. Why? Because, when you've seen a ghost, you generally—though not always—*know* it. Something sounds a very special alarm inside you. The living recognize what isn't living. You might say it's part of our evolutionary history. The elephant on the veld mourns the death of her mate or offspring . . . but then she joins the herd, and moves on. The dead *must* be left behind. Our instincts know it. So I would recommend, in fact I'll insist, Seth, at this stage, that we all treat your mother's words with respect. If she is speaking through pain and disability, as it seems to me she must be, then she is still fighting to speak, which isn't easy for her. She may be garbled in some particulars—believing, for example, that you all must have known about what attacked her. Some victims seek to place blame elsewhere to avoid blaming themselves for the harm done to them. The truth is this: no one is to blame in cases like this, no one but the ghost itself. *We* are where we are supposed to be. *They* aren't. I'm here to make sure everything is in the right place. And before I leave, on your behalf as well as that of your future visitors and neighbors, I will make sure it is."

Such elegant speeches you make, Mr. Pratt; a murderer practiced in his murders.

"Mr. Pratt, you are masterful in your explanations," Mary praises him. "Thank you very much."

"Thank *you*, in advance, for your patience as I work to sort all this out."

"We're sure you will, to all our advantages. I suppose if we see anything we should let you know right away?"

"Please do, Madame Mayor."

"You're good." John Berringer narrows his eyes. "But we still need to see your credentials."

"Of course."

Pratt pulls back his sleeve and shows them the etched metal cuff welded to his arm. His weapon against us, and his badge.

"Well, friends." Pratt tugs his sleeve down and stands. "If you don't mind, it's been a long day, and it would be nice to find my room."

"Of course, dear!" Mary agrees. "I'm sure we're all feeling tired by now and ready to be on our way. Seth, I assume you'll be heading to your mama's house for the night? Harold will go with you and let you in. He has the key. Since it looks like there's a little break in the weather before the next dump arrives, John and I will make our way home, too. Martha, you call us in the morning and let us know if anything might be needed. Such a pleasure to meet you, Mr. Pratt, and so glad you're here." She holds out her hand.

"The pleasure is all mine. One of the joys of my profession is getting to visit places that are new to me. This is a beautiful old hotel, and I'm sure the town will be quite beautiful when I get to see it in the morning."

"You tell him all about the hotel and the square as you take Mr. Pratt to his room, Martha."

"I will. Be careful going back across, you two. Bill, you go with Mary and John. Call me when you get over."

"Any word from Rose?" Bill asks Martha, eagerly.

"I believe she's left us. Our last guest of the season." She turns to Pratt, smiling. "Well, no, looks like you'll be that!"

"I'm not a guest. An employee," he reminds them.

"Except it's hard to think of people like you, who perform such a service, in that way."

"He didn't say," John Berringer mumbles, "who he was an employee *for*."

"For the good of the town," Pratt answers. "But I hope for the greater good, too."

"Huh. Could swell your head a bit, seeing yourself that way," the old man humphs.

"Come upstairs, Mr. Pratt," the mayor leads him on. "I'd be proud, too, if I were as good as you."

For the second time in my afterlife, I find myself shadowing Pratt as he climbs the stairs of a house, a haunt, that has no wish for him to be there. Martha is telling him about the old saloon, the madams and the miners and their tastes in rose glass, the little speech she gave me two days ago.

"Of course, we're family-friendly now. White Bar is a simple, serene place, Mr. Pratt. Peaceful. Peace is our byword. Don't let the noisy weather fool you. Storms can be quite restful."

"What a pretty second floor this is. And no problems with haunts in this building?"

"None in recent memory."

"Because of earlier cleanings?" he asks.

"That's correct."

"And you do regular checkups."

"I can't say that I do. Should I?"

"Depends on how attentive you are to accidents that might not be accidents. Would you say, Mayor Hayley"—he studies the closed doors down the long hall—"that yours is an attentive community?"

"Oh yes. We try to take good care of each other. That's how I knew something was wrong with Ruth."

"Is Ruth Huellet a friend of yours?"

"A dear friend. I've known her for many years."

"Has she ever done anything that might be considered inappropriate? Out of line? Say, stolen or misused something from the museum? From the past?"

"Good heavens, no! Ruth is as honest as the day is long."

"Yet you assume she's mistaken about any hauntings here."

"Because she has to be . . ." Martha falters.

"Why?"

"Because there just aren't any. That we know of."

"The dead are serene here, too, you're saying?"

"Strictly speaking, we don't have any dead here. The cemetery's at Dutch Gap. The next town over."

"I see. But the dead aren't always interested in graves, as I mentioned. A cemetery can be one of the safest places on earth."

She ignores this and takes out a key.

Pratt points to it. "It's a room with us they're most after."

"Here's yours." She fits the key to the lock.

"You said there was another guest?" Pratt watches her.

"She just checked out."

"When?"

"After the accident. I guess she didn't like all the upset. Will this be all right for you?" She holds back the door. "Not overly green?"

She's put him in a room just like mine, only all is curtained and carpeted in a fine emerald.

I flit up to the canopy above the bed, floating on it like a sea.

"This is lovely. Did your last guest know about the possibility of a haunting?"

"She was just passing through, for a few days. Do you see everything you need, Mr. Pratt?"

"I do. And breakfast is at eight, I think you said."

"If you don't mind it being a little dark, still. But then I suppose your work is mostly in the dark."

"Not necessarily. It's often in the light I make the most progress. Good night, and thank you."

"Good night."

I hover over him as he stands at the dresser and makes his final notes of the evening. After a moment, he sits on the bed, wincing—and the smile he's been wearing falls slack. A tired look comes across his face, settling on his brow as though he's been carrying a heavy thing on his back but now it's lurched forward and dumped its weight on his head.

I don't care. He's come to do his dirty work, and though it would be a pleasure to stay here, cold and judging him, watching him ache and moan, I've left a body on the roof above us, and that's the flesh I care about, not his.

The snow is whirling as I top the hotel chimney and look down.

There are four children, staring down at the body I've left there, all of them pale and softly keening with the wind.

17

Four of them. The children are as clear as crystal behind the screen of the hotel's false front.

They're angry, looking down at the abandoned body in front of them. Their anger is why I can see them. They shimmer.

I must let some of my own anger and grief and pain come to me now, too, so that they can see my form as well.

I float down to them, slowly, whispering so they'll know my voice, letting all the bitterness I've been holding back this night flood and color my soul.

"I'm Emma. I died in 1915. I drowned unjustly. I haunted a mansion for more than a hundred years, until a man tried to put me down again. Some of you have met me before. I'm sorry if this sad corpse has . . ."
Reminded us.

They don't move. They stare at death. Three boys and one girl.

One of the boys, the oldest but still young—Anton he must surely be—his jaw hard, keens, "Why is she left alone in the snow?"

I've heard it's the wisest thing to answer children's questions as truthfully as you can.

"She died, this summer past. It wasn't her fault. I took her body up to keep her from being shut moldering in the ground. And so that I could get away."

They look up at me, at my skirt, my red-ribboned hair, my father's cleft chin, and I see their confusion. Not the face they knew, melded with the body on the roof at their feet. A different one.

They back away. Mistrusting.

"I can show you," I say.

I bend down and will myself to join her. The feeling ... it's like diving, deep, then rising into a safe harbor.

Merged, I stand.

"You're magic?" little William asks, less afraid.

"You're William," I say. "And you're Anton. You're Adelaide, Addy. And you're Jack," I say to the redheaded, bruised boy I'm meeting for the first time.

There is one missing. The ghost of the flowered sleeves.

"Ola," I say. "Where's Ola?"

"She's run away," Anton whispers. "Ever since Ola—our teacher—" He stops himself.

"I know all about Mr. Longhurst. Is he here?"

"He's gone after her," the boy says, still whispering. "He'll find her. He'll find all of us. Mr. Longhurst keeps us in line."

"How can I find her first?" And then I think quickly, *How can I get them all away, away from Longhurst, before their anger betrays them to Pratt?*

Will sobs, "Where is Ola?" and he holds up his ghostly arms to me.

He's just a quivering, frightened child. I can't say no to his arms—though I don't know, and it's plain to see the others don't know either, what will happen when our spirits meet.

164

I lift him.

And I see, feel so much.

Maman. Maman!

I'm bending over my little bed in my small, lean-to room.

Bonjour, mon petit!

She lets me go play. A puddle in the mud of the square. It makes rings like flapjacks when I poke my finger in it.

A man passing and shouting. Horses. Hammering and sawing whoosh, whoosh, whoosh.

Kicking my boots under the school desk.

We burned.

Ola says don't be afraid. This will be our new school now.

Other children come to this school, too. We have to be quiet. Make no noise. Stand beside them.

Hush, be quiet, Teacher says.

Ola isn't quiet.

I am quiet.

Where is Ola?

Where am I?

Adelaide pulls him from me before I'm able to see more.

"You're not Ola," the girl says coldly.

"Where is Ola?" I ask again.

"Teacher will find her."

"But what did she do?"

"It's broken," the blond girl says. "Ola broke it."

"What did she break?"

"The bargain is broken."

A sound of slamming comes over the air to us. I lean over the roof's edge. Pratt is coming out of the hotel, his head down. He limps to his car, fetches something out of it, then turns and drags through the snow again.

I turn away and say with the wind, "Listen, children. That was a ghost hunter down there. He's dangerous, and no matter what he does, no matter how he tries to hurt or anger you, you mustn't listen to him. Keep together, now. Keep away from him, go cold, and hide. Hide from everyone, and keep away from the places they might think to look for you. When I find Ola, I'll bring her to you, we'll find you, and we'll all get away. I'll show you how. I promise. Hide and wait for me. I'll find you. Ola will find you. Trust me."

A low hiss from the blond girl as they fade into the snow.

"We don't trust anyone. We burned."

18

But how will I keep my promise to these children?

They disappear and all goes blank. The snowstorm comes so thick that when I hold up this body's hand I can't see its fingers in front of me.

The few lights on the square are dim sparks. The world careens under a dome of ice.

I don't know how much coldness even a cold, dead body can manage. I slide down the gutters of the hotel. I tunnel—that's what it feels like—through the blizzard, across the square, listening for the call of the wind chimes.

There's only one other here that I believe I might trust for help.

When I reach Su Kwon's door, I beat on it, again and again, and don't stop till she's let me in.

"My God! *Rose!*"

She pulls me in. She's wide awake and dressed in tight stockings with a nightshirt worn over them. Her hair is braided.

She pulls me toward the glowing stove. "Where have you been? What are you doing, my God, don't you know you could die out there?"

She takes my coat and rubs my hands, and can't know she'll never warm them. It's never the living I'll be able to touch and know, not in the way I touched and knew little William.

There's nothing I can do about that. But it feels good, somehow, to be set down in a chair and have a heavy blanket wrapped around these shoulders.

"Hot tea. You need hot tea!"

"No. Stay with me." The fading of the children has left me feeling so alone again. "I'm better now."

"Then you weren't out for very long. Where have you *been*? You left when, when, at the café—did you *hear* any of it? What went down in there?"

"There are ghosts here. And all the people here are—"

"—holding them hostage. It's awful. It's disgusting. I don't know how else to describe it. It's sick. Keeping them here to . . . you didn't hear it all, Rose. It's worse than you know."

She tells me what she believes I haven't discovered. That the black-mailed dead are kept caged and afraid here, to make the living feel powerful. That the living are soothing themselves with the dead.

"They said anyone who breaks this *bargain*—that's what they call it—will be hunted and hounded. I don't know exactly what they mean by hounding. I'm worried it means the dead are forced to turn on anyone who speaks out. That to save themselves, the ghosts would have to become . . . horrible."

It's true. Sometimes, to survive, you have to become, they make you become, the terrible thing they want you to be.

"And the ghosts are children, and the teacher who murdered them," she goes on. "Kept in some horrible limbo together, in the schoolhouse.

Once a year there's a ceremony, apparently, when the bargain, the pact between the town and them, is sworn again. If the children agree to go on acting like docile pets, the town shelters them. They, the Berringers, Martha, Bill, all of them, they're all in on it, the whole town, and here's the part they didn't say, but it's so obvious: to keep the 'tradition' going, they rope in likely converts—castaways, outliers, orphans, misfits, like you and me, they think. Only they made a fucking mistake with me. I am *no one's castaway*. You?"

I'm Irish born and Irish stubborn. Raised to be staunch in the face of wounds. I am no one's castaway either.

"Say something, Rose. Let me know you're okay, what's happened."

"I'm fine," I say. "I've been hiding out."

"Because of what you heard, what you thought they were going to do to Seth? I know. I thought the same thing. But I stopped it. Or at least the worst of it." She paces between her artworks. "I saw him going into the Huellet House just now. He looked like a prisoner. Harry was with him. My God, even Harry! People that you love, you think you love, and then . . . They were coming from Martha's. The hunter, he's over there. You remember what I told you about my Uncle Bao?" She stops. "I *will not* stand for this. I don't stand for hunts and cruelty. I have to do something, Rose. I've been waiting to see what happens. If they can convince this Pratt guy there's no haunting, that will call for a certain kind of action. But if they decide to give a ghost up to him—that's what they're actually talking about—then a different action has to be taken, and it has to be quick. Are you following? Am I making sense? I know this is a lot to take in."

I ask, my rage rising, "Which ghost would they hand to the hunter?"

"I don't know. If need be, they'll say it's whichever one Ruth saw. They're all described in the letter. Do you still have it?"

"It's in my pocket."

"They're looking for you. They've basically given me the job of finding you. I told them I was out looking for you, and I was—but not to drag you into this shit. They think they've hooked me into it, got me. Right. As if I'm some Asian orphan that needs adopting. Me!" She slams her desk. "While the ghosts, the actual orphans—"

"They won't get any of them," I assure her.

"How can you be so certain?"

"I won't let them."

"How? Oh, I don't care, you are a friend sent from heaven." She squeezes me. "All right. It's *our* pact. And listen, I think I might have a plan."

I now have a plan, too—though it's one only a ghost can know. "What is your plan?"

"Mind staying hidden a while longer?"

I do, very much, but don't say so.

"My idea is you stay here, at my place, while I see if I can start to unravel this. I think Martha might be unhappy, Rose. I've been watching her pretty close. She seems like she's mostly following orders. She's a prisoner in a way, too, ever notice that? Like Ruth. They're always having to obey the Berringers—Ruth because she's stuck with that museum and poor and has no place to go where she would be anyone, and Martha because being mayor means something to her. That's what they do, they find some way to hold onto you. But I think Martha can be won to our side. If Martha can be brought to see how she's being *used* by the Berringers, maybe she can get Bill to see it. Bill respects her. And if Bill comes along, maybe he can get more. But first we have to convince Pratt there are no ghosts here—which is, at least, exactly what the Berringers want. Once Pratt is gone, we good guys simply take charge of the Bar. All of us with decent consciences. We find out what the *ghosts* really want, each one of them, like with Uncle Bao. We *listen*. And take things from there. And it won't make a bit of difference to the success of the town. The tourists will still come. They never knew the schoolhouse ghosts were here to begin with, so what's the worry? And we'll be truly welcoming. To anyone who wants to come and move here. No more misfits-only policy."

A fine plan it is. "And the Berringers?" I want them brought to justice.

"My hunch is when we push back, they'll threaten to tell the state. They'll say we'll all be thrown in jail, and hounded by devils. But we won't believe it. The Berringers aren't going to want to end their days locked up themselves or in a town with an ugly reputation no one wants to come to anymore. They'll want to go on believing they're special. Power comes from pretending to what you don't really have. They're pretending to be powerful people." She paces again. "They think they're gifted. They aren't. They're just people who inherited some sick traditions and think it takes talent to keeping them going. It doesn't. It's all shit pretending to be gold. No, it's worse, it's banking human souls, and acting like it's diamonds and not corpses you're wearing around your neck."

Oh, what a marvelous thing it is to see good, living anger, and the person feeling it not afraid to be seen feeling it.

"And Pratt, too," I insist.

"Absolutely. That's why you have to hide, Rose. Because I'm going to say, I'm going to *convince* the Berringers to say and everyone to say—hold onto your hat here—that *you* were, are, the ghost. I know, it sounds insane, right—but hear me out. You just showed up out of nowhere, right? Nothing bad started happening till *you* arrived. *You* were in the museum the day Ruth fell. *You* fled the scene when Seth came in. And I've been looking into this Pratt fellow. Turns out he's obsessed with what he thinks is the world being taken over by ghosts that look like living people. He's looking for some sort of zombie, he's got some sketch up on the internet he's trying to get people to take seriously. And get this: it looks just a little, maybe just enough, like you. I think it'll be easy to convince everyone, even the Berringers, to go along with this ploy of saying, 'It's Rose you need to go after.' All they want is for Pratt to leave. They'll be perfectly happy to put the blame on you, they'd rather keep their own ghosts and not lose one of them. I've been up all night thinking about this. It's really a miracle you showed up, because the only thing that could have shot the idea down was you not knowing about it. But now here you are! And after Pratt's gone, boom! You emerge, you're not a ghost, you're everyone's hero, even the Berringers'. We can even say it was your idea. And by that time, with Martha and all the rest, we've gotten the real revolution under-way, to make this town a good, a better place. What do you think? It's just fantastic enough," she says, breathing out, "that it could work."

If I make myself the target; if I let them pretend that I am *what I really am*. That's what she's asking, and doesn't know it. I must make myself the bait.

"He can't hurt you—Pratt—is the good thing. And I swear to you I'll never let a bad thing come to you out of all of this. I'll take all the heat, if it comes to that. I'll be the bad arty girl who dreamt all this up. I'll do whatever it takes to protect you."

Long ago, when I was alive, I had a best friend. Her memory is still dear to me. Now it seems the best can be born again. When you don't expect it, a soul rises to remind you what a fighter, what spit, really looks like.

"I'm in," I say. "There's one spot of trouble, though."

"You mean more than illegally impersonating the dead in order to launch a bloodless coup in a remote mountain village?"

Spit and fight. "Only this." One important, secret thing. "What if a ghost did startle Ruth? Ruth could describe them. He—or she—could be out there loose for Pratt to find."

"I've been thinking about that, too. It is possible. I think it could have been Longhurst that scared her in the jailhouse. Though that doesn't make sense. The way I understand it, he has his own prisoners. He gets to keep them, have power over them. That's another sick part of the arrangement. It's all so sick. I have to wonder, though, if it was one of the children who scared Ruth . . . If it is, then the teacher has to get them back in line. That's how this all works. Like a pyramid. He keeps them in line, and the town, the bargain keeps him safe in power in the schoolhouse."

"If Pratt comes after any of them," I say quietly, "I'll take care of it."

"How will you do that?"

"I'll leave some ghostly-looking clues to fool him."

"Brilliant."

"But there's something you need to know about him."

"So you've been boning up on this guy, too?"

For a long time, now. "He has a sixth sense. He's not like other hunters." He uses the same tricks, I tell her, the cruelty they all use to anger the dead and make them appear. But he has more than that up his sleeve. Pratt raises his hand to his heart when he picks up the sensation of a careless soul. He's been doing it since he was a boy, he claims. He's not easily fooled, nor easily put off.

"He doesn't stop," I finish, standing.

"I was reading about just how tenacious he is. He basically bullies ghosts into the ground, they say. Sometimes he doesn't even have to fire a weapon."

But in the end, he always does fire it. Imagine that.

"How does he do that, you think?" she asks, puzzled. "Get ghosts to put *themselves* down?"

"He gets them to give up."

"But how?"

"By making a ghost feel worthless—worse than cursed. By getting a ghost to believe that everything the ghost touches becomes cursed. So that a soul begins to worry: might it be true?"

"Jesus, Rose. That's some insight. But we can beat him, right? We'll start in the morning. I've got a loft up here you can sleep in tonight. Nice and warm under the rafters. You're still chilly, I can see. That's your core temperature knocked down. We've got to get it up. I'm surprised you're not shaking like a leaf. Come on up with me."

She pulls back sheets for me on a low bed surrounded by small pictures in metal frames.

"But this is your room, Su."

It's a room with us they're most after, Pratt said.

"No biggie. I'll sleep on the couch in my office downstairs."

"No, no."

"Shut up about it, Rose. We need you healthy for what's coming. Lie down."

"Who are the people in these pictures?" A family.

"My mom and me. The frames were some of my first designs. I don't do small things anymore, though I'm still proud of these. I go big these days. I make and sell great big things, and I send them out into the world and never see them again. It's the making that matters, as well as the bigness. And being willing to let go of, to lose what you love." She looks at the woman in the picture. "Go big or go home, you know what I mean? Sleep well. Coup starts in the morning."

A ghost doesn't sleep or dream. But she can lie very still and listen and picture the storm's size outside, and tally the odds, and wish, and place her bets.

19

In the morning, my friend—is it fair to call Su Kwon that, now, when I know what she is, but she doesn't know me?—moves quickly. When I come down to her, she's having her breakfast, reading, and dressing all at once. Her gallery is filled with a sudden, clear light. I go toward the window, though keeping back from it, and see why.

The Bar is completely buried in white. Snow has filled the streets around the square, swaddled the cars up to their cheeks, circled the ankles of the statue of the Prospector, and leveled the porches. So that the earth seems, suddenly, even.

"Snow's stopped," Su says. "For now. The passes are still open, apparently. I'm glad. We want to make sure Pratt can find his way home, wherever that is."

"I don't know that he has a home," I say. In that much, at least, we are alike. "They travel, these hunters. They move from place to place." Like locusts. Ah, but what happens to an insect, in the cold?

"He'll have fun moving around today, unless he's with someone on a snowmobile. The Berringers told Pete not to plow the roads. They want to control where Pratt goes. Okay." She pulls the shades down over the gallery windows. "You hide out here. Make yourself at home. Make some breakfast. I've texted and volunteered my services as a guide to Pratt. The Berringers are very happy about that, about how *on board* I am. He wants to go to the museum first, to see where Ruth fell. If it seems perfectly natural, as though the idea's just occurred to me, I'll start dropping a few mentions about a visitor who passed through here and how strange it was that she disappeared right when Seth arrived. Not too much, you know. I'll need to play dumb a bit, let him think *he's* the one starting to put the pieces together. God, I hate playing dumb with men." She looks in a mirror beside her desk, adjusting her scarf. "Even in a good cause."

"You're getting him in your sights," I tell her. "You're the hunter."

"Right on." She puts on her gloves, pulling her sleeves over her wrists. "You know what pisses me off? Have you ever seen one of their weapons, that tech they wear, the cuff?"

"I have."

"It's made of an alloy and etched with all these lofty symbols, and made to look artistic, like—what?—like shooting something that can't shoot back is so damn creative?"

We look at one another, Su and I, before she goes.

She says, "Will you be okay here?"

Other than the fact that Pratt's to be told I've been in White Bar, and that soon I'll be described to him in great detail, I'm in fine fettle.

"It's not my first trick-or-treat," I say. "You go on now, Su."

"When I've planted the hook in Pratt, and he's seems to be taking it, I'll fill the others in." She goes to the back of the gallery. "Here's how you lock this back door. Don't let anyone in. I'll leave the workshop unlocked. There shouldn't be any reason for you to leave the gallery, but if you get uncomfortable or worried for some reason, there are lots of places to hide in out there. Just be sure no one sees you crossing the alley." She takes a pair of metal baskets from the wall and begins attaching them to her boots. They make her look tangled in two nets, like a caught animal.

I don't like the feeling I have, suddenly. I'm worried. Is she doing too much?

"Also, there's extra snowshoes in the closet there, if you need them. All right. Wish me luck."

"I wish you every good thing in the world."

"If only we didn't have to slog through so much shit to get to it, right?"

She goes, pulling the door tight behind her.

I don't like what I'm feeling. Pratt can do her no harm with his weapon. She's on the bright side of the line, the side of the living—it isn't that. It's that the boundary where the dead meet can be treacherous.

You are a curse, Pratt once cried out to me, *and curse everything you touch.*

No. I mustn't believe it.

Though I wear the body of a woman who died while Pratt and I fought.

Among the metal artworks hanging from the walls around me is a mirror framed with salvaged wheels and gears. I go and stand in front of it. The face I see might be one I willed and shaped out of misfortune and terror, but the misfortune wasn't my doing, I tell myself, and the terror wasn't at my hand. I put a hand up to the glass, this soft palm pressing against its reflection, and press this forehead, too, against the slippery coolness. All I wanted, when I took this body, was to try some new way to outlast pain and injustice. Then along comes the world, and wants to punish you for the trying. For wearing this sleeve on your heart.

"I won't have it," I say aloud. "I won't be called a devil for finding my way out of hell. And listen to me, Ola, fellow spirit," I call out, for we must find a way to each other again. "I know what it means to lose even while you last. I know you lost someone dear to you. I know about the red hobbyhorse." I must get her to trust me for my plan to succeed. "You're not alone in your sorrows. I'm here. I'm looking for you. I want to find and help you. But we must be quick. The teacher is looking for you. Another is on the hunt as well. You needn't fear me. I'm all alone here. I wait for you. I wait for you, and no one else."

Beneath the palm of this hand, I feel the mirror warming. Burning. I lift my forehead away from it, yet leave my fingers against the glass.

A mirror is also a door.

"You burned. But before that," I say, "you were alive and strong. I saw you be strong. With the horse in your hand. Can you see me?"

A hand presses behind the reddening glass—as it did the first time we met.

This time, I don't hesitate, I don't fear. I make sure my hand stays steadily against hers.

Her face and body appear on the other side.

Now, I hear her voice say, *I will tell you.*

20

My name is Ola Varga. I am not from this place.

I wasn't born here. I came across the Great Salt Desert with my parents. I had a little brother, Karl, who didn't survive the trail. We stopped the wagon and buried him under a little pile of stones, in the middle of an empty plain.

My mama, she broke that day. She said to my father, if we don't become rich in California, then our Karl has died for nothing.

The way she said it, I knew it wouldn't matter if we found all the gold of all the kings. She would never forgive my father for reading a newspaper story about the riches in the West and selling our farm and taking us to the Rush.

Later on, when she was cruel to him, I understood the devil hands a broken heart the hammer that smashed it, then tells it to smash the next heart closest.

We came to California and tried to make what in Hungary my parents called tiszta lappal, *a clean sheet, a fresh start. Our cabin was at the edge of the camp and had only a canvas roof, with no windows. It was hot in summer and cold in winter. We worked very hard no matter the color of the mud. It was a long walk upriver, each day, to the piece of streambed Papa bought from a man who said it would pay well but who hadn't stayed to work it himself. My father and mother dug and shoveled and I carried the dirt by bucket to the river and the long-tom. My eyes learned to pick out the tiniest flake in the slurry.*

Mama's eyes were always hungry. At the end of every day, she would ask, What do we have? At the end of every week, she would ask, What do we have now? We might have an ounce, sixteen dollars, but eggs were five dollars, a bag of flour three, and lumber and nails swallowed most of the rest. By the end of the year, we had only enough to winter through to the next spring. I begged to go home, but Mama said no, we must work harder, harder, dig more, buy another claim. My father could find none to buy until some foolish men grew drunk. They thought there was gold underneath the river, and when they died by dynamiting it, my father took one of their claims and called it his own and said the man who could die so foolishly was too weak to find the "color."

Then it was two claims we worked. Mama and me at one, Papa at the other. The camp was no longer called Eno Camp, but to honor the men who died called White Bar, for the rushing falls they made. I thought it a poor thing to name a town after men who were drunk and stupid. My father said to hush about it. There was nothing more to be done, and I shouldn't say anything like that at the diggins or in the square or in the mercantile. The men had erred and that was that, and we should be grateful we had profited from some misfortune without being the cause of it.

It was then I knew my father, and my mother, too, were not the same people they had been in Iowa. They were hard people now, and hungry, and frightened that they would have nothing to show for my brother's dying.

That was in our second year, the year I stopped begging them to go home. I had grown stronger by then, and bigger, and was less afraid than when we first came. Though the work was hard, I slowly came to like it better than my farm chores. You never hope for gold to fall out of a cow's teat. Slow though it was, I grew to like the life of the camp, for there were things you could never see on a farm, like a bear being led down the street on a leash, or a picture-taker with his velvet cape, or a passing preacher jumping onto a whiskey keg to give his sermon about damnation, or drunken men dancing together on Independence Day.

The one happiness I missed from the old life was going to school. But then came some good news. My father came home from the saloon and said men had cleared out that part of the camp where the drunken men and others had lived, and scraped it clean and made of it a meadow, and there they were building a schoolhouse, for now we are a town and are like to have some of the things a good town has. Wouldn't you like going to school again, Ola?

I said very much. Papa said I could go as long as I helped at the claims in the morning and after. And so I came to the school in the meadow with the few other children of the camp.

It was nothing like the school at home, being a cabin of logs with a short steeple and a kettle fixed with a clapper for a bell. You stepped on a crate to go inside; to your right hung the rope from the belfry tied to the wall, and then in front were three rows of desks the brothers Huellet had ordered made, and then the stove for heat and the teacher's desk. There were four who came along with me to school. They were so much younger. I felt at first stupid and back-ward, like I had missed some chance and it had come around again but too late and wearing a coat too small.

Yet soon enough I liked my schoolmates. I still missed my brother Karl, and until then had spoken to few people excepting my parents. So I was sure to be friendly with the others. I liked Will because he was like my brother had come out from under the pile of stones where we left him. I liked Anton because he made me think of what Karl might have been had he lived. I liked Addy because even though she looked so fine in her blond curls, she was kind to Jack, who might as well have come out from under stones, so bruised he was. Once I asked him why he was so marked, and he said he helped his father work a claim and it was hard work and not for layabouts. I told him I worked hard, too, but not in a way that turned me black and blue. After that, for a time Jack didn't speak to me. I had made some mistake I didn't understand. But then I gave him my turn to ring the school bell at the end of the day, and that made him happy.

At first I liked Mr. Longhurst, too, because he had been a prospector as our fathers were and he put on no airs, though he was one of those people who when words come out of their mouths they sound like a newspaper or the Bible. His coat wasn't the best, and his trousers had seen mending he'd done himself or that maybe a woman had done. Every day he made us stand by our desks and say our names and the word "present." He did this when we were alive and then later when we were dead. When we were alive, he said it was to remind us that no matter where we find ourselves or what might happen on the journey to knowledge, we must always stand awake and straight, look ahead, be good-mannered, and do or say nothing that would bring shame on us or sorrow to others. And we should not be proud or arrogant, but praise persistence and the weathering of storms. And so we said,

"I'm William, and I am present."

"I'm Adelaide, and I am present."

"I'm Jack, and I am present."

"I'm Anton, and I am present."

I stood in the back, the oldest, the last.

"I am Ola, and I am present."

I wanted schooling as much as some want gold. Even when I was alive, and had a choice in the matter and could have stayed away, I came to school every day. I never wanted to fall behind Anton and Addy. It isn't only numbers and spelling and history and drawing and manners that you learn at school. My favorite lesson, even if it was for the little ones, was when Mr. Longhurst, who hadn't fought with the men of the town yet, would bring to class a penny, a clear glass bowl, and a pitcher of water. He would put the penny in the bottom of the bowl and fill it from the pitcher, and then he would show us how, if you looked at it from above, the penny seemed to be in one place—but if you looked through the side of the bowl, it seemed to be in a different place entirely, or even that there were two pennies in two different places.

"Are there two pennies?" Willie would always ask, wanting to be sure.

"Are there two pennies, sir," Anton would correct him. He's the rule-follower.

And Mr. Longhurst would say, "No, William, it looks as though there are two pennies, but there is only one. Because water bends light. The water is not without its effect. The water might be clear, invisible. But it is not without presence, without force. Neither is the penny. The water and the penny act together with the light coming through."

Once Jack asked which we thought was stronger, the penny or the water. Anton said the penny, because you can buy a thing with it. I said the water, because water can push metal around in a sluice. Jack said it was neither. He said it was a trick, like when you thought you saw gold in the Eno and you bent down to grab it and no, it was nothing, just the light.

That's as far as we got in our learning when we died, in 1852. That winter was called the Lean Winter. There wasn't enough money left, nor supplies, and the wild game had all been hunted, and the prices were too high. Papa had managed to put a wood roof over our cabin, but it was still cold and the fireplace smoked. He was weak, too, and many people in town were getting sick with a strange fever and some were dying. The undertaker kept coffins lined up outside his door. My mother nursed Papa with Doctor Huellet's Tonic and said I must go to school so at least there would be more air in the stuffy cabin for Papa to breathe. I wrapped myself in my shawl and a blanket and walked through the snow, afraid to leave my father but glad to go, because the blue-jarred window in the schoolhouse let in some colorful light, and because Mr. Longhurst had taken the rope and bell down and stuffed the belfry with a quilt so the snow and wind and pine needles wouldn't get in, and the iron stove warmed nicely, and there were lessons to learn and biscuits to eat because

Mr. Longhurst was using his own pay, he said with a strange heat in his eyes, to be sure that what we ate wasn't tainted by the quackery of powders and tonics. Mr. Longhurst was every day more feverish himself, until finally he bolted the schoolhouse door and wouldn't let us go out again. He said it was for our own good. After we died there, my parents went away, quickly, and my heart was broken. I think they couldn't bear to lose me so soon after Karl, and I didn't know how to stop them. I didn't know, as I know only now, that I can both move and be still, like the penny.

I've been still for so long. I am the oldest in school, and after we were dead Mr. Longhurst said the best work for my soul would be to protect the others and make sure they didn't stray. "If we all behave and keep to the bargain," he told me, "we can go on. But if any one of us betrays it, they will tear the new schoolhouse down and we'll have nothing, no home, no place in heaven or on earth to bide in. Remember that." On one anniversary, not so long ago, we learned about the hunters, men who'd tear our souls apart and drive us into the ground if we made even the slightest trouble. But how can we be any less trouble than we are now? I wanted to know.

Mr. Longhurst said for me to be quieter still. And then we saw what the hunters could do. In front of the schoolhouse, we saw one chase an Indian woman with a baby in her arms. I won't say what happened next. I don't speak of terrible things. When I try, my thoughts go shut and dark.

Jack was always shut like that. Until this summer past, when he started whining he was hurting, he was being stepped on and kicked, we all were, he said, he said he could feel the living bruising us, walking all over our ashes. They were walking on our ashes in our meadow, which they should have left alone, he cried. Before we knew it, he was throwing himself against the tall windows of the new schoolhouse and Will and Addy were clinging to the ceiling, and while Mr. Longhurst was trying to settle Jack before he screamed so loud that all would be lost, all of a sudden I could stand the madness no more. I flew up and out the steeple and to where I knew the meadow was, and Jack was right, there was a man in a hard yellow hat there pointing and kicking at things, and he pointed at a big hole being dug for I know not what reason, where our ashes had lain. From behind him where I couldn't be seen I pushed him down into that hole. I didn't cause him to die. I only wanted someone else to feel what it was like to fall into the pit.

And then I looked around and realized I was out. I'd broken the bargain. I was free.

Now Mr. Longhurst thinks he'll find me and bring me back. But we've been still for so long, so long, while all around us everything moves. Not just the living, but machines, new things, full of freedom and excitement and promise. I can hold still no more. It's so dull being dead. Learning the same lessons over and over, day after day after day. And if you must only behave, and never speak out, what does learning matter at all?

I'll never go back. I only worry about the others. I'm the oldest, I'm sup-posed to watch over them. But why do I have to be the one to keep them still, a stillness that's death inside death?

Her face wavers in the heat of her anger. Even as I press my fingers in the mirror hard against hers, she starts to go, unwilling to stay still.

I understand.

"The others, the children, they aren't still," I whisper into the glass. "They're moving, too. They're trying to find you before he does. Can you find them? Can you find them and bring them to the old stables behind this place? I can show you how to be free. Do you want that? If you do, stay cold, and make the others stay cold, Ola, and let no one see you. I have a plan."

Not a flicker in the glass left nor a sound anywhere.

I hope she's heard me.

And more: I hope the escape I imagine will be possible.

21

Out of the Jailhouse Museum the hunter comes with his notes in his hands. He's wrapped himself in his heavy coat and wears stiff black boots that seem to help his limping body keep upright.

I've had to leave the weight of a body behind again, in the cold. I need to be a free spirit to follow Pratt and learn what he's found.

Su has come out of the museum, too, and points across the square. Pratt nods and follows the line of her arm and walks ahead of her, sinking into the snow, while she puts on her snowshoes and then tramps easily over it.

I flit across, reaching the porch of the Huellet House before they do. Gone are the rocking chairs where the doctor-brothers once sat and surveyed White Bar. The gingerbread carpentry that was once so fine is cracked, so frail-looking the ice might pull it down. The plaque on the house is a small one and says nothing about the men or their medicines.

HUELLET HOUSE
1852
HUELLET FAMILY RESIDENCE
FIRST PLUMBED AND ELECTRIFIED BUILDING IN WHITE BAR, 1896
CALIFORNIA HISTORICAL ASSOCIATION

Pratt beats the knocker on the peeling door while Su frees her feet again. I keep close to her shoulder, so that Pratt, with his extra sense, will think any quiver or pulse coming from my soul is hers.

She says, as their breaths fall in quick puffs against the door, "Harry's probably still here with Seth, keeping him company."

Pratt makes a note. "Harold Dubois. The former marine."

"How'd you know that?"

"I do my homework at night."

"Harry doesn't have anything to do with what you saw in the museum, does he?"

Pratt wipes some ice from the plaque. "The clues aren't just in the dead, Ms. Kwon. They're in the living. The ones being haunted. Your museum yielded so little because there's no one left there to haunt. The action"—he taps his chest—"is where the beating hearts are."

"How interesting." She smiles pleasantly at him.

The door is opened by Seth. Harold stands close beside him.

"Uh, sorry," the young man says and squints, "it took me a minute to come down. I was upstairs . . . um"—he looks at Harold—"napping."

"May we come in?" Pratt smiles his flattering smile.

"Been expecting you. Mr. Pratt." Harold swings the door wider for them. "Come right in. Handling the cold okay?"

"With some able assistance, yes."

Su comes into the foyer with them, looking behind her, toward the Berringers' house. She's anxious to put her plan into motion, I see.

"You want me to take off now, Mr. Pratt?" she asks him. "I don't want to be in the way."

Pratt, handing Harold his coat and muffler, shakes his head. "You aren't in the way, Ms. Kwon. If you don't mind, can you stay? I welcome your recent knowledge of the town."

"Of course. I'm here to help." A smooth one she is. Steady. "Harry, anything warm to drink for all of us? It's bitter out there."

"Coming right up."

"Late riser?" Pratt smiles at Ruth's son.

"Usually."

"But things aren't usual for you right now, are they?" He pats the boy's shoulder. "I can tell. Don't worry. All will be put right soon. I have just a few questions for you. And also"—Pratt peers into the great musty darkness of the house—"if I sense anything in this house, I need you to know I'll be taking some readings. Since it's your mother's residence, and she was the target of the recent assault."

"If it even was that," Seth says, quietly.

"Yes," Pratt says, tilting his head at him, "there are always 'ifs' when it comes to a haunting."

"Must make the work interesting," Harold says, coming back with the coffees. "This should hold you for a bit."

"If I sense anything here, it will be a longer visit, Mr. Dubois."

"No problem. Right, Seth? Ruth would want you to be thorough and complete." Harold leads them into a half-empty room with velvet paper curling on the walls. "Discover anything at the museum, Mr. Pratt?"

"Nothing at all. It was quite dead."

"That's kind of odd, isn't it?" Harold invites them to sit on the two sagging couches. I rise into a damaged chandelier above them.

"Not at all, Mr. Dubois. Spirits move. When they do, they take their anger with them."

"Like we do," Su says.

"No, not exactly like us. Their anger is all they carry. Like a flag of a single stripe. While we're three-dimensional."

"A flag has three dimensions," Su says and stirs her coffee.

"Well noted." Pratt smiles again. "The dead, in point of fact, lack any dimension at all."

She smiles back at him flatteringly, yet from above I see the tightness in her shoulders.

Harold goes to open the curtains, heavy moth wings over the windows.

"Thank you, that's better," Pratt says. "Not so gloomy. An interesting house. It looks largely original."

Seth shakes his head. "Pretty much a dump now. You can hardly see what it used to be. It's mostly empty. I've been through the whole place. With Harold."

Harold says stiffly, "Your mother just lived in a few rooms, to save on heating."

"Well, I don't see what she saved." The boy slouches beside him. "There's hardly any furniture left or anything valuable. The plaster's coming down, and the whole place smells of soap. She made, makes, perfumed soap. Smell it?"

"I did notice." Pratt sips his coffee, watching him.

Su rises and goes to the windows. "She always kept these drapes closed. No matter the time of year. Like she didn't want to see out. I wonder why."

Harold says, "We always tried to get Ruth to turn this into a bed-and-breakfast and make some money from it, but she never would. Inns are a staple business here, Mr. Pratt. We live and die by our visitors."

"Ms. Kwon was just telling me about a visitor who came through town right before Ruth's—accident—and then disappeared right after."

"Well, we're sort of a one-night town this time of year."

"Are you going to see my mother?" Seth interrupts, turning to Pratt.

"Yes, I've been cleared by the hospital to see her this evening. You should accompany me. Alone, if you don't mind."

"Well, uh." He looks at Harold. "I don't know. There's a lot to tend to here. I mean, I didn't know my mother was living in this crappy way. There's a bunch of decisions I should be making."

"What decisions are those, son?"

"Harold says—I guess I have to agree now—that things around here go a long way to showing her mental state, and why she might have been confused about what she saw. The way she was living, Mom must've been having trouble in the head even before she hit it. I need to decide what to do about the property. Harold's been helping me clean up a bit."

"Least I could do," Harold offers. "I really care so much about Ruthie."

"How about a tour?" Pratt stands, leaving his cup. "So I can see if anything else needs to be . . . tidied."

They move slowly, following Pratt. I keep close to Su, whose neck stays taut.

"This"—she stops, surprised—"was her soap manufactory?"

Harold nods somberly. "Used to be the dining room."

"Mom left a mess." The young man curls his nose. "But it's not as bad as before Harold and me started on it."

Harold points. "See, she was bringing the butter and oil in from the kitchen there, and looks like she added all the herbs and flowers on the table here, then did the cooling and wrapping over there." He shakes his head. "Some of it was actually rotting when Seth and I got to it. We threw a lot away, so it's a bit better now."

190

"I didn't know," Su says, lowering her voice, "she was struggling this badly, Harry."

"I guess it was hard keeping the Huellet legacy up."

"Tell me about the Huellet legacy, please, Mr. Dubois," Pratt asks, making his scribbling notes.

"Sure. So . . . her ancestors were a big deal in this place back in the 1850s and all the way to the middle of the last century. They got rich with their tonics and tinctures and powders and whatnot. Over the generations, though, the family didn't keep up with the times and sort of lost their fortunes. I don't know, but I always thought it made Ruth feel ashamed and anxious, and that's why she worked so hard in the museum and at this soap stuff, trying to get back some of that Huellet magic. I think you can feel guilty when you can't keep things up. This house was a lot of upkeep. Once upon a time, the two doctors, they were the brothers who started it all, both lived in and raised their families here, which is why it's such a huge house. It was real plush—you'll see in the photos upstairs, in Ruth's room. Follow me."

They reach a bannister and a grand staircase with spindles missing. I float above them along the high, stained ceiling, and looking down at them I have the feeling, as I sometimes do, that the living are so poor and earthbound, always straining for something just out of their reach.

"Why *didn't* Ruth turn this place into an inn?" Su asks, clearly upset by the poor state of the landing, the threadbare carpets. "It would have been perfect."

Seth shrugs. "My father says Huellets never apologize, even if they admit a mistake. He said that's why they're hell to live with."

Pratt lays a hand across his chest, the way he does when he's trying to sense something.

Careful now, everyone, I think.

"Where are the Huellet family buried? Dutch Gap?" Harold answers. "That's right. It's a bigger town. Nice church there. Fancy cemetery. All that. We don't have any dead here."

"You can see how my mother lived, just in her room," her son says, turning. "It gives you a sense of how mixed up she was."

It was clearly once a fine room, with a marble fireplace and a carved bedstead still something to wonder at, heavy mahogany and four-posted, though the embroidered canopy above the posts droops sadly.

The rest of the room is a jumble of papers and photos and clothing mixed with medicine bottles on a nightstand and on the mantelpiece, and shoes thrown every which way, and bits of food left uneaten.

"We haven't gotten to this room yet," Harold apologizes. "We didn't know if we should."

Su stares. "But she's so organized at the museum."

"Private chaos," Pratt notes, "can be masked, can't it, by public control." He studies the photographs on the wall, the well-dressed families, the children beside their ponies or posing next to touring cars, or playing in meadows checkered with picnic blankets.

"I have to let some light in here," Su says. Opening the curtains, she sees the bedroom's outside balcony, its railing in pieces. "Well that looks sad. And unsafe."

Pratt winces.

Are you remembering your fall, and how you were wounded?

"What's this?" he says, looking away at a picture beside the window. The photo. The one of the town all gathered on the wintry square.

"That's the original of one that's copied in the museum and all over town," Harold says. "It's famous here. A town celebration. Dated 1852."

"If it's a celebration, why is no one smiling?" Pratt asks.

My own wonder. It irks me when I share a hunter's thoughts, even for an instant.

"Never really thought about it," Harold says.

"Look at the angle," Pratt says and then looks out the window. "I do believe that photo was taken from this very balcony."

Su looks, too. "Was it?"

Yes. The hunter is right. The vantage, it's exactly here. Who was it, then, that took the photograph? Would it have been the doctors themselves?

"I sense something here." Pratt taps his chest. "Close by."

I've come too near to them. Felt too much. *Foolish.* I scurry behind the fireplace irons, go cold as gray ash, and wait.

"Close by," he repeats, excited.

Harold frowns. "Really? I guess that doesn't make any sense to me. Why would any ghost do that? Come so close to someone like you?"

Pratt's eyes slowly trace the room. "In my experience, the answer is either overconfidence or lack of awareness. Everyone, step away from these walls, please."

"Okay"—Harold steps backward—"but if you're right, why are you letting it hear you say that? Isn't that warning it away?"

"The dead aren't intelligent, Mr. Dubois. When they die they leave all living intelligence behind."

Keep calm, Emma Rose, I tell myself and draw deeper into the marble hearth. *He's baiting, fishing.* He doesn't know who might be here, or why. A man can feel his heart beat and still not see or know a thing outside it. Pratt doesn't know what he's scented. He only hopes an unwary spirit will grow angry at his words and show herself.

Instead, all he's done is betray himself. *Why, Mr. Pratt, it seems you've forgotten a thing or two since last we met. When you raised your weapon at me all those months ago, I saw something flicker, if only for a moment, in your eyes. It was a brief wonder, a moment of doubt, hesitation, mistrusting yourself and what you were doing. But you've driven away the memory, I see. You haven't learned the memory of our errors is all we ever have to learn by. All we ever have to guide us, in the end.*

He turns abruptly. "Is there a restroom I can use?"

"Uh, excuse me?" Harold blinks.

"A bathroom. Please?"

"Sure, follow me," Seth says. "There's only one that works on this floor."

"A moment, my friends." The hunter smiles.

He leaves Harold and Su by the door, puzzled. Harold watches Seth go with him.

"So what do you think?" Su whispers.

"I think we'll have to go with John and Mary's plan," Harold mutters back. "We're not going to be able to convince Pratt there's nothing here. He *knows* there's something loose. We'll have to give him one of them."

"We should give him Rose. He was already starting to ask about her. We need to—"

"Rose? What on earth are you talking about?"

"Get out your phone. Google Pratt and 'fugitive.' Look. See? Rose looks like one he's been trying to catch."

He stares and whistles. "Is this for real?"

"Does it matter? Rose is gone. It looks like her. Let's use that fact."

"Well, of course it matters! If she isn't *it*, it won't work. Rose could come back any minute. Martha says she never really checked out. Sweetie, you're so new to all this," he says, patting her shoulder as though she were a child. "We're lucky to have you with us, of course, but let the pros and old-timers handle things, okay? John and Mary have already figured out which one to give up. Then we can keep the rest. Safe and sound. Everybody's happy."

He's in my sights. I could do as I like to him, with this fireplace iron.

Su says, trying to stay natural, "Which one are they planning to give up? And what about Seth?"

"Shh! They're coming back. Let me handle this. Seth's a nonissue now. I'm taking him over to the Berringers after this. Watch and learn."

Pratt returns with the boy behind him.

He taps his chest, and again I see the etched weapon flashing at his wrist. "The creature didn't follow me. That's why I went. I believe it stayed here with you."

Harold starts. "I thought you said they weren't clever, Mr. Pratt."

"I said they weren't intelligent. A thing can be clever without being self-aware. Think of a puzzle. A puzzle doesn't understand itself, but it can still be tricky to solve, yes?"

He's still goading, baiting what he hopes to rouse. He's trying to be the most cunning soul in this room. But is he?

Harold asks, "Any idea who this ghoul might be?"

"At this point I'm keeping an open mind."

"Something else they can't do, right?" Seth laughs.

"So what now?" Su asks.

"Now we go back downstairs."

"But you just said there's a——"

"Come, everyone. Cleaning is a process completed by degrees. And trust me, it takes time and patience to do the job right. I do have a few more questions." Pratt begins leading them out of the bedroom. "Meanwhile, we're learning something about this haunting with every step we take. Notice that we, the living, must always lead the way—not the dead. Now, friends," he says when they're out the door, "*why* do you think the dead would come to Ruth Huellet?"

"I left my cell phone back in the bedroom," Harold says, feeling his pocket where I emptied it as he passed me. "Be right back."

Su says, "Are you asking, Mr. Pratt, if we think she did anything to deserve this?"

"That's exactly what I'm asking."

"I haven't lived here as long as some others, but I never saw her do anything that would anger a ghost. And I don't think anyone like Ruth, no matter what they did, *deserves* to be knocked down and paralyzed."

"It might not have been her actions, Ms. Kwon, that brought the attack on. It might have been her blood."

"I don't know what you mean by that."

Pratt checks the other rooms, cold and empty, on the landing. "I don't know yet either, to be honest. I'm simply wondering why your mother"—he turns back to Ruth's son—"who could have lived, as you say, more comfortably if she chose to, punished herself by living in quasi-poverty instead and spent her days with oils and lye, making what scrubs and cleans stains away?"

"That sounds awful pop-psych," Su says sharply. Some of her calm is slipping. "Especially from someone who calls himself a cleaner. Do you do *your* work to wash some stain away?"

Pratt flinches.

She's cut him. Good.

"No, Ms. Kwon, I don't."

It's the last I see of them before I close the door and lock Harold in with me.

A pity they won't be able to see what happens next.

22

I never terrify the living on a whim. Fear should serve some purpose, I say. Fear: surely it was first meant to teach us something—how to survive—before it was twisted and used to punish, instead.

It will serve a good purpose now.

Harold is pounding on the bedroom door, calling out, confused.

How can it be shut and locked so tightly, so fast?

Now he turns. Remembering.

Pratt said something was here.

A bead of sweat stands out on his tanned brow.

The room begins filling with a sweet, soft scent.

The old marine presses his back against the door, as if he hopes it might turn into a raft.

"What's happening?" he whispers. "What's that?"

It's a mist. A fog, unfurling from the opened curtains, slinking down to the floor, filling the room up, from below. The faces in the photographs stare glassy-eyed, unmoving, as the vapor thickens and the ceiling drops down, lowering on him, lower, lower, squeezing the scent of fear out of him, mixing it with the pale pink fog as it snakes around, finding its

197

way into your mouth, Harold Dubois, your throat, the odor filling your lungs, like smoke, but not really, it's not that, what is it, what is it?

What is that smell? I hiss in his ear. *Scream it out loud, so the others can hear. No? Too late, then. It's inside you now. It has you. It's in you. It can pull you down. I'm drowning you with my perfume, sailor. A mermaid with a name. What is it? Say it now. What is it? What is it?*

"Rose!" he screams. "Rose! Rose! Rose! Rose! Rose! Rose! Rose!"

23

"Let me go! Please, *please!*"

So polite the wicked are, when they're trapped. As if they imagine manners were their only failing.

I let him go. Harold Dubois has done what I need from him.

He flings open the door and stumbles out onto the landing, falling to the carpet, shaking and coughing and spewing.

"Harry!" Su bends over him.

"Dude is soaking wet!" Seth marvels.

"Harold? Quiet, both of you, please. *Harold!*" Pratt takes the weight of the heavy man in his arms, steadying him. "He's been contacted. Harold! Good job. You got it to manifest. Wonderful. Excellent. What did you—"

"Rose," the frightened man croaks.

"Rose?"

"Rose. She told me to say her name. I said it. Didn't you all goddamn hear me shouting for help?"

The hunter grips him around the shoulders, happy, grateful.

Why, when I was the one who did all the work?

"Are you sure?" Pratt breathes out, excitedly. "That the name was Rose?"

"I'm sure. And the air. It stank like roses."

Pratt stands him up and rushes back into the room.

Too late, hunter. It's stale as a bone in here.

Yes, Pratt, it was Emma Rose. I can see by your flushed face how gleeful you are that we're meeting again. You've longed for this moment, haven't you? Yet now you can't feel or find me, for I'm as cold as a burial stone.

Su hovers in the doorway, confused. Not understanding that I've helped her, put meat on the bones of her plan. I've given myself away to make certain none of the other ghosts are or will be discovered. But she still falters. She's lost. She thought it was going to be a clever trick, saying her friend was dead, and now . . .

"Harry," she says, turning to him, "I don't understand what you're saying."

"Rose tried to choke me!"

He won't come any closer to the door, preferring to clutch the broken landing rail. Well, it will take him a little while to get his sea legs back.

"Did you *see* her?" Pratt hurries out of the room. "Was there a form? A body?"

"No. Just mist. The smell of it. And I recognized her voice."

"Did she say anything else besides her name?"

"You mean that wasn't enough? Why did she have to go for *me*?"

"Because you weren't me," Pratt says quickly, "and you were handy." He turns to Su. "Can you take him downstairs, please?"

"I can, but what are you going to do?"

Harold straightens and comes back to life, swearing. "Show it no goddamn mercy!"

"All of you, please, go down," Pratt orders, his eyes flushed and alight. "I'll join you when I can. Go on. Please. I have everything under control here."

Do you really, though?

He's like a man who believes because an engine stops he's the one steering the train.

When they've gone, he comes back into Ruth's bedroom. I stay cold above the broken canopy. Now that we're alone, he runs his hand through his thick hair. He looks sharp, even if he doesn't know where to look.

"Given up grave-robbing, Emma Rose? Or did what you cruelly stole rot on you?"

Keep still. Pratt isn't the game, I must remember. He isn't the prize.

He strokes his chest and sniffs the air for some fresh sign.

"Are you still here, Emma Rose?"

He sits on the bed below me, with nothing to shield or protect him, his weapon down. As if he suddenly needs to rest.

"Just tell me," he asks in a more ordinary voice, "what have you done with the body? Let me find it at least. Let me bury it, or whatever's left of it." He sees Harold's telephone, where I left it on the nightstand. "Let me call someone, for her. If you've left her body somewhere . . . She doesn't deserve to be treated that way. We both caused her harm."

No. Don't you take that tack, I think. *It's you who's to blame.*

"There's no reason for you to cling to her now."

He looks up at the photographs on the wall. The dead are all long gone, yet their bodies still glow. The light in Pratt's eyes deepens.

"I have to admit I'm impressed. How can you have been sighted as a body and move invisibly, too? Unless . . ."

It dawns on him.

M DRESSLER

"You can take the body or leave it, as you like."

Nearly enough to drive you mad, isn't it? Just the thought of how free I am. What I can choose and do.

He jumps up and paces, limping, his body a prison he's trapped inside. "This won't last. I promise you that."

He stops. Another dawn breaks over his face.

What is it now, hunter?

"You're still nothing, you know, Emma Rose. Haven't you figured that out yet, you poor girl?"

I'm invisible. Cold. Safe. He can't hurt me. He's the one who looks like a ghost, whitened, rippling with anger, now.

"Do you hear me? I say that you have nothing, Emma Rose. You reach, and have nothing. You cry, and have nothing. You steal, and have nothing. You terrify—and still, look, what have you gained? Nothing. You rage and have nothing. You move and have nothing. You hide and have nothing." His rough voice grows louder. "You *wait* and have nothing. You *speak* and have nothing. Do you understand me? No matter what you put on. Or don't. You're still nothing forever accompanied by nothing. And no one."

I long to shout, to lash out: *And you, Mr. Pratt? You who, I notice, arrive always alone, and hunt alone, then leave alone, return alone, stand in rooms like this one and talk alone, to those you're unsure are even there, tapping your chest to make sure that—what?—you're still alive? You're feeling something? You who have no one, either, to warm your chest?*

Tell me again, which one of us it is who has nothing?

He waits, his head cocked, as if he's still hoping for some crack, some bargain in the air around us.

"You won't win," he finishes simply.

Then he hitch-steps, hurrying from the room, toward the stairs.

I follow him. Though I don't want to, yet I have to. For the others. For no other reason would I stoop to follow what I've already escaped.

"Change of plans," Pratt says, bright-eyed, when he reaches the others at the foot of the staircase. "I need to go see your mother now, Seth."

"Uh . . . why?"

"Harold, how are you feeling? Better?" The hunter is smiling, throwing out a caring look.

I know that look. All he cares about, now, is what he hopes to do to me.

"How am I feeling? Pissed as hell, Mr. Pratt."

"Good. That's exactly the right response."

Rage, thought to be ugly on us, is allowed as handsome on others.

"Ms. Kwon." Pratt turns to Su. "Can you update the Berringers on our progress?"

"I was just—" She pauses. "About to go there."

"Excellent. Now, how do I get to the hospital?"

"I can snowmobile you up to the mountain road," Harold says. "The county plows it, and the town council keeps a truck up there this time of year, with keys in it, just in case. I'll take you and Seth to see Ruth." He wants, I see, to keep an eye on Pratt around the injured museum keeper. "We should be able to get our own roads plowed by tomorrow. But you won't be able to get your car out till then."

"If you're up to the trip, I'd appreciate the snowmobile lift."

"Absolutely."

"Sounds like you're anxious for me to do my work."

"You bet. That's one sadistic bitch I just met."

The three men leave by the front door. Su follows slowly behind, turning back once to look at the house, hesitating in the doorway.

She whispers, halting, at a loss, "Rose . . . ?"

I want so badly to show myself to her. All that I really, truly am. But she's frowning. Angry. Is she bitter? Dismayed? Does she feel betrayed by me?

"Are you one of them? Did you lie to me?"

What is there to say?

Bending to put on her snowshoes, she whispers, "If you did, good for you. Now let's go get the bastards."

24

Yes. Let us go. I've given myself away now.

A strange feeling—to know you've chosen the end.

Su crosses the square, heading off to tell the Berringers why none of the schoolhouse ghosts need to be touched. The town's so quiet, all at once. As if waiting. Not a breath of breeze. The square lies snouted in snow, the weather biting down, the white roofs seeming to bend to meet the white stoops. Only the statue of the Prospector looks merry, a small apple of snow balancing on the brim of his slouch hat.

Sometimes time almost seems to stop.

For a moment.

The living, they divide time up, as if by measuring spoons. Months, seasons, years—they tell themselves that because now there's snow, this season is different than the last, the warmer one. They try to make of time a solid thing, a cupboard or a chest, carve time into drawers, in which this or that might be stored. They lay in goods.

But time isn't a cupboard. It's a river. And pours only toward one sea. There's nothing solid to it. It holds no compartments. Little to slow it. A body, I know, I remember, can build a little dam against it and stem the rush, for a while; until, at death, the dam is swept away. And then there is only time, again, as it always is: a single flood. Even when it carries on its back, as this day does, a tiny apple of snow.

I stare at this tuft on the Prospector's hat. It moves, as though pushed. It hangs suspended, round in the air, without falling to the ground.

No. Not an apple of snow. That is the shape of a glowing fist. A pale fist is being raised at Pratt and his companions as they motor away on a roaring sled. The hand freezes, and now a black coat flaps behind, around the Prospector, as if in the wind.

The muffled flap of a tattered black coat.

Longhurst, I whisper.

All I can think is that I must lead him away from where the children might be already hiding. I knew it wouldn't be easy to win this race between us, find the children and get them clear of him and his mad bargain. Still, to show himself, here where the entire town might see, if anyone were looking—that's bold and a gamble, I'll give him that.

But why is he doing it? Perhaps to show the children how powerful he is, in his anger? To frighten and win them back?

Time, it starts again. I fly invisibly up to the balcony of the Huellet House. There I lift my own angered fist, my ghostly shape at him. With any luck, it will pull him away from the others and toward me. He can do nothing to me, after all, who's so far survived death and everything after it that's been flung at my head. I haven't come so far, all these months, to these mountains, and given myself away to Pratt, for it all to be for nothing.

I feel him land on the balcony beside me, a ripple in the cold light. We've both cooled ourselves, are invisible now to the town. Yet surely he feels, as I do, the danger perched and balanced between us.

"How do you do, Mr. Longhurst," I greet him.

"How do you do, Miss Finnis."

His voice is as I remember: crisp with book learning and the accents of the East.

"We should go inside," I say, "where we can safely talk."

In a twist of the light, the wintry air seems to bend and bow to me. "Apologies. I won't enter the house of any Huellet."

Fair enough. "We needn't move," I say. "As long as we're careful." As long as he's away from the children.

"How is it"—the whisper beside me changes, becoming interested—"you move, you travel, the way you do? Inside a body and out of it?"

More than curiosity in that voice. Envy. I must be cautious.

I don't answer his question. "You tell me you won't go into the house," I say instead. "Is it because this is the balcony they hung you from? Where all the town gathered, in the photograph, to celebrate, and see the sentence carried out?"

The ripple of light beside me wavers, but doesn't grow stronger. He's keeping himself invisible and in check.

"It wasn't here I was put to an end. They noosed me on a tree by the falls. It was the custom then to carry out a sentence in a place close to the crime."

My first day at the Bar. Standing beside the river. A rippling light, then shadowy footsteps had come from a swaying tree toward me.

"Close to the crime? Did you kill the children by the falls, Mr. Longhurst?"

"No. That's where our ashes were scattered, into the water. The ground being too hard in winter for any burial. It was also the place where four other men died. The town thought it worthwhile to clear that account, as well."

His whisper is even and calm now. A man speaking of his own death as though it were no more than a bill delivered. To be sure he needs, as I do, to keep cold so as not to be seen—but can a man truly recall his guilt so quietly, without even a tremor?

All at once I want to see his face, so I'll know, as I have with Pratt, how better to deceive it.

"We have both been equally," I say kindly, "at the mercy of others."

The light shimmers beside me. "Come to the jailhouse," he says, quivering, "and I'll show you."

He can do nothing to me, I remind myself, as I feel the air behind his coat swoop away like a blackbird darting toward the square.

The snow in front of the museum is trampled where Pratt's boots have limped through it. I slip through the keyhole of the iron door. Inside, all of Ruth Huellet's trinkets are gone. The walls are bare stone. A table and six spindle-backed chairs are the only furnishings standing on an unswept, earthen floor.

Longhurst stands in damp, stained garments inside the shadows of the jail cell, his fingers wrapped around the bars.

He nods, looking past my shoulder.

Behind me, the iron door opens.

Snow crumbling from their boots and from their bent, hatted heads, half a dozen men shuffle into the jailhouse. Pistols flash at their belts. They wear heavy leather pouches. Two of them, this vision reveals to me, are the men who rocked haughtily in their chairs at Huellet House. Another wears the badge of the law on his coat. The rest are unfamiliar to me, unshaven and red-cheeked from the cold.

"Gentleman," Mayor Caleb Huellet says, dusting off his beaver hat, "on this grim day, we must call this court to order. Berringer, let's get on with it."

The sheriff comes from stoking a potbellied stove and sits at the wooden table. The others take chairs in front of him, the Huellets in the first row.

"Court is convened," Berringer announces.

Longhurst calls calmly from his cell, "This is no court."

The mayor snaps, "Lynch law is your cellmate, now! Go on, Berringer."

The sheriff folds his arms across his chest. "I affirm that these men here present have the authority to render judgment and pass sentence upon you, Landon Albert Longhurst, on behalf of the town and encampment of White Bar."

"And what"—Longhurst grips the bars—"are the charges against me?"

"You know well enough." The Berringer badge glints in the light from the stove. "Luring children to their deaths."

Dr. Huston Huellet takes his white hat in his hands and shakes it. "Killing innocents! Their poor families are wailing all over town!"

"I've heard them," Longhurst says quietly. "I'll never stop hearing them. Nor should you."

"The criminal will speak when addressed!" Caleb Huellet commands.

"I say then, you should address yourselves."

"Let's just get on with it," a man in the back says, as if frightened. "Before cold and fever take us all."

Longhurst faces him. "You can thank our local charlatans—forgive me, our leaders—for that."

"We'd have you whipped for slander but the rope will break your neck first," Huston Huellet snorts.

"Let's just string him up and go find our suppers," a weary man calls out, "and give the Bar some peace."

"My actions," Longhurst says, "could have been prevented if these brothers had only had the decency to quit camp after seeing their poison only hastens the deaths of those already sick."

"A fine speaker, ain't he?" the mayor taunts. "Got that schoolmarmish wheedling voice down. Says whatever cowardly, womanish thing it takes, don't you, Longhurst?"

The sheriff turns nervously toward him. "No need to defend yourself, Caleb. This man can't escape his fate by any means."

Longhurst nods slowly, as if in agreement. "Only the unscrupulous can do that—including you, Berringer. I've watched you look the other way as these tricksters created pestilence where there wasn't any, then offered up a false cure. How much were you paid to do it? And how many bodies have you, undertaker," Longhurst calls to the man at the back, "put in coffins at a tidy profit? And why are so few others from town here, I wonder? Afraid to leave their houses because of the sickness in the air? How many will survive this lean winter? Ask yourselves why the good doctors, if their medicines are as potent as they claim, have suddenly told their wives not to come West. You might also ask them why Brinks, Collum, Tanheuser, and Smith would drunkenly set dynamite along the river for no good reason. Did you put the powder there yourselves, boys? Or merely get the men drunk on your poison and send them on their way? Or was it both?"

"Spare us your ravings," Berringer cries and leaps up. "No one's paying them any heed! And it's a fact, generally speaking"—he turns to the rest, quickly—"that someone guilty of a crime will try and shove that guilt onto someone else, if he can. Kiersten," he calls to the undertaker, "why don't you show us what you have with you."

The man in black draws sheets of paper from his pocket, all the while keeping his head lowered. He stands up from his chair and brings them forward to the table.

"It gives me no pleasure to do this, gentleman," the undertaker says, clearing his throat, "but here you can see we have a sample of the murderer's handwriting, in this letter, unsent by him. And here, a second letter, in a matching hand, bragging of his cleverness in killing the men to get land for the schoolhouse and his own reward. We all know, Longhurst, your claim was played out, and you had no money to move on." The man keeps his head bowed, uneasy, as he sits down again.

Longhurst shakes his head. "I wrote no such second letter. The first was purloined from my lodgings—was it by you, postmaster?" He looks at another man sitting with his eyes averted. "My handwriting was obviously copied. No logic accompanies these accusations. How could I have organized such a murder? By what farseeing trick could I have predicted the meadow would be cleared, and a schoolhouse—not by me but by the doctors—proposed?"

"It establishes a pattern!" Berringer slaps the table. "And let us all note this murderer has yet to express remorse for the killing of five children!"

"You're wrong, Berringer. You've seen me do nothing but mourn and lament in this cell. Yet you've denied me the chance, when I've asked, to speak to and beg forgiveness of the families. I've been allowed to see no one, apologize to no one. I'll forever carry the horror of those small, snuffed bodies in my heart. You'll never understand or accept what drove me to my desperate actions. You've made that clear. This is no court. This is more lust for murder."

Longhurst steps back from the ghostly bars and straightens his tattered tie. "My remorse is known to my soul only," he goes on. "You"—he stares at the brothers—"know none. You have been the architects of our town's misery, laying down bones to build your mansions. Your snake oil does nothing for ailing people except keep them from seeking a real cure. You knew this, and did nothing. You are cowards in every respect, not only you but every man in this room—my God, the children as they died were far braver than any of you, stronger than you! They showed more will in their smallest fingernails than you can find in all your empty profits. Unending remorse for me, yes. But unholy shame for you. And may the trail of your shame follow you from now through all eternity."

"Enough of your curses!" The mayor stands, stung. "It's time, it's been long enough. We'll string him up near the meadow. At the falls, yes, men? To honor the children and all the men who suffered at his hands."

The postmaster mumbles, "March him through the snow and let's get it done."

"But," the undertaker whispers, "as with the children, there can be no burial. And like the children, he might be carrying the fever, too."

The men recoil.

"Then we hang him and you publicly burn the body, Kiersten," Huston Huellet says.

"Sir? The town's not likely to come to witness it. Not if there's more contagion."

"Can't be helped," Berringer says. "They'll be grateful, in the end, for what we've done for them in absentia. Pass the word to everyone— Longhurst was dead within a day of those precious little ones passing and being laid to rest. Enough. Let's go. We have a winter still to meet. Let's finish this."

Like a rope cut, the vision Longhurst has shown me ends.

I stand alone in the museum—with the silent Indian arrowheads, the baby carriage hanging overhead, the prospectors' metal pans.

The schoolmaster is invisible. Yet I feel him in the room, still.

I must think. Think.

Is this vision all true? But what does it matter, if even now he still clings to the children, wanting them behind bars with him, is hunting for Ola and the rest, to put them all back in the schoolhouse again?

The undertaker's writing was on the letter Ruth was given. The writing read: *Letter found among the possessions of and in the hand of the deceased, Landon Albert Longhurst.* The letter Ruth Huellet would have been holding in her hands, when her head was struck.

"You struck Ruth Huellet in revenge," I say.

"No." I hear only his voice. "I swear to God. I showed myself in anger to the woman without meaning to. I'd been searching for the children ever since they flew away to chase Ola. I flew into a rage when I saw the letter. I hadn't seen it in years."

It doesn't matter. "You killed the children."

"Yes," the voice says.

"Then let them come with me."

"I'm all they have," he pleads. "They're all I have. We have no other place."

"They must come with me."

"Where? How? And how could you possibly help them?" His voice is full of judgment now. "They're not like you. It would only torment them to be with you, a stranger, and drive them mad with jealousy to see you, them lacking the flesh, the form you've grossly stolen. You'd exile them from their only remaining home. And all the while the brutes here, heirs to the sins of this town, they'll be free of us. They'll have won the field."

I see the outline of the black coat again, crawling along the beams above me. He's growing angry.

I keep my own temper. "I'm no thief. Nor will I let anyone tell me what form I may take. Not you. No one. A hunter is here. You've seen him. Will you give the children no way to escape him? You have a chance, now," I say quickly, "to atone for your crimes. When the hunter returns with his weapon, you can—"

A pair of screams.

Not from Longhurst. Or anyplace here in this cell.

Outside.

On the square.

The children.

25

Motorsleds are whirling in from every direction.

Lights flash. Horns blare. The living of White Bar are racing on sleds and on foot. The Berringers come from their porch into the snow, the mayor stumbles from her hotel, Bill, others, come floundering through the snowdrifts. Su steps out of her gallery, her jaw dropping.

The children. From the roofs, the balconies, they fly.

Shrieking.

Below the Prospector, a statue unmoved, the living tumble and fall together. The children swoop and keen around them, dancing, diving down. Ola dives with them, then twists like a sheet and lands atop the statue. She raises her burning hand.

There's nothing I can do, I think. Every ghost's fury is her own.

Longhurst appears on the roof of the General Store, livid above her. She points away from him.

"There!"

"What have they done, Ola?" he calls, clearly.

"They're talking about choosing one of us to teach us a lesson."

"Who is talking?"

"*All* of them."

"And which one of you did they choose?"

"Anton," Ola cries. "They chose good Anton!"

I follow her blazing eyes. Toward the one who would cause the town the least trouble. The obedient, rule-following boy.

Anton, shimmering, hovers a few feet above the roof of the jailhouse.

"No!" Su cries out from her porch. "Wait! I told the Berringers it was Rose—"

The plan didn't work. Why?

"Then the bargain is broken completely!" Longhurst's raging voice echoes. "Do you hear that, White Bar? You've sundered the pact. It's done!"

The ghosts, keening, rise slowly from their roofs and perches. They rise in a white foam and surge together, like a falls. Then they drop and disappear. Scattering, hiding from all of us.

"You *said*"—a woman sputters and claws her way out of the snow, pointing wildly at Martha—"*you* said this was under *control*. You call this is *under control*? This is ridiculous, a nightmare, a disgrace, a, a—"

"I don't understand." Martha struggles to wade toward Mary Berringer. "Didn't we decide to say it was Rose?"

"The cleaner wasn't going to swallow it." The old woman straightens calmly now and brushes off her coat. "Pratt's with Ruth. Harold's with them, and he's been texting me. Ruth is telling him it was a male spirit that attacked her. Harold will try to stop her from saying there's more, but she likely will. They'll need to give up one of their own if they want our help."

"But why one of the children? Why not the schoolmaster?"

"He keeps the rest in line."

"That's *not*," someone shouts, "what he did just now!"

"Just get the hunter to blast them!"

"And lose our traditions?" Mary shouts back. "Our rights?"

"I'm not letting any spooks make a fool out of me like this!"

"Least of all *them!*"

"They don't deserve our charity!"

"Ungrateful!"

"After all we've done for them!"

"You blast 'em"—John Berringer shouts now, standing under the Prospector, leaning against him—"*they* win!"

The square quiets down, obedient.

I wait and listen, for my kind.

John Berringer wipes the ice from his chin. Squinting at the townspeople around him, he says, "That what you all really want, huh? Think that's what *they* really want? To have no place to go? Don't be fooled by all this . . . *spectacle.* This is a tantrum that'll blow over. It happened at the very beginning. Before the first bargain. Which put an end to such dramatic displays. Those who don't have any choices, and got nowhere else to call home, always come home to their senses in the end."

Mary Berringer stands beside her husband. "My dear John is right. No need for us to overreact. None at all. Children will have their outbursts from time to time. Then they remember what's best for them—with a little help. John and I have been here longer than any of you!" she calls out. "We know what to do, good neighbors and friends. We know the history of the Bar. We know how to get through this, and keep what's ours."

A man stands up, shivering. "And just what do you propose we do right now? Freeze our asses off outside our own homes because they've hounded us from them and won't let us back in them, until—what?"

"They drove me from my own kitchen!" another calls.

"From my TV!"

"From my bed!"

"It's simply time to renew the bargain," Mary Berringer announces. "A little early. Pick up your flashlights, everyone," she says, for night is descending. "Bill, get some torches from the storeroom. Everyone. Stand up. Turn on your sled lights. Time to put everything back in its place. As any lost thing will know is best."

"Everything back where it belongs!"

"I like the sound of that!"

"I'm with Mary and John!"

"This is our home. Our way of life!"

"But it's not," Martha whispers to Mary, "the anniversary yet."

"I think we can move things up by a week, don't you? Sometimes in life, dear, you have to adjust."

"But what about the hunter? He'll be back soon."

"Then we have no time to lose, Martha. Now come. You're our mayor! Be mayoral. Lead us. Go up on the Huellet balcony, as you've always done. Begin the recitation."

She gives Martha a little push toward the Huellet House. The mayor wipes her hair, then wades through the snow, a slow crossing, to the porch. There she looks back, uncertain.

"We're all with you, Martha dear."

The townspeople turn on their beams, and the lights flood the darkened mansion. Martha goes through the front door. A feeble light turns on inside the house. Next a brighter one, on the second floor. At Ruth Huellet's bedroom one of the tall windows is thrown up, jerkily. The mayor tucks underneath its sash and climbs out onto the ragged balcony.

The faces of the town look up at her. Solemnly.

She closes her eyes, as if trying to recall something.

"People of the Bar—"

She stops.

"People of the Bar."

She opens her eyes, trying again.

"It's okay!"

"Go on!"

"Do it, Martha!"

"You can do it!"

She sets her shoulders. She shouts: "People of the Bar! I thank you for gathering here. Let us begin the ceremony. O, spirits from beyond the grave: we now join with you. The perils of the world are many. And the way is hard. Who among us is not without sorrows?" She looks down. "Who among us does not know the pain of loss, or the wish for retrieval? There will be errors, accident, tragedies, and dismay. But so long as our hearts are good, and made of good intentions, our consciences will be clear and our purposes certain. Let us not seek ways to tear each other apart, but in politeness and civility make our bargain: that we will dwell together, each keeping to our own place. We have built for you a house, spirits, a monument to you, where you will find a home, and be forever cared for and entertained and educated. You will acknowledge what we have built for you, and cease your ravaging our homes and shops. Your families are gone, o spirits. They left, tearfully, when you were taken from this life. You have no other family but us, to honor and care for you. It is a time for a rebirth. If you will keep to your house, then we will keep to ours, and never let your peace be disturbed, as you will never let ours be. All things are possible with order and the rule of law. All things will be torn down with vengeance and blame. Anger is futile. Peace and correct behavior an endless reward. We will now proceed to your domicile and raise our lights to you. Come, and show yourself at its windows, so that we may know you are content, and all may go on in fitness and right-ness, with glory to God. These words first spoken by Dr. Caleb Huellet, mayor of the township of White Bar, 1852, in the presence of all those of right-thinking civilization. Let us now proceed to the offering."

The gathering in the photo. Not a hanging.

The bartering of souls.

The citizens of White Bar turn the iced noses of their sleds and plow and walk with their lights through the shadows on the hill, up to the schoolhouse. They'll find nothing there, surely, I tell myself, hurrying invisibly along with them. I'm certain of it. The children have shown they know now what it is to move freely. They've chosen freedom for themselves. Unless . . . unless . . .

Longhurst.

I wing over of the heads of the mob, looking down for Su, her bright scarf. She isn't with them.

Inside the schoolroom, empty desks. I wait for the gathered people of White Bar to top the hill. No one is here to greet them, I see, relieved, but me. And I'll do whatever must be done.

The parade of lights and torches comes no farther than the edge of the schoolyard. The people of White Bar unmount and stand and face the locked and chained school, their faces half hidden by the flares they hold in their hands.

"This house"—Martha stands just in front of them, still reciting—"is a house of dignity, built by humanity, in the shape of what is holy. Show us you are like us in dignified breeding and humanity—or if you are mere animals, creatures of the devil. We believe you are not. We believe you to be marked by charity and good manners. Let us see each other, and make and resolve this bargain from this day forward. Show yourself at these windows of wisdom."

No one comes.

"No one's at the windows," someone whispers.

"I told you. It needs to be the actual anniversary," Martha says to Mary Berringer.

John Berringer steps forward and lifts his chin at the steeple, into the darkened air. "Just to be clear," he shouts. "Return to this house, and we'll manage this hunter, and any who come after him. As we always have. That could change, however, whenever we want it to. If you stay in line, we'll take care of him and the rest. If not . . . well. We're returning now to our homes, *un*molested. We'll come again in the morning, and look for your answer—unless you want the hunter to be told about each and every one of you, down to the smallest. And if any one of these good people"—he points behind him—"are made to feel even the least bit of discomfort tonight, you'll all be destroyed."

"You see, we have to show strength." Mary nods at Martha. "It's the only thing they understand." She turns to the others. "Now, if any of you don't want to preserve our traditions in the way John describes, speak up or forever hold your peace."

Soft murmurs come.

"All right."

"Give 'em one last chance."

"If they're blasted, it'll be their fault."

"Not ours."

"Give 'em some time to think it through."

"We're probably being too generous."

"But let's go."

Inside the schoolhouse, I feel faint vibrations behind me.

I know it's the children. With Longhurst.

I don't turn away from the windows to look at them. I stay frozen. "Keep still and cold," I whisper to them behind me. "Be clever. Wait. Listen."

"We won't be sacrificing the oldest boy to Pratt?" Martha is saying to Mary.

"No, of course we will, dear. Some price must be paid for what they did tonight. And to keep them in order."

The vibration grows stronger behind me.

"Stay calm," I say. "The hunter will be back at any moment. We must keep to a plan. Ola, do you remember where I said to take the children?"

Her voice rises out of the silence.

"Yes."

"Good. Mr. Longhurst, will you help me distract the town?"

I feel him move closer to me, away from the children. Good.

"You have some plan, Miss Finnis?"

I have an end. "I need more time. I know this hunter. I know what to do. Will you help me, for the children?" To atone for your murders, I don't say, but let the thought vibrate through the souls around me.

A pause.

"I can," says the schoolmaster.

"Then I'll trust you."

Trust no one, the children once said. *We burned.*

They sometimes frighten me, they stare at me, the schoolmaster said.

"We all know what to do, then," I say quietly and rise through the steeple, the children's eyes following me, looking up.

26

I've never taken to the air with another like me. A strange comfort to it, in spite of everything. After the coldness of the children.

"There they are," Longhurst says of the townspeople below.

"You'll keep them on the square?" I ask. "Don't let them go back to their homes."

"And you?"

"It's Pratt I have to take on."

"You know him. You've met him before."

"Yes."

"It's good to know your enemy. I'll keep them busy. As long as I can."

I leave the schoolmaster to take on the Bar.

I alight on the roof of the hotel, where the body I've protected waits for me under its icy cover.

"A little longer," I whisper, "and I'll return for you. I promise."

I pass down the chimney.

In Pratt's room, nothing is as it was when I last saw it. Papers are scattered all around on the floor. On the bed, an artist's sketchbook lies open, sheets torn from it. Across the bedspread, in scrap after scrap, a face is charcoaled over and over again, each drawing stricken through and dismissed, it seems, and a new one tried. Yet he can't quite remember. He can't quite capture what he saw, months ago. Two faces, blurred into one. One small and round, the other with eyes that seem too large for it, and the shadow of a cleft in her chin.

I'm glad I've been haunting you, Philip Pratt. You might think me a monster, yet here, with every line, you've been trying to grasp me.

Outside the window the statue of the Prospector groans and falls. Longhurst, showing off his rage and vengeance and power. The townspeople cower in the snow, fallen, too, their knees curled into their chests.

On the dresser, below the town's famous photograph, Pratt has made more sketches, of buildings and plunging bodies with arrows drawn beside them, pointing up and down. I see after a moment what Pratt's doing: he's mapped the course of what happened when last we met—what he did, how he lifted his wrist and turned it to fire his weapon, too late to save a life, too late to strike me down. He's haunted by this, by the error he's not sure he made.

Dates below, and scribblings, notes different from the ones I saw him make in front of Harold and Su and the others.

"First sighting—San Francisco—Fisherman's Wharf. Ferry crossing."

"Second sighting—near Davis—moving East."

"Third sighting—Lake Berry—attack on driver. Still East."

He's been following me, closer than I knew. Chasing the error.

Well, now we each have a weapon.

Longhurst is done flinging the Prospector to the square. He rises, spreading his black coat wide. The cries of the town go up and now, added to them, is the shrieking of a fresh motor. I go on looking through the curtained window. Harold and Pratt are returning by sled. Harold's mouth is all agape below the window. Martha is running toward them, stumbling into Pratt's arms.

"Help us! Please!"

"You're all right." Pratt grabs and steadies her as he watches Longhurst's coat flap away into the night. "Listen to me. You're all right!"

"It was the schoolmaster!"

Yes, the new part of my plan.

"I know," Pratt says quickly. "Ruth told me. Mayor Hayley, pull yourself together. Where is he going? What lies that way? The school?"

"Schoolhouse Knob! Yes! Yes!"

The children will be gone from there by now. Longhurst will be leading Pratt there for me.

"Harold, I'm taking the snowcat!" Pratt shouts. "Take care of Martha!"

And now we'll all race to see who's fastest, whose aim the sharpest.

Pratt rattles the chains at the schoolhouse door. He can't get in. He kicks it with his good leg, breaking it in, falling forward inside. He swings a beam of light across the slanted desks and the slates tossed to the floor, over the cold stove, across the neat alphabet on the chalkboard, reflecting now with dust and snow.

"No need to stay," I whisper to Longhurst. "Go."

"I wouldn't dream of it," Pratt says, misunderstanding me.

The hunter hunts quietly now, moving slowly between the desks. I see him breathing, sense his heart pounding. He reaches for his own chest. "Ruth has told me about you. What a long, sad road it's been, Landon Albert Longhurst." They try to use our names to call us out. "She told me she wants to end this long curse, this burden and suffering you've all been sharing for centuries. She's lying in a hospital bed, at this very moment, wishing you peace." He adjusts his wrist with one hand, carefully, twisting the mechanism. "The hospital where *you* put her. But she bears you no ill will. She's tired and frustrated, as you are. It's time, at last, for a new beginning. And peace and rest that can be shared by all. Not just by some. Rest is so close. Why don't you show yourself to me, and let me help you toward a happier place than this mad, maddening one?"

A slate rattles at his feet. He sees it. Stares down at it for a moment. Then bends, inching—is it because he's in pain, or because he wants to show how little he needs to hurry?—and lifts and turns it over.

I've written across it: *WE ARE SO TIRED.*

"I understand. So there is more than one of you here?"

I whisper, in a childish-sounding voice, *Yes.*

"Are you all here?"

Yes, my whisper comes, as another slate slides across the floor to him. It reads: *ARE YOU TIRED, TOO?*

"It's kind of you all to ask. Ruth says you were always polite ghosts—before time began weighing so heavily on you. You're right." A hand still at his chest, he looks around the room. "I am tired. I wouldn't mind a bit of rest myself." He sits at a small desk, his bulk nearly too much for it. "Ah. It's so dreary, isn't it, children, always having to do your duty. It's so heavenly—for teacher and students both, I imagine—when school lets out. No more being bound by rules." He sighs, deeply. "I don't miss school at all. I didn't go to a school, myself, exactly like this one. But then, you didn't attend this schoolhouse either, did you? Your school was burned, Ruth told me, when you died. This is just a tomb. A room that's never meant anything to you. It isn't really your home. And never really felt like it. I know. I understand. I can imagine. You've been trying to imagine you're at home, inside death, and that these walls are real to you, and that all the long days and years, the centuries, that have come and gone are real, watching others more real than you come and go, while you stay, and go nowhere. The nights are too real, too, aren't they, the most real thing of all. They stretch so long, with nothing to fill them. You understand all the days and nights are real. But you know, in your hearts, you know that you can never be real again, no matter what tricks you try. And it makes you feel terribly sad. So terribly sad and alone. With nothing but more sadness ahead of you."

This is what he does. He tries to worm his way into your soul—though you've kicked and scraped and fought off worms. He tries to make you doubt your heart is real because there's no beat to it, doubt your wishes are real because they haven't come true. And should you find, by some miracle, a body to put all your wishes and dreams in, a body at this moment waiting saved and cold, he'll want you to believe that miracle isn't real, either, and that you don't deserve it. It's all the same, what the powerful want to do: trick you into thinking so little of yourself, you'll come out and hold your hand up, like a child asking to be slapped.

I slide another slate across to him, from a different part of the room. *YOU SHOULD HAVE*, it reads.

"I should have what, friends?"

He stands, baring his arm, gauging the distance the slates have crossed. I keep calm, move away.

SAVED HER, the next says.

"Saved who?"

The last of the slates, now.

THE ONE WHO FELL. EMMA ROSE TOLD US.

"What?"

A piece of cold satisfaction—if a small one—to see the certainty on his face slip away. It needs no slate to speak what's written in that man's eyes. The living might not know, but the dead know you for what you

227

are, Philip Pratt. That's what you're thinking, isn't it? You're imagining six ghosts in this room with you, seeing you, though you can't see them, all of them seeing you for what you are. This room knows, Pratt, that you used a young, living woman to try to catch a ghost and got her killed in the process. It was later called an accident—but let's call it what it was: a bargain *you* made. And now you know, as your eyes widen, that you'll never be able to fool anyone, not in this room, with your lies and tricks. And more: if you want to finish your business here so you can go off and chase me, the rose with the thorn that cuts because she reminds you of what you cut down, you'll have to aim, now, recklessly, wildly, again—as you did on that day the young woman whose dead body cools not far from here fell and died, glass piercing her neck. I've worn her scar.

The dead know all wounds. We remember everything. We know all.

And you want to kill us for it.

My name is Will, I whisper in a childish voice, *and I am present.*

My name is Adelaide, and I am present.

My name is Jack, and I am present.

My name is Anton, and I am present.

My name is Ola, and I am present.

My name is Longhurst, and I am present.

Pratt's fist clenches. He raises his hand.

I dart away in fear. Knowing what comes next.

I hear his weapon burning as I break free of the steeple. He'll aim to finish six ghosts at once, blasting and blasting away at the schoolhouse walls. Not caring if he aims at nothing, or everything.

It's not my business to teach you, the living, that it's all the same darkness inside you—whether you strike at the nothing you can't see or at the something you don't want to see.

To her body, remembering all those who have borne terrible blows, I fly.

27

The square is a ruin, the statue tumbled, boot tracks mazing across the snow, running in all directions, leading at last to the café.

I walk past the shadows of the town hiding behind Bill's curtains, and go to Su Kwon's door.

She opens it, and looks afraid.

I'm not what she thought.

Then her face changes. Just like that. As if she simply decided it.

"Right. Come in, quick, before anyone sees you." She lets me in, then turns to face me. She looks at me. Closely. "They're all over in the café, hiding. Rose. My God. One of these days you're going to have to tell me everything about . . . who you are."

"When there's time, yes."

"I'm not going to be freaked out." She tries a little laugh. "But I am seriously impressed."

"I'm so sorry I lied to you."

She shakes her head, never taking her eyes from me. "Don't say that. I haven't been perfect myself. I've let us both down."

"You haven't."

"I have. I went to the Berringers, exactly the way we talked about. And I told them you were a ghost and we could use you to protect the others, especially since you seemed to have moved on and with Pratt clearly more interested in you than in anything we had going. But Mary and John still wanted to make an example out of one of the kids. I came back here feeling—my skin was crawling—disgusted—there isn't a strong enough word—ready to nail them to the wall and now not having any way to do it. But just now I got an idea. Can you come back to my desk with me?" she asks, tugging my arm in her old way.

There are hands, in this world, who hand you all the hope in the world.

"At first I was thinking I'd report their asses to the state for harboring ghosts. Then I realized all that would be doing is following orders I don't agree with. Because you know and I know who it is who'll really end up being blasted and punished, and who won't. So I put my problem-solver's hat on, wanting to figure out my own punishment for them. Nothing came to me. Then, outside, I see people screaming and ghosts flying—then the ghosts disappear. Then more screaming and a black coat flying and the Prospector tossed off its base like it was a paperweight—great, fine by me, I've always hated all that Conquering the West bullshit—and then the black coat disappears. And I thought, 'That's always what ghosts are having to do, what we want them to do, just go away.' They want you to disappear. Then I knew what I wanted to do. I want to turn the tables."

She sits in front of the great gleaming slate on her desk, and taps it quick and hard.

"I told you my father runs a tech firm, right? And how he expected me to be his partner, was grooming me, all that."

I trust everything she says, I think, *even if I don't understand it.*

"Well, I wasn't being perfectly honest. My father owns a very large internet security firm. My father was one of the best hackers on the planet back in the day. Probably still is, though he keeps a low profile now. Luckily, he taught me everything about his business. If you're not familiar with what I'm getting at, here's the gist: to know the ways you need to protect who a person is, you need to know all the ways someone might *steal* who they are or make them disappear. I've been busy at that for the last two hours. Now all I have to do is hit a few keys, and everyone in this town, every name I have listed here, every single one of them, I'm going to turn them into ghosts."

I don't follow.

"Not like you, of course," she goes on, her voice hard, sharp. "It's not so much of an action, in some ways. Except that in this world, it basically *is*. If I wipe every trace of a person's existence, right here"—she points—"every account, social security number, licenses, birth certificate, titles, records, property—bam, they have nothing, own nothing, are nothing, have no record of their being. They become nothing. They are, to all intents and purposes, dead."

I still don't follow, so I ask, to be sure: "They die?"

"So to speak. No trace left of who they are or what they claim to have. No way to prove who they are, or that they ever were. In the modern world we—" She stops herself. "Shit, I don't even know what I'm saying. Are you, um, modern, Rose?"

"I died in 1915."

"Man, I *so* want to know all about that one day. Okay, for now, let's just say, if you don't have names and numbers here and here and here and here"—she points again—"you're technically gone."

"And then . . . what if you really died?"

"It would be hard even generating a death certificate. Your family would have a hard time inheriting anything from you. But, of course, we're not—Rose, you don't mean that you—"

A shadow crosses her face. A pang of fear, looking at me.

Pain. Pain is all the same, no matter who feels it.

But what pain, I want to know, is owed those who were ready to destroy a meek child to keep others bowed down, meek and afraid? Ghosts who were only fighting not to disappear?

"Would you like to meet them?" I say suddenly.

"Like to meet who?"

"The children."

"What do you mean?"

"We made a plan, the others and I. Let's see if it worked. This way."

She follows me, uncertain, across the windswept alley to her workshop and what I hope to find there. Inside the cold barn, no one. Only her covered motorsled in the corner. The Ghost Door stands without a quiver. My soul falters, now.

"Hello? Are you here?" I call into the nothing.

A fearful quiet.

Then, from under the tarpaulin, they appear.

Addy is holding Will's hand.

Jack keeps his bruised head close to slender Anton.

Ola stands a little apart from them, in her patterned dress.

And Longhurst. He's hovering tall over them, still keeping them close.

Su stands beside me, breathless, amazed.

"These are friends," I say.

"Uh. Hello. Hi." She nods. She's confused, doesn't know what to do. "I'm glad you're here. I'm glad to know you. I think I need to thank you.

You—you didn't come after me, when you chased everyone else out of their houses. Why is that?"

"We know who you are," Ola says. "We've been watching you."

"I don't know if that makes me feel any better, but thank you."

Longhurst ignores her and looks at me. "The hunter?"

"At the schoolhouse. Finishing his cleaning. Or so he wants to believe."

"Are we going back there?" Anton asks, shrinking.

"Never!" Ola say firmly.

I agree, and say so.

"But where *do* we go?" Willie whimpers.

Ola bends down to him, taking him by his ragged little waist. "We have to be brave, Will."

Addy shakes her head. "But we're not brave, Ola."

"We *are*. You saw what we did to them out there!"

"Yes, but what we did was very bad," Anton frets.

"We've been bad again. Like when we burned," Jack says.

I don't understand them and their words. "What are you saying?" I ask Anton. "How were you bad? They will try to make you feel cursed, but you mustn't believe it."

"Mr. Longhurst, he asked us to hold on, and we didn't. That was bad. We brought all this down on ourselves."

Longhurst. Of course. I turn on him. "You—"

Before I can say more, he kneels to the floor, to the boy, surprising us both. "Beloved Anton, no! What are you saying? I never said any such terrible thing to you."

"You said we had to be strong and hold fast."

"Yes, I did, but this is something else now, children. If we let go of this place—"

"We didn't hold on before," Anton insists. "We know. We went wrong."

"No, never—"

"That's why you said, hold fast here. Hold fast and be good. Stay in the schoolhouse. Hold on, you said. Stay."

"Children, yes, no, it's not the same, I never—"

Willie begins crying. "I want to go back. I'll be much better. I promise."

"So will I," Addy says.

"So will I," bruised Jack says.

"*No!*"

Ola shouts them down so powerfully the harp of the Ghost Door quakes.

Her voice burns with rage. "It's too late now to hold on! Stop it! All of you!"

"Rose, look," Su whispers.

The Ghost Door's metal is turning red.

Longhurst doesn't see. His eyes are fixed only on the children. He begs,

"No, no, you don't understand, pupils! You were *never* wrong. You *must* believe that. You must trust yourselves and that you are brave, now, just as brave as Ola says."

Ola wheels on him accusingly. "How? They don't know how to be brave. You never taught us to see how we were."

She's strong. She doesn't need my help. I don't move.

"Then I'll teach you," Longhurst says, desperately. "Remember the penny. All of you? Remember?" He tries to gather them to him. "The water? There are different ways to see—what lies under—"

The Ghost Door glows, whispers and hums. A wind escapes it.

Understanding, I say quickly to Longhurst, "The door is calling for you. This is how I came to you, into the past. You must answer to it. By walking through this opening."

"What the—?" Su blinks. "*How?*"

Ah, if only I knew how all the pieces of the world fit together, I'd draw a map and hang it in every square. But there's no time.

"The door is calling," I say again. "You're meant to go back. I know this."

Uncertain, he turns to the children, kneeling down beside all of them.

"Shall we all go through this door, as Miss Finnis says, to the past?"

Anton shakes his head. "Why?"

"So we can see how it was, in truth."

"I'm too afraid," Willie says.

"I am, too." Longhurst says. "But we must stop being afraid of ourselves, children. We lost each other, once, twice. Now we've found each other again. And now we must face together what we must. This is the way. I believe this. Miss Finnis has already walked there. Will you"—he turns to me—"show us how, now?"

They move toward me in a ghostly circle. All but Ola, who hangs back.

She doesn't need the past. I see it in her face. She wants only the now.

"I think I should leave this form"—I stroke these cold arms—"and travel with you all. But I'll need a spirit to keep this body safe until I return. Ola, will you help me?"

Her eyes are their own answer.

"How?"

"Close your eyes and imagine I'm a safe harbor." As I did, the first time, daring to believe I had the right. "Can you swim toward me?

As we did in the mirror, we stroke and touch.

A fine, strong girl sobs, looking down at skin, at herself.

"My God," Su says as I step away. She looks not at Ola but at me, seeing me for the first time—my white skirt, my ribboned hair, my face, only nineteen years old when I died.

I ask her, my spirit asks, "Su, will you stay with Ola?"

"Yes. Whatever you say."

Anton has crept closer to the metal door, lifting his eyes to it, not so frightened as he was before. The world can seem full of possibility, once it's shown to be that way.

Jack comes to stand beside him, full of wonder. "It's from our meadow, Anton. I can feel it. Are we really going in there?"

"We are," the older boy says firmly.

Longhurst hesitates. Ola is stroking her cold hands, amazed. I see a flash of longing, of envy blaze through Longhurst's spirit, then quickly die out.

"Come on," Anton says. "This way."

28

The timbered door of the log-framed schoolhouse is locked, bolted from inside. I'm standing in the middle of a schoolroom I stood in once before. But it's dark now, lit by lanterns. In the yellow light, I look down and see flowered sleeves on my arms.

I don't understand, then do. I'm to take her place, on this journey through time.

I'm Ola.

My arms are busy helping to pile blankets in a corner, then wood beside the stove. My braids lie thick against my chest and the neck of my dress feels tight. The young ones are busy cutting cornbread in tins on the woodstove; Jack is peeking into a covered kettle of beans. The air smells of fat and smoke. The two lanterns swing from the rafters. The belly of the stove glows. Outside, a glinting beam comes through the jar-filled window. A rattling wind shrieks. I hear shouting. Women's voices, crying out.

"Do you think you have enough, Mr. Longhurst? Is it enough?"

"We should be all right until the fever passes!" Longhurst cries in answer through the jars. "Take shelter from the storm now, please!"

"*Êtes vous sûr?*" a high voice calls through the wind. "Are you certain this is the best thing?"

"Until the fever passes, madame, it must be!"

"Keep them safe!"

"I will. I promise you. You must go now, and heed what I told you. The Huellet family's medicines are poison. You've been sold a lie. Keep away from it. Go home, now, mothers of White Bar. See to your dead."

Their sobs and cries fade away. Now there is nothing but the wind picking at the mud between the logs.

"Is my father dead?" Anton asks.

Longhurst puts his hand on his shoulder.

"He isn't well, son. I can't lie to you." The schoolmaster's face falls, drawn. His whiskers are damp.

"My *maman* isn't sick yet," Will whispers. "Will she come back to get me soon?"

"Not for a while, Willie," Addy murmurs, nodding sleepily. "We can't leave yet."

"But she will come back," Longhurst says. "They all will. Until then, children, come, let us sit near the fire. All will be well." He shivers. "The pass, they say, is blocked. We'd be stuck together till the spring, anyway!" He tries a laugh.

Jack mumbles, "I want to go home to Missouri."

"Jack, you must try to understand what's happening now. You have been entrusted to my protection. We must stay in the schoolhouse till the storm passes and the contagion lifts."

"Why can't the doctors make everyone better?" Willie frets.

"Sometimes a peddler isn't what he appears to be. His bottle doesn't keep the promises stamped on its face." Longhurst turns away from the blue glass of the window and reaches for Addy's pale wrist. "Addy, when were you last dosed?"

"This morning." She blinks, dully.

A creaking sound pierces the wind. Jack jumps.

"What's that?"

"It's just the trees at the edge of the meadow," I say. Ola says. As she must have then.

"But they never sounded like that before."

I say, "We've never been here at sundown before."

"Night is falling, children. This is all a new … adventure." Longhurst smiles, sweating.

"I want my mama!" Willie cries.

"Don't care if my pa comes or not," Jack says.

"You all had your suppers before you came here, yes? And your clothes are warm enough?" He tugs at Will's high collar, and seems comforted. "We won't have lessons so late in the day. We'll busy ourselves with rounds and carols until it's time to make our pallets and go to sleep. First, some instruction: there's water over there in the bucket to ladle if you're thirsty. And another bucket behind the hung blanket, there, for any private necessaries. I'll keep the stove stoked, and each of you will help until you've gone to bed. I will see to the fire during the night. In the morning, we'll have a meal and our usual lessons and recitations, and will continue our study of—"

"Do we ring the bell in the morning?" Jack asks.

"Yes, I've told all your pare—" Longhurst stops himself. "I have told those remaining in town that we will pull the bell rope in the morning to let them know we're still safe."

One of the jars inside the window begins to shake, like a loosened tooth.

"Will they hear us through the wind?"

"Yes, Jack. Well, isn't it a fine night for a blizzard!" Longhurst straightens in a cheerful way. "Now, everyone—to our carols. Before we sing, let me check each of you to see if you are not too . . . nervous."

He moves around the room, feeling each of our foreheads with his palm. When he comes to me, a strained look passes over his face. As if his eyes are longing to speak across centuries, but can't, trapped. His hand feels smooth and sticky.

He turns, squaring his shoulders in his thin coat.

"All right. What shall we sing? Of Clementine and her herring-tin shoes? Or 'I Dreamt I Dwelt in Marble Halls, and You Loved Me Just the Same'? 'The Days of '49'? How about 'Long, Long Ago'? Addy, that's your favorite, isn't it? I think it must be 'Long Ago,' you sing it so well, dear Addy, and it will help you to keep awake." He feels her drugged forehead again. "Will you sing it for us, to help us warm up, and cheer us on this cold night?"

She stands, obediently, beside her desk, and in a voice soft with sleep, sings:

Tell me the tales that to me were so dear,
Long, long ago, long, long ago.
Sing me the songs I delighted to hear,
Long, long ago, long ago.
Now you are come my grief is removed
Let me forget that so long you have roved
Let me believe that you loved as I loved,
Long, long ago, long ago.

Do you remember the path where we met?
Long, long ago, long, long ago.

240

Ah yes, you told me you ne'er would forget,
Long, long ago, long ago.
Though by long absence your truth has been tried
Still to your accents I listen with pride
Blessed as I was when I sat by your side,
Long, long ago, long ago.

Now you are come, my grief is removed
Let me forget that so long you have roved
Let me believe that you loved as I loved,
Long ago
Long, long ago.

Longhurst blinks in the lantern light, as if the dampness has reached his eyes. Then he helps Addy to sit again. Next he calls for rounds of "Frère Jacques," with a bow to Will.

Are you sleeping, are you sleeping
Brother John? Brother John?

Our schoolhouse fills with waves of song. As the last, quavering notes die away, our teacher seems to sag, his shoulders drooping. He says it would be best now to prepare our beds for the night.

"Boys to the left of the stove. Ola, Addy, girls to the right. Jack, help Will pull that horse blanket down on the floor."

We pack ourselves in together, tightly. The floor is rough and cold, much harder than a desk, and the wind whistles and seeps through the boards.

Jack frowns at Longhurst sitting straight in his chair. "You're not going to sleep, sir?"

"I must keep the fire going. You get your rest now."

"Is the storm getting worse? It sounds like it is."

"It does, doesn't it? But we're as snug as can be. Off to dreams, now."

No sleep comes to me. Peering over the edge of a quilt smelling of horses and smoke, I watch our schoolmaster. His chin is in his hand, his brow furrowed over it. He starts, then tires, then straightens again. His eyelids flutter. My own begin to close with the weight of the blanket and the heat of the stove. I don't want to sleep, there's too much that's unknown, but as the others begin to breathe slowly around me, their blankets rising and falling, a deep rest comes. The air beyond my wool collar grows colder, and the whistle and whipping of the wind in the trees twists into one long hum. My eyes shut, and I dream I'm falling, falling into darkness. I dream of a great crash and of powder falling into my eyes, and when I open them, my arm is on fire.

"Ola!" Longhurst is shouting. "Children! Help, help!"

A lantern lies crookedly on the floor beside me, its oil leaking out. The other lamp has fallen on top of me. Longhurst kicks it aside. Snow rushes in from what should have been the schoolhouse roof. My arm is beaten with a blanket, and when I lift my head only a few inches, I see Anton and Jack and Addy fighting with their bare hands against a tangle of limbs and boards and branches lying across my feet, while my arm screams with pain beyond bearing. Longhurst cries, "It's out, the fire's out, see if she can stand, Ola, Ola, please, you must stand!" He lifts my shoulders under what's left of the lantern light, as Addy grips Willie and the blizzard pours through the gaping ceiling. I pull my skirt free, I'm free, free, I can stand now. By no more than a moving flicker of light, I see our shelter has been torn open on one side, too, and gapes into the night, with snow coming so fast it stitches the eyes and fills the mouth. We cling to each other and to Mr. Longhurst, who as the last feeble light is dying out shouts, "Rope, rope, bell rope, hold on, don't let go, follow me, hurry, hurry—"

I understand. We must hold and go, or we will freeze and die.

I feel no pain in my arm. Longhurst is groping among us, blindly, his hands checking that this hand, my hand, has a hold of the rope. I'm oldest and last. I understand. We bend our heads against the wind and the rope tautens, pulling. I hold fast to the end. There's never been such wind and snow, but we must hold, hold on in the dark, our teacher has gone forward into the blizzard and we must follow him, though the snow strikes the face so hard it cuts like a blade. *Hold on, hold on*, I hear the shout and cry, but the snow is so deep I sink, I'm sinking, slowing, falling, I must let go so I don't hold back any of the others. Hold on, hold fast, I try to shout to Anton in front of me, and don't know if he hears me, but I don't feel any pain at all now, not even cold, only my mouth sinking to the ground, warm. Which must mean the storm is melting. It's melting all around, warm, so warm, but now I feel too warm, hot, my clothes are on fire again. I think, *You'll burn, you'll burn*, so I must take them all off, no, no, that wouldn't do, a girl must keep her manners and at least there is no pain, no more fire nor cold, only a blanket that starts to come over me, soft and heavy as a horse. How strange it is to be so still. No more pushing against the wind, though the wind is there, somewhere, far away, roaring and going up and away. And here are Mother and Father at our farm loading provisions, but finding nothing to put inside the wagon—neither my brother nor me, though they call and call for us. Through an opening in the snow, they drive the horses away. *No, don't leave me*, I cry out, *it isn't right.*

I awake. I hear voices.

The children. Oh, my God, the children!

Longhurst, he's over here!

Turn him over!

He's still breathing!

Dig them all out!

Get back! I recognize one of the doctors' voices. *Give us room. We must examine them!*

I'm awake but I can't open my eyes. How unusual.

Caleb. My God.

Listen to me. They were already sick, brother. Remember that. It's a mercy, in a way, for there is nothing that could have helped them.

It was so, truly.

Kiersten says they'll have to be burned, this time of year. Or floated in the river till spring.

Burning's best for any contagion.

So we'll say. We'll do it here where they lie, in this meadow, where their poor bodies dropped. We'll make a pyre. Best for all. The most fitting place.

And the schoolmaster?

If he survives, his is the crime.

Putting them in such danger. Madness!

Here's Berringer. We'll get him to carry the duties out with solemnity.

Sweet angels.

Longhurst is the very devil.

Clearly, brother.

We'll make him pay.

We will. For all of it.

I'm ash in the wind. Ash falling into water.

How long did we stay in the deep? How long does any ghost wait for what's right? However long, too long. One by one, we floated to the surface. We found each another. Mr. Longhurst came at last, too, and told us these falls were no place for us.

"We must rise, children, and show them we're still here."

His face is ablaze with anger.

"We will sit at their tables—if there are any left here still known to us. We'll sleep in their beds. Follow them through the streets. Stand at their windows. Lie in their wagons. Do you understand me, children?"

His voice rises. I feel my own soul burning, understanding.

We were left by the town to burn in the cold. Then shoveled into the river, like muck.

Yet as I stand here by White Bar Falls, I feel, I know, all of this has happened before.

All these words have been said before.

It's what I must say now to Longhurst. To help him.

To help myself. Ola. All of them.

"All of these words"—I look at him—"have been said before."

"But what is it that hasn't been said, you're asking?"

He nods, and faces the children.

"Beloved pupils." He speaks to them where they stand ghostly beside ghostly waters. "I am so sorry. Please forgive me. You must put blame in all the places where it belongs, and be no more afraid. Nor ever doubt yourselves again, or your courage. You didn't let go, you see. You held on. Did you *see*, this time? The rope was pried from your hands by fiercest cold and wind. You did nothing wrong. You *were* brave. You held on, for as long as you could. You must trust yourselves, now. And I hope you will trust in what I say: *I* led you to this end. I led you to fall in the storm. I meant to help you. I tried. I tried again, when we rose from the waters. When we made the bargain with the living, and gained a schoolhouse forever. But then I said to you, Now children, you must set your suffering aside, and be good and hold fast and make no trouble. I said you must be silent about the past, and what was done to you. Is it any wonder, then, Jack, when they desecrated and dug a hole in the place where you died, that you cried out in pain? Your wounds were never mended. I only bound them more tightly to you. Do you understand? I do, now."

We're no longer beside a ghostly river, beside a bank where drugged men died, where fever took hold, where gold was hungered for, and never enough of it found. We seem to be nowhere. In empty space. Neither dark nor light.

"We need to be getting back, sir." Through the emptiness, Jack holds out his arm, shyly, as if for a handshake. Longhurst, surprised, takes it. "We shouldn't stay here, sir. Addy, what do you think?"

"I say so, too," Addy takes Will's hand. "Willie?"

"I say so, too. Anton?"

"We're done here. Miss Finnis?"

They all turn to me.

Never in all my life or afterlife have I seen faces, souls, so sure of themselves.

"We're done here," I say. "Now come."

29

She who made the Ghost Door is there, waiting for us as we glide into the barn.

There is so much that must and will be said between the two of us, Su Kwon and Emma Rose Finnis, one day. Words of thanks. True words. Perhaps there are more among the living, like her, willing to arc and bend what is hard to bend. I don't know. I do know her.

Ola comes forward, glowing inside the freed skin she's so well filled. I know, too, that feeling: to have a chance handed back to you again.

"Well, what now?" Su asks.

Longhurst bows to her. "You have given us more than we can ever express."

Su nods simply at the door. "Thank you. We were talking about what we should do, what the door means—Ola and I—all night long. How we have so many questions. But we decided the only answer you ever get is by doing and not waiting for directions. Doing is the answer."

I see Longhurst look again with envy and yearning at Ola. Again, he seems to catch himself, pull himself back, let some pain go. Did he, does he love her, I wonder? And still long for hope and love? How many of us are alike in that way, our paths strewn with errors and loss, and yet still we'll never say, the part of me that aches is dead?

So many questions.

But first, my plan.

30

We wait. We bide our time. Time is what ghosts have, and the living do not.

"They're all still at the café," Su says. "I just got a text. Pratt's coming to present his assessment to the town."

Yes, he would do that. He'll want to trumpet his accomplishments, real or imagined. If we're to have any chance against him, there's this still to do:

We must help him.

How different the townspeople look than when I saw them meeting with Su in this café. Then, they were full of their stories of finding peace and power in the mountains. Now they look battered, unkempt, their certainties all gone. Everything now depends on the hunter Philip Pratt, they think. They need, want him to erase all their troubles.

The hunter sits in a booth by the window. The snow has stopped, and a twinkling morning light, glittering, silver, like the spoon in his coffee cup, hovers outside. A machine has plowed a narrow road out of town.

"I call this meeting to order," John Berringer announces, hoarsely. "We're here to hear from you, Mr. Pratt, that this job is done and we can be sure we won't be made fools of, or harassed, anymore."

"Mr. Berringer, I can only assure you that—"

"Because if I see one hide or hair—"

"Let him *speak*," Martha, sitting on her stool at the counter, says desperately.

"Thank you, Madam Mayor," Pratt says. "Mr. Berringer, everyone: I have completed a thorough sweep. I left no corner of their confirmed lair untouched. It was—" From where I perch, above, on the doorbells, I see his hand stirring his coffee steadily but slowly, as if he's searching for some truth in the water, not sharing the search with them. "It was quite intense."

"And your proof the job is done?" Berringer asks.

"Will be in the coming days. I will be staying with you for a surveillance period. Have you had any disturbances since last night?"

Mary Berringer asks the room, "Anyone?"

"None," comes the sullen answer.

"Optimistically," Pratt says, "the infestation is at an end. But only some time will tell."

"Then maybe," Martha says, looking down into her own cup, "we should have a moment of silence for the passing of the sad souls who lingered here for so long."

"You're not serious," Bill says behind his counter.

"Well, as your mayor, I do feel that—"

"No, there is nothing to say!" Mary Berringer snaps from her booth. "Except for this: Mr. Pratt, we are now prepared to double your fee from the township, if you will agree, in return, and as we do, that this matter is now at an end, and no business of the state's or anyone else's, and so no need to report it to the authorities."

Pratt unfolds his napkin and seems annoyed. "We have had no discussion of what my fee buys, Mrs. Berringer. You're making assumptions." He looks up and around the room, frowning, disappointed. "Assumptions that don't reflect well on you."

"But Mr. Pratt"—the old woman twists her face into a smile—"since we are, as I now understand it, the *first* to hire you after your rather *unfortunate* performance at the coast—where that poor young woman died, and you let the ghost you were cleaning get away?—you are making assumptions yourself, wouldn't you say? We have the power of review. We can praise—or, I suppose, we could find fault with your work, if you choose to make our private matters public. We could note, for example, that you let matters get entirely out of hand here—or maybe you didn't notice us being chased like rats across our own town square?—while you were off wasting time in Dutch Gap where that hideous boy Seth still is and that, that, that vegetating—"

"Ruthie," Martha says quietly. "You're talking about our Ruthie."

"In your absence, Mr. Pratt, we were *assaulted*. Why, it's a wonder John and I can even walk! And perhaps it was because your work was a bit sloppy. And too slow."

"You mean thanks to the obstacles and obfuscations you put in my way?"

Harold jumps to his feet. "Every community has the right to always act first in its own best interests!"

"Sit down, Harold!" the older woman orders him. She turns, her jaw tense, back to Pratt's booth. "I wonder if what Mr. Pratt is implying is that maybe, even now, he's still unsure of his work. If so, I think it best you stay on for a week, cleaner—at the increased fee, of course—in case there is any . . . mopping up you need to do. Harold and Bill will make sure you are . . . comfortable. Mayor Hayley has just graciously consented to keep her hotel open for a while longer—"

251

"I have?" Martha asks.

"—and we'll do our own inspection of the schoolhouse, now that the weather is clearing, to see if, in *our* opinion—"

"I am," Pratt interrupts, "perfectly willing, Mrs. Berringer, to accept a higher fee if you would like me to stay on for a longer period to monitor and confirm results. But that's all I can accommodate. I must report the haunting of White Bar. Hauntings are a matter of public record."

"So are the public's reviews, Mr. Pratt. So are newspapers. The internet. Television."

"I don't frighten easily, ma'am. And you don't frighten me. There's only one thing that does—that should frighten any of us. And it's not the rather ordinary, dirty little secret you all have been trying to hide here. It's the great change that's coming. The line, the border that's being crossed, every day, the disruptiveness and the brazenness the dead are starting to show. No one cares, let's be frank, about a town in the middle of nowhere, or what's happened here, or about how you've been able to keep your ugly little zoo for so long. What people care about, and what I know how to bring down, is big game, the greatest threat. And it's here. Without your knowledge. Probably watching us at this very moment. Its name is Emma Rose. You know her as Rose. What I'm known for is finishing what others don't know how to finish. The work ahead is difficult and dangerous. It's work some others aren't even trying to or want to confront, because it means admitting we're facing the greatest existential threat to our established ways of life that we have ever seen. What I am saying, Mrs. Berringer, is that your threats don't impress me. Because they're nothing compared to what else is here, with us, nothing compared to what needs to be done, what else I must do, which exceeds anything you can imagine."

It's time.

I ring the bells above the door. My signal to Ola.

Dressed in the body of the woman whose life Pratt couldn't save, she passes right in front of the window where the hunter sits.

He sees her.

His whole body electrifies. It isn't every day you observe a man's conscience, as well as his hope and desire, parading in front of him. He leaps up, shoving his napkin aside, slipping on it.

Ola runs, runs as we planned, up the cleared road, toward the bridge, into the trees.

Her name is Ola Varga. Perhaps it's the last we'll ever see of her. She'll be all right. Pratt's weapon can't be used against flesh.

He grabs his coat and lunges out of the café, limping.

"What on earth—?" Martha goes to the jangling door left open behind him.

Behind her all of the town comes, too, following her out onto the porch, into the morning, staring, as Pratt starts his car and roars his tires into the plowed lane and out of the valley.

Ola, I think, *best of luck I send with you, as you fly through the world and with new hands touch and taste freedom.*

As for me, I have much to look forward to now, with company to see it.

"What the hell is that?" John Berringer points to the square.

It's the rest of my plan. They've discovered it. What's been put in place of the fallen Prospector.

The Ghost Door, gleaming in the twinkling mist.

Bill whistles. "What is it?"

"How did it get there?" Martha says.

Harold frowns. "And when?"

Su's sled tracks lead away from her gallery. There's no other sign of movement.

"Is that thing making some kind of *sound?*"

"What is it? What's it doing?"

It's an experiment, I think.

It won't hurt, I assured Su. Not in that way.

From the rooftops, we, I and all the ghosts of White Bar, now come down, bearing down on the townspeople, our mouths gaping with no sound, driving them forward. Stumbling from the porch, into the square, driven by all of our memories, our righteous rage, our justice, they go. One by one, corralled by us, the living cry out and are herded through the Ghost Door's arc, and disappear. The last face I see is Martha's, her lost eyes turning back toward me, tearfully wide, as if she'd say something, if there were anything left to say, with judgment already passed.

When it's done, we, the ghosts of White Bar, watch from the café porch as Su Kwon sleds out again from the alley and, with her face wearing its mask and her tool that spits fire, cuts the frame on each side from its granite footing. A sculptor, she told us, is always letting go of what she's made. She lets the metal fall away, broken, to the snow.

And now we'll see, good people, if you can find your way back.

Epilogue

Yo, everybody! It's Brin and Ky here! I know, I know, we haven't posted to this blog in a long time but it's because we've been having TOO MUCH FUN BEING IN LOVE and trying on the whole mate-for-life thing. It's awesome.

But here's the latest: WE'RE HEADED BACK TO THE PCT! Some of you remember we started on the trail last year but cut things short when the weather tanked. Now it's spring and we've decided to pick up where we left off. We're staging here again in the town called White Bar, getting our gear in order and ready to book it back up to the high range. This pretty little town is even quieter than the last time. There's nobody here except one really cool artist who's filled the whole place with chill wind sculptures and big, funky pieces. She's running the hotel now and we asked her where everybody went, and she said sometimes people have to leave, in a small town the population just sort of comes and goes in waves. We also asked if we could see the museum since we didn't get to see it last time, but she said the woman who ran it was paralyzed and in a home and her son tried to sell her stuff but couldn't and left with the key, oh well. We asked her if she could put us back in the same room we had last year, and she did, which is great because it really makes us feel like we're picking up *right* where we left off. Ky says the only thing that looks different in here is this old-timey picture they have hanging over the dresser. Ky says he has a *perfect* visual memory for everything including the first time he saw me (I LOVE YOU BABY) and he says he could swear there are more people in this picture than there were last time (here's a shot of it). See in the back this blur that looks like a bunch of people with their arms up waving, like they're trying to shout over everyone in front of them or want to be seen by the camera? Ky said it wasn't like that before, and he asked the cool artist about it and she said no, it was exactly the same as it's always been, it's a famous photograph, the same one all over town. I asked if she did photography, too, since she was obviously such a good artist and she said no, photographs are like prisons, she said in some cultures people believe you can get stuck in them, frozen, and she prefers to make art that moves. But I managed to get her to take a shot of us with all our gear and HERE WE ARE!

Back on the trail in the morning. We are so stoked. You never know what's going to happen out there. We just know it's good to do it with SOMEONE YOU LOVE ALL CAPS.

Okay. I want to get serious now for a minute. We love all you guys and we'll miss you. Keep us in your thoughts and hope we'll stay safe. We're about to start the toughest stretch. We'll post and text when we can. If you don't hear from us for a while, don't worry, not right away. We'll be out here, doing our thing. It feels good to be getting away again. Free. If we don't make it back (pro tip: we will), just look for our spirits on the other side of the range where someone's been saying there's a whole trail of ghosts moving around and shaking things up. I say, SAVE THE GHOSTS. Who doesn't want to stick around forever? (Ky says he loves me forever but please give it up.) For real, though, we *love* all you guys. Be good. Or not. Peace out.